VACLAV AND LENA

VACLAV

AND

LENA

A

NOVEL

HALEY TANNER

WILLIAM HEINEMANN: LONDON

Published by William Heinemann 2011

2 4 6 8 10 9 7 5 3 1

First published in Great Britain in 2011 by
William Heinemann
Random House, 20 Vauxhall Bridge Road,
London SW1V 2SA

www.randomhouse.co.uk

Addresses for companies within The Random House Group Limited can be found at:
www.randomhouse.co.uk/offices.htm

The Random House Group Limited Reg. No. 954009

A CIP catalogue record for this book
is available from the British Library

ISBN 9780434020447

The Random House Group Limited supports The Forest Stewardship Council (FSC), the leading international forest certification organisation. All our titles that are printed on Greenpeace approved FSC certified paper carry he FSC logo. Our paper procurement policy can be found at:
www.randomhouse.co.uk/environment

Book design by Barbara M. Bachman

Printed and bound in Great Britain by
CPI Mackays, Chatham, ME5 8TD

Gavin, my partner in crime, my lovely assistant,
my comrade, and the very best husband a girl could have,
you are still my rising sun.
You fill my life with wonder and joy and
possibility every day.
You were always on every page of this book,
and now you're part of the big, wild, gorgeous universe, too.
I know you're having fun out there, I can feel it.
I love you.

TOGETHER

NO ASSISTANT,
NO MAGICIAN

. . .

"Here, I practice, and you practice. Ahem. AH-em. I am Vaclav the Magnificent, with birthday on the sixth of May, the famous day for the generations to celebrate and rejoice, a day in the future years eclipsing Christmas and Hanukkah and Ramadan and all pagan festivals, born in a land far, far, far, far, far, far, far distance from here, a land of ancient and magnificent secrets, a land of enchanted knowledge passed down from the ages and from the ancients, a land of illusion (Russia!), born there in Russia and reappearing here, in America, in New York, in Brooklyn (which is a Borough), near Coney Island, which is a famous place of magic in the great land of opportunity (which is, of course, America), where anyone can become anything, where a hobo today is tomorrow a businessman in a three-pieces-suit, and a businessman yesterday is later this afternoon a hobo, Vaclav the Magnificent, who shall, without no doubt, be ask to perform his mighty feats of enchantment for dukes and presidents and czars and ayatollahs, uniting them all in awestruck and dumbstrucks, and thus, one day in the future years, be heralding a new era (which is a piece of time) of peace on earth. Ladies and gentlemans, I give you, I present to you, I warn you in advance of his arrival, so that you may close your eyes or put your hands on your face if you are afraid, Vaclav the Magnificent, Boy-Magician."

"Eh," Lena says in a grumbly voice.

"Lena, what we are having here is perfect introduction to the act. It is long and perfect and made of only the best and longest thesaurus words," says Vaclav.

"After third sentence, say, 'Magic is art of control events using supernatural powers,' " says Lena. This sentence is a favorite of Lena's—she memorized it from *The Magician's Almanac,* which is a big old black book with gold around the edges of the pages, all about magic and tricks and illusions. Vaclav kept checking the almanac out of the library, so last year for his birthday she put it in her backpack and took it home with her, so that she could give it to him for a birthday present, and it could be theirs forever.

"That sounds good, but is not belonging in the act. I already told you. This is the introduction, complete. Seal it now with the magic birthday candle." Vaclav folds the notebook paper on which the introduction to the act is written, and he holds it out to Lena. Lena does not take it from him. Lena holds the magic birthday candle in her left hand and rubs its spiraled ridges with her thumb. In her right hand, she holds the lighter with which she is to light the candle. The wax-dripping paper-sealing is an important part of anything Vaclav and Lena write, and it is Lena's job, exclusively Lena's, to light the magic birthday candle, to hold it high, and to then let the wax drip onto the folded paper, sealing it for all of time.

Under Vaclav's bed, next to a forgotten sock, among many

gatherings of fuzzy, dusty things, is a shoe box full of pieces of notebook paper folded and sealed with Lena's wax drips. The things written on them are important declarations, pacts, lists, and other artifacts of the lives of the young magicians.

"We write and finish now, Lena, and tonight I will ask permission to have a show."

"Impossible," Lena says.

"Possible. I can make this happen. Maybe not tonight but soon. And so we seal the introduction, which means we can begin on the act. Once we have permission, we perform. Light. Melt. It is done."

"Unfold. Write. Magic is art of control events using supernatural powers."

"I will not, Lena, no. This is not part of the introduction of the act; this does not belong. It is very good English, but it does not belong. This is the introduction, which we must seal, so that it will be, and so that we begin work on practice the act."

Lena looks at the lighter she stole from the pocket of the Aunt's robe. Lena knows it is not right to steal unless you need something really badly, and the person is not home, and won't even realize the thing is missing. Stealing the lighter felt scary, and it felt good, and brave. Lena feels very brave with the lighter in her hand, very grown-up.

"Why you are the boss always?" Lena asks.

"For one thing, I am magician and you are assistant. Assistant is second to magician. There is no assistant without magician," says Vaclav.

"Without assistant, no magician," says Lena.

"I am one year older than you," says Vaclav.

"Ten is only little more than nine and eleven months," says Lena.

"Magician is more important than assistant, because . . ." says Vaclav, getting ready to say one more thing to prove that he should have authority over Lena. He wants to win this argument, even though he knows they will have this argument again. This fight is a fight they have over and over again. It is like the famous argument between the chicken and the egg, about which came first, and which one is more important and better than the other. This fight is never resolved, because it is impossible to prove which came first or which is better when actually both things are the same thing.

There is a knock on the door. Lena and Vaclav look at the door with wide, terrified eyes. There are three loud knocks, and then the doorknob jiggles but does not open, because the door is locked.

Vaclav is filled with regret. Locking the door was a terrible idea. A locked door indicates to Vaclav's mother that something illicit may be happening in the bedroom of the young magician.

"Vaclav! Open the door right now or I'll open it for you! You wanndo this hard way or the easy way?"

Lena and Vaclav shove their magic things under the bed, hide them behind the eyelet-perforated dust ruffles of the bed skirt.

"Coming, coming!" says Vaclav, scrambling to his feet. As soon as Vaclav unlocks the door, it bursts open, pushing him backward.

Rasia's eyes search the room. Rasia doesn't know what she is looking for, but all the time she is worried. Every day at ten-past-five she rushes home as fast as she can, because her son is growing and changing every second and she has only so many hours to mold him like clay. She has only so many hours to show him that it is important to do homework, to have dinner like a family, to not do drugs or to steal or to be a lazy person or a cheat. She must protect him from pedophiles, from strangers, from bullies, from guns, and from carbon monoxide poisoning. She is worried, because he comes home to an empty house after school; he is what they call the latch-key kid, and she is a working mother, and they live in an urban area, and Vaclav attends a crowded public school, and all these things are the ingredients of disaster, if you are listening to the news, which she is, carefully, vigilantly, always to see what next to be afraid of.

"I do not like what I see here. What is going on here when I am not home?"

"Nothing! We are doing nothing! Homework. We are doing nothing but homework," Vaclav says.

"Nothing and homework for three hours? This I do not believe. I want to see all homework after dinnertime." Rasia backs away toward the door, keeping her eyes on Lena. She's worried about Lena because of the well-known occupation of the Aunt. This is unfair and also fair at the same time.

"Okay, nothing and homework and, also, maybe a little practicing the magic act," Vaclav says. Rasia steps back into the room.

"Maybe a little practicing the magic act?"

"Actually, yes, we are practicing the magic act," Vaclav says, trying to look earnest. "Maybe, also, if it is okay with you, because all homework is done, maybe . . ." Vaclav looks up at his mother, and Rasia looks down at her son, at this dancing around what he wants, at his Velcro sneakers digging nervous little circles in the carpet.

"Maybe what?" says Rasia.

"Maybe, before we are eating dinner . . ." says Vaclav.

"Say what you are saying," says Rasia, narrowing her eyes.

"Can Lena and I do for you a magic show, in the living room, before dinner?" Vaclav says, very fast, all in one breath.

"All homework is done?" she asks.

"Yes, all is done," Vaclav says, even though his homework is only mostly done.

"Lena, you are staying for dinner?" Rasia asks.

"Da," says Lena.

"English!" says Rasia.

"Ye-us," says Lena, with a growl.

"Before any magic is happening, homework must be done," Rasia says.

Vaclav smiles, because he knows that this is her way of saying yes.

Rasia scowls at the room for one extra minute, just to eradicate any funny business that may or may not be happening, then, satisfied, she finally leaves the room, pulling the door almost shut behind her. As soon as she is gone, Vaclav and Lena jump up and down and squeal with excitement, and then start scrambling frantically to prepare their magnificent act.

LADY AND GENTLEMAN

. . .

Vaclav and Lena turn off the big-screen television in the living room. They push the big mahogany coffee table back against the wall; it is a perfect stage, black and solid and shiny. They have moved the coffee table this way many times; it is easy to push across the big threadbare Persian rug.

Vaclav and Lena stand onstage, waiting for the audience to take their seats.

"Dad," Vaclav shouts, "come on, we're ready!" Rasia is already sitting on the big black leather sofa, waiting for the show to start. Vaclav's father comes in with a glass of vodka in his hand and sinks down into the sofa.

"Okay, so I am here. What are we watching? What are you going to show?" Vaclav's father says.

"Only watch, okay?" Vaclav wears his school clothes, jeans and a green T-shirt, with his bow tie hanging around his neck and his magician's top hat on his head. Lena wears only her normal clothes, jeans and a T-shirt, because she has not made her costume yet.

"First, welcome to my lovely and intellectual audience. Lady and gentleman, you are in for quite a surprise. I am Vaclav the Magnificent, and this, my assistant, the Lovely Lena." Vaclav swings his left arm out to indicate Lena, who takes a long, deep, serious bow.

Vaclav and the audience wait in silence for her to return to an upright position.

"Tonight we have for you a special treat which will astound and amaze you. May I please, from the audience, give someone the honor of volunteering a quarter to give to me to be involved in a magical trick?"

"This is scam," says Vaclav's father.

"Dad!" says Vaclav.

"Oleg, give it," growls Rasia, and with much moaning and groaning, he reaches under his butt and into his pocket and retrieves a warm quarter, then hands it to his son.

"Thank you, kind sir. Much appreciate." Vaclav holds the coin pinched between his forefinger and his thumb, and holds it forward for the audience to inspect.

"Lena, if you will, the paper." Lena produces a sheet of paper from behind her back. She steps forward and shows the audience the front of the paper, the back of the paper, and the edges of the paper. She holds the sheet of paper up to the light, then steps back.

"As my lovely assistant is showing, this is a normal piece of paper—no holes or rips or no tears. This is just a normal paper. Thank you, Lena." Lena nods.

"Please watch carefully. I am now folding the paper around the coin." Vaclav folds the paper several times, so that the coin is contained within it, as in an envelope. Rasia scoots a bit forward on the couch, following her son's direction to watch carefully. Oleg crosses his arms. Oleg has sleeping marks like deep scars on his face and neck, and hairs bursting out of the top of his shirt.

"You can see that the coin is completely sealed within the paper." Lena steps next to Vaclav and extends her hands sideways to draw the audience's attention to the mysterious coin wrapped in paper.

Focusing carefully, Vaclav passes the paper-wrapped coin from his left to his right hand. He doesn't explain this movement. Lena puts her arms stiffly up in the air and twirls around and around, coming dangerously close to the edge of the coffee table. Rasia gasps, afraid that Lena will fall.

"Using my magic wand, I will now make the coin disappear from thin air," Vaclav says, holding the coin packet stiffly in his right hand and nervously slipping his left hand into his back pocket. Lena attempts to shimmy, twitching her bony shoulders back and forth.

Vaclav keeps his hand in his pocket for a moment of Lena's shimmying, and then removes it, smiling, and shows the audience his magic wand.

Vaclav's magic wand is one of his most special things. It is a real magic wand, from a real magician's-supply shop in Manhattan. His mother took him, and they had to ride on the subway for more than an hour to get there. At the store, they asked the shop owner for help picking out the best wand, and afterward they had lunch at a restaurant, and Vaclav held the wand in his lap the entire time.

Vaclav taps this very wand three times on the paper packet.

"Abracadabra!" he says with the final tap. "The coin has disappeared!"

"Lena," he says, "my lovely assistant, if you would be kind, please take this paper envelope and tear it into two complete pieces." Lena takes the paper packet from him and effortlessly tears it in two. She then shows the paper pieces to the audience, and once the audience has seen sufficient evidence of the disappearance of the quarter, she throws the pieces of paper up into the air for dramatic effect.

Vaclav and Lena bow so that the audience knows to begin clapping.

"Fantastic!" says Rasia, although she is not sure which part of the trick was the trick. She is almost certain that she was not supposed to see Vaclav tip the coin out of the paper packet and into his open hand, and that she was not supposed to see him put the coin into his pocket when he went to take out the wand.

Vaclav and Lena bow again.

"Bravo!" says Rasia. Vaclav and Lena step down from the coffee table.

"Where is my quarter?" says Oleg.

"A magician never reveals the secrets," says Vaclav.

"Oleg," says Rasia to Vaclav's father, meaning *do not ask about the quarter again.*

"Thank you," says Vaclav. "I am glad you like. Lena and I will perform this on Saturday for fans at the boardwalk of Coney Island." Vaclav is beaming.

"Vaclav." Rasia takes a deep breath. She's been trying to ignore this idea of a performance at Coney Island, but Vaclav won't forget. He's too persistent. He doesn't know that this is a very bad idea.

"This is not such a good idea," she says.

"Why?" asks Vaclav.

"It just is not." How can she tell him the truth? She can't tell him that the drunks and the teenagers at Coney Island will laugh at him. She can't tell him that he will humiliate himself. She can't tell him that no one will clap, that no one will do ooh and aah.

"Why?" asks Vaclav.

"It is not safe." This is maybe close to being honest, she thinks. It is not safe, for Vaclav, out in the world, with his eyes open to everything and his heart beating right on his sleeve, with his dreams in his hands, ready to show and tell.

"That's not fair! We must practice to do the show for a *real* audience!" he yells. This is fine, she tells herself, to let him think she is being the meanest person in the world. Let him think that she does not want him to perform his magic.

"That is the final word. I will not discuss," she says.

"I cannot believe!" says Vaclav.

"Go wash your hands and get ready for dinner," she says. "Lena, you too."

Rasia stands at the door as Vaclav and Lena march toward a dinner that is not the thing they are hungry for.

DINNER

...

The kitchen in Vaclav's house is very hot, and the air is thick. Breathing the air into your nose is like sucking a milkshake through a straw. Once Lena is in the kitchen, she already feels full, like the smell is filling up her belly all the way to the top. Dinner at Vaclav's house is always like this. The smell is enough to have for dinner; you don't even have to eat.

"What's for dinner?" Vaclav asks.

"Is joke?" Rasia asks, because her son must know what is for dinner. The house is so full of the smell of borscht that you would expect the air to be tinted a little purply-red; you would expect that there might be condensation of borscht on the ceiling and on the walls and on the windowpanes.

Lena opens a drawer next to where Rasia's large behind vacillates with the stirring of the borscht. She takes out four forks, four spoons, and names each one in her mind so that she's sure she has one for each person. Mother spoon, father spoon, Vaclav spoon, me spoon. She says *mother* and *father* in her brain, but she means the mother of Vaclav and the father of Vaclav. This is not confusing to her because her own brain would never confuse the mother of Vaclav with the mother of Lena, because Lena has not seen her own mother since before she could have even remembered her.

Lena thinks about her own mother in a very different way from the way she thinks about Rasia. Rasia has a smell like strong perfume. She's a big woman with a big rear end who wears faded, worn-out dresses and leather loafer-shoes on her feet and who makes smelly soup that she stirs and who makes chairs creak when she sits on them. Lena's mother is an idea. Lena's mother is a mystery.

Lena sets down the silverware and sits in the same place she always sits, next to Vaclav, across from his father, next to his mother.

Vaclav makes quick work of doing his job, setting out napkins and putting one water glass in front of each plate.

Lena sits while Vaclav fills her glass first, then Rasia's, then his own. She watches while Vaclav fills Oleg's glass with vodka.

Vaclav and Oleg sit down next. Vaclav quietly, Oleg with a low, embarrassing groan. Rasia will not sit down yet; she'll remain standing until she has served borscht with meat to everyone, and then she'll sit.

Rasia holds the pot of borscht to her side with two hands, her dark armpit exposed above it. She thuds the pot on the kitty-cat-shaped steel trivet on the table, then plunges the ladle into the borscht and brings it back like a piston. The ladle is white, stained with brown. The borscht is the color of the carpet in the school library, Lena thinks. Rasia fills her husband's bowl. The borscht is the color of flowers. Rasia plunges the ladle into the soup again and again, serving Vaclav. The borscht is the color of a dress a queen might wear. The borscht floods Lena's bowl. The borscht is the color of blood. The borscht is the color of blood, and in it are not pieces of meat but moles that have fallen off the many chins of Rasia. Once Lena's mind has taken this turn, she cannot turn back.

Rasia sits heavily on her chair. She arranges her large belly above the waistband of her pantyhose. She holds her spoon above her bowl and lowers her head, but before she takes a sip, she glances at Lena. The air in the kitchen is wet and thick. Each breath Lena breathes is of borscht, of the sweaty spot between the folds of Rasia's belly, of the breath from the back molars of Oleg, of the bits of moles floating about in the soup.

"Eat! Lena, eat!" Rasia is focused on Lena. Lena lowers her spoon into her borscht. She angles her spoon to try to get a spoonful with no moles.

"What is your problem? Can I give you personal invitation?" The yelling startles Lena, and she plunges her spoon into the borscht.

"She is so skinny like children on the streets of India. It is not cute, this skin and bones!" Rasia says, and then slurps her borscht.

Hot stomach stuff is rushing to the back of Lena's throat, filling her mouth. She stands from the table, thinking maybe she can make it to the bathroom, where no one will see her, and she will rinse out her mouth and come back to the table maybe with her cheeks a little hot but otherwise no one will know anything. She's thinking the bathroom is so close, the bathroom is so close, and if she can just keep her mouth closed, everything will be okay. But then there is another hot hiccup, another bubble, and she can't keep it inside her mouth the way she thought she could, and it bursts out and onto her shirt and onto the floor, and she is barely three steps away from the dinner table.

Rasia rushes to her as Oleg throws his napkin down on the table and pushes his chair backward. Rasia's back softens as her big, squishy arm extends around Lena, and she leads the girl, shaking, to the bathroom. Oleg takes his big glass and goes into the living room to sit on the couch and watch soap operas from Russia on the big-screen TV. Once he finishes the glass, he will start to snore, and he will snore on the couch until it is time to snore in the bedroom.

Vaclav pulls his feet up onto his chair to keep them away from the puke and looks down at the floor. Lena's puke is not like his puke. His puke, behind the swings at school, when he has eaten too much and swung too much, is substantial and often borscht-colored. Lena's puke is like the sea foam on the beach at Coney Island, frothy, stale, and not as yellow as pee.

Vaclav rises from his chair, careful not to step in the lovely puke of his lovely assistant, and reaches for a dishrag with which to clean up Lena's too-small mess.

In the bathroom, Rasia dabs at Lena's face with a wet washcloth. Are Lena's eyes really so dark and huge, Rasia wonders, or do they just seem this way because her skin is so pale, her face so small and delicate? Lena sits on the seat-down toilet, holding her pukey T-shirt balled in her hands. Rasia decides, while cleaning Lena's frightened face, to clean and dry Lena's shirt, and not to mention the incident to the Aunt.

Rasia wonders if anyone has talked to Lena about the girl things that she would talk to a daughter about if she had a daughter. She wonders if one day Lena will have to ask the Aunt for a training bra to train her breasts to do what breasts are supposed to do, or if she will save her allowance money and go by herself to the department store. Rasia wonders if Lena misses having a mother, and then tells herself that this is stupid. Of course she does. It is hard, in your mind, where to put Lena; it is hard to know what to do with so much pity. Rasia tells Lena to wait in the bathroom while she fetches a clean T-shirt. Lena sits on the toilet, shirtless, arms crossed against her rib cage, staring at the tile.

HARD TO KNOW

...

When Rasia walks Lena home, she notices that Lena holds her hand harder than usual. Maybe this is all in her mind. It seems, also, to Rasia that Lena is skinnier than usual, but with children, it is hard to know.

When Rasia opens the door to take Lena inside, and turns on the light, and looks around, she sees that everything is the same as it was the night before. Rasia's best guess is that the Aunt has not been home, not to clean up the mess or to add to it. Lena has been left alone. There is no doubt in Rasia's mind that this is not a place for a little girl to live. Of this she is sure, and this, this is hard to know.

VACLAV DOES EXCELLENT THINKING IN THE BUBBLE BATH

...

Vaclav wakes up early, without any help from his alarm clock. This morning, Vaclav has a clear, steely resolve to win his campaign for permission to perform a magic show on the boardwalk at Coney Island.

Still in his pajamas, he sits at the desk in his room, takes out his thesaurus, and begins a list.

EVIDENCE TO PARENTS OF THE TRUSTWORTHINESS OF VACLAV FOR PROMOTING PERMISSION TO PERFORM MAGIC SHOW ON THE BOARDWALK OF CONEY ISLAND:

1. *Room cleaning*
2. *Chore doing*
3. *Table setting*
4. *Homework finishing*
5. *Grade achieving*
6. *Extracurricular accomplishments*
7. *Devotion to career of magic*

Vaclav replaces his pencil in his pencil cup, pleased for the moment with his list. He then pads gently to the bathroom to brush his teeth, careful not to wake his snoring mother and father.

Vaclav runs a bubble bath, because a bubble bath is where he does excellent thinking about his magic. He lies back, submerging himself only to the ears, and listens to the sounds of his body, the sounds of his house, through the water. His heartbeat is the same as the thump of something too heavy and hard in the clothes dryer of Mrs. Ruvinova upstairs. The gurgle of his tummy is the same as the gurgle of the pipes in the wall.

Vaclav closes his eyes, and the roar in his ears is the roar of an excited crowd. He is big and tall, now a man. He is dressed in a tuxedo that shines black and blue in the stage lights. Behind him, a curtain lifts to reveal Lena, in her own future adult body, strapped to a spinning wheel for the knife-throwing act. The audience gasps. Vaclav, from thin air, pulls out a handful of sharp knives. He fans the knives like playing cards and holds them up to the audience, to increase their anxiety. To demonstrate the sharpness and realness of the knives, he cuts a large gash in the curtain behind him. To make the audience think of the terror of such a blade piercing Lena's beautiful skin, he throws a tomato into the air and slices it in two. Lena, spinning on the wheel, looks afraid but is not, really. Really she is trusting in Vaclav, and trusting in the precision, the perfection, of the act, for they have fine-tuned it over many years of practicing together.

Still, she is attuned completely and totally to Vaclav's every muscle twitch, every blink of his eye. Even invisible signals he may give her with his mind—she listens for these like a radio that hears the silent songs in the air.

There is a loud knock on the bathroom door.

Oleg often needs to pee suddenly in the morning, because big glasses of vodka do not sit happily in the piss belly of a fifty-year-old man.

Vaclav is always telling his father that the word in English is *bladder,* and his father always responds that learning how to name piss and shit is not why he came all this way from Russia. He came from Russia, he is always telling Vaclav, for Vaclav to learn about stocks and dollars and American business, and to buy his papa a hot tub full of American Hooter waitresses one day.

Vaclav hoists himself out of the tub and plants one dripping foot on the bath mat, one dripping hand unlocking the door, the other dripping hand covering his you-know-what, so that his papa will not make fun.

As soon as the door is unlocked, Oleg bursts in, without giving slippery Vaclav any time to plunge back under the cover of the bubbles and water. He sees his son holding what he should not be holding, and lets out a roaring laugh.

Vaclav plops back into the tub and sinks down while Oleg pees, groaning with relief. Vaclav dunks his head under the water, to hide from the yellow smell that is in the steam, that is everywhere.

Oleg finishes his peeing and puts everything away inside of his pajama pants. Then he looks at the tub, looks at his son submerged under the water, his eyes squeezed shut. Oleg grunts and leaves the bathroom but does not close the door.

It is not easy for Vaclav to return to his vision of the future, but he keeps this vision in his mind, in the back of it, so that his dream is never far away from him. He dries his body and wraps himself in a large bath towel, then pads into the hallway, slowly, listening and sensing. His father has already fallen back to sleep; he can hear his parents snoring together in their bedroom. This is good. He will have time to lay the groundwork for his plans.

Vaclav takes great care to comb his hair, to tuck in his shirt, to wear an outfit for school that will please his mother. He tiptoes into the kitchen, and without turning on the lights, he silently sets the table. He even fills the teakettle, and puts it on the stove, and lights the stove, carefully. Because his mother has taught him that it is possible to turn the knob of the stove and leave gas pouring out with no fire to burn it up, and that this will explode the house like Chernobyl, he makes sure that the hiss of the gas meets the snap-snap-snap that makes fire to heat the water for the tea. Vaclav even slices bread and makes toast, and arranges the toast nicely on plates, and puts out his mother's favorite jam for breakfast. Then Vaclav sits at the table and waits.

He can hear the alarm clock buzz in his parents' room, then his mother clunking around in the bathroom, and finally his father coughing his morning cough, so Vaclav knows he won't have to wait long.

When Rasia enters the kitchen, she takes in everything with her eyes. Vaclav can see her catalogue the room, and he can see her begin to smile. But her smile is the wrong sort of smile right away. It is not a happy smile, it is a nervous smile, a smile that goes straight across her face instead of curling up at the ends.

"Vaclav, we have to talk about what is happening in the bathroom," she says.

Even though he does not know what, Vaclav is sure that he has done something wrong. He suddenly feels embarrassed and anxious, because Rasia is staring at him and looking nervous, and this is not good.

"I know now about your bath time," she says, trying to speak softly and gently. She wants to have an open, supportive conversation with her son, because everyone says to talk to kids about these things so that there is no secret and no shame. She means to sound warm, nonjudgmental, but straightforward. Like Oprah.

"You go in there at nighttime so no one will know? Is this happening every night?" Rasia can feel that she is not sounding like Oprah.

Vaclav knows now what she is talking about, and he knows that he was not doing this thing in the bathtub. Vaclav knows now that when his father came into the bathroom, and he covered his *mekki* with his hand because he was embarrassed for his father to see it, his father thought that he was doing masturbating in the bathtub. Vaclav knows about this from talking to boys at school who know a lot about it from their older brothers or from television stations that they have at their homes.

Rasia takes a deep breath and tries again.

"Where did you learn this?" She is still meaning to make this conversation a nice conversation, but it is coming out all wrong, and she is sounding like a KGB commandant instead of a cool American mother. She doesn't want to have the same horrible conversation that she had with her own mother. She doesn't want Vaclav growing up like she did, believing that if you touch or even scratch yourself for an itch your buhguhgie will rot and fall off on the ground and shrivel up like an old potato.

Vaclav knows that no matter what he says, she won't believe him, and that if he argues with her, she'll talk more about it, and she'll ask more questions, and he'll die of being embarrassed. If he denies it, she'll think that he's a liar in addition to being a person who does masturbating in the tub at night. Vaclav knows that it is best to just stand and be quiet and be still.

"Vaclav, this is okay to talk about; you can tell me."

"Okay," says Vaclav, and, grabbing his backpack, he bolts for the door without even bringing up the question of permission to have a show on the boardwalk of Coney Island.

"Have a nice day of school!" she shouts after him, grateful herself for his escape.

FAMOUS AMERICANS

...

Only after Vaclav runs out of the house does Rasia notice that he made toast for her, that he set the table so nicely, took out her favorite jam, that he even put up water for tea. Rasia turns off the stove and sits down at the table. At first she has a panic because she thinks the list is homework that Vaclav has forgotten, and she is about to run out the door to give it to him, until she sees the words *parents* and then *magic show* and stops. She reads his list, all the reasons he should be allowed to do a magic show.

She wants him to stop with the magic, all the time magic. But she understands.

They spent a long time waiting to come to America. A long time she waited to have Vaclav, because things were so terrible, and then there was glasnost, and just when Rasia thought things were going to be getting better, they got worse, and everything came apart.

She went, eight months pregnant with Vaclav, to wait in line to get on a list to go to America. Oleg had a good job as an architect, he didn't want to leave, but he said if she wanted to wait in a line and put their names on a list, then fine. She didn't realize it then, because she was still a young person and still in love, but he was the same then that he is now, his tuchas always stuck to whatever chair he's sitting on, no matter how uncomfortable.

They told her there was a limit to the number of Russian Jews America would take, that it could be years. They told her they could get her on a plane to another country the very next week. She told them thank you, and that she would wait. Vaclav was born, and Oleg lost his job just like everyone else, just like she knew he would. Now he was a new father who couldn't pay for his son's diapers, and he went out every day to complain with the other men. He came home smelling of vodka, but Rasia thought if she could get him out, if they could get to America, everything would be fine, and he would be sweet again and make his jokes again.

The economy got worse, and Vaclav got bigger, and they

kept waiting. In the meantime, she bought books and tapes and learned English and taught Vaclav. She didn't want him to be scared to leave his home, like she was, she wanted him to be excited to be American. She paid a small fortune for black-market English books for children about famous Americans, about Abraham Lincoln, Rosa Parks, George Washington Carver, and Molly Pitcher, but his favorite, the one he asked her to read again and again, every single night, was the book about Harry Houdini.

Vaclav especially liked the part of the book about how Houdini came to America when he was four, just like Vaclav, how he became America's most famous magician, how he amazed President Theodore Roosevelt with his magic and performed at the World's Fair, about how he could escape from heavy chains, how he could jump, handcuffed, from bridges. He liked the parts about how Houdini struggled with his act, how he practiced and never gave up.

Rasia thought that this Houdini person probably drove his mother to an early grave, worrying her with all his death-defying feats and doing Chinese water torture, and was not someone Vaclav should be so interested in. But Vaclav wanted to hear a story about a little boy who came to America and became a big, brave, magical man, and this she understood.

Every night she read Vaclav the book about Houdini, until he knew every word. When they finally got their papers and Rasia told Vaclav that they were moving to America, he already knew all about the place they were going to live: Brooklyn, the home of Coney Island, where Harry Houdini performed his first magic show. It was coincidence only—Rasia knew someone who was in Brighton Beach and could give her a good job doing bookkeeping and help them to find a house—but to Vaclav, it was a sign.

For Oleg, in America, it was worse. He didn't have the right license to be an architect in America; he would have to go to school, take tests to prove that he knew what he already knew. He told her that he would drive the cab until he could pay for it, but all he ever spent his money on was the satellite on the roof for the Russian TV channels and vodka to drink while he watched it. He hated going out; he hated when the store clerk treated him like an imbecile because he didn't know words for drain cleaner or cotton balls. Rasia remembered the Oleg she fell in love with, who was a charmer, who was famous in a small-town way, flirting with old ladies, always giving gum and toys from his pockets to children, who sang songs to make her laugh. She knew now that she would probably never get him back.

LENA IS IN A MOOD OF LAUGHING

...

Vaclav counts the steps as he walks along Avenue U, from Thirteenth Street, to Twelfth, to Eleventh, all the way down to Seventh, where he turns the corner and sees Lena sitting on the stoop outside her house, swinging her string-bean legs. He is always excited to see her, but today he is especially excited, because he has a big plan to share with her. Vaclav smiles, and waves, and trips a little bit on the sidewalk right in front of her, but he does not fall down.

Lena tries not to, but she laughs very loudly at Vaclav. Vaclav is glad that Lena is in a mood of laughing, because this will make it easier for him to persuade her of the new big plans.

"Did you get permission?" Lena asks Vaclav, as she hops off the ledge.

"Is very good English, Lena!" says Vaclav. Lena rolls her eyes at his flattery, hands him her stack of books, and they begin their walk together toward Public School 238.

"Okay, okay. Sheesh. Tough audience. Getting permission is not the best way to go. Getting permission is not for this. This, which is part of destiny. Not permission needed."

"You no get," Lena grumbles.

"I can have this permission if I want, but it is not the way. This is a test, of the universe for us, and we must prove ourselves and overcome this adversity. We should be thankful for adversity, for giving us chance to forge our strength, like Houdini, who never gave up trying, and was always adding to his escape act more chains and more locks." Lena rolls her eyes again, because Vaclav is saying this about Houdini and adversity and destiny all the time.

"We do by ourselves. Is less trouble. Is better, okay?" Vaclav stops walking and pleads with Lena with his eyes. Lena plants her hands on her tiny hips.

"No. Your mother must give permission."

"Lena!"

"I will not do without permission. Is trouble," Lena says, and stomps ahead of Vaclav.

"Lena, no trouble, will not be trouble," Vaclav pleads. "We will plan by ourselves. No one will know. We will have secret show, on Coney Island, with secret acts, and we will plan in secret. No trouble. None."

Lena likes to have secrets, this Vaclav knows. She slows down her walk and tilts her head just a little. Sunlight glows around the black fuzz of hair that has escaped her French braid.

"Lena, since you are the best secret keeper, of course, you will be in charge of the secret planning of the secret act. You will be the master." Vaclav knows that this will please Lena, that this is the key. Vaclav also knows that he will still be the master of the secret planning.

"No."

"What?"

"You are thinking that you will still be boss. No, is fake, I will not do."

Vaclav quickens his step, thinking about this worst-case scenario. This is a list that he did not write down but a list that he composed only in his head.

WORST-CASE SCENARIOS:

1. *Permission is not given to have show on boardwalk*

AND

2. *Lena will not agree to show without permission of parents*

Vaclav thinks about doing the show without Lena, but the show cannot go on without Lena, even as the show must go on. There is no show without Lena. Lena is necessary for all the illusions; they have already accomplished so much together. Lena is irreplaceable. Even if Lena was replaceable, no girls at school will replace her; none of them even speak to Vaclav or look at him in the hallway.

"Plan is not good, Vaclav. . . ." Lena says, trying to be gentle but interrupting Vaclav's thoughts anyway.

"Don't think now. We'll talk later. No more talking now," says Vaclav.

Lena makes a grumbling in the back of her throat, and they continue down Seventh Street toward Avenue P, toward school.

THE WAY THINGS ARE AT SCHOOL

...

P.S. 238 is a school that was built very long ago, with big bricks and enormous doors and windows. There is a huge door in the front of the school, where parents and teachers and visitors can enter. The students, including Vaclav and Lena, must use the side doors.

Each morning, students play on the side playground, which is just blacktop with lots of lines drawn in different places for hopscotch, and four square, and basketball, and marbles. Kids also play cards, sitting on warm asphalt. When the bell rings, the boys line up at the boys' door and the girls line up at the girls' door. The boys' door is on the right, and above the door there is a stone plaque that says BOYS. The girls door is on the left, and above the door there is a stone plaque that says GIRLS. The school hasn't used the separate entrances in an official capacity for years, but the boys still refuse to walk through the GIRLS door, and though the girls dare one another, giggling, to walk through the BOYS door, no one ever does.

When Lena and Vaclav arrive this morning, they have missed all the playtime because they dawdled on the walk, talking about the act. Vaclav joins the end of the boys' line, and Lena joins the end of the girls' line. The lines slowly feed into the building single file. Vaclav and Lena look at their feet. There is no girl for Lena to talk to and no boy for Vaclav to talk to.

Inside, they both climb two flights of stairs to the third floor. Vaclav goes to Mr. Hunter's room, and Lena to Ms. Walldinger's room. They will not see each other until ESL class, when they will both descend two flights of stairs, with all the other kids who have stinky lunches.

In Mr. Hunter's class, Vaclav is the only stink-lunch ESL kid at the green table. The other boy is Ulysses, and the two girls are Nachalie and Genesis. Each table has two boys and two girls; no table has more than one stink-lunch kid.

On the table is a Do It NOW! worksheet. There are always four Xeroxes of the Do It NOW! worksheet on each table, and the children are to begin work on them immediately as they enter the classroom.

Vaclav thinks this must be the best part of the day for Mr. Hunter. During this time, Mr. Hunter stands outside the door to the hallway, one foot in, one foot out, looking for straggling students, even when everyone is already sitting in the classroom. Next door, Ms. Troani also straddles her classroom threshold, and they talk to each other like people on TV, with lots of jokes and gestures and winks and laughing.

Vaclav focuses his mind, trying too hard not to think about Lena or about getting permission, and reads the Do It NOW! There is a paragraph about fires. Then there are questions about fire safety. There are directions to the children to discuss with their group what they would save from their homes in case of a fire.

Vaclav knows what he would take, and it does not help at all to distract his mind from his problem with Lena.

"Hey, V! What would you bring?" The kids in Vaclav's class don't say his whole name, just the first letter. Vee. Vaclav doesn't know for sure if this is a friendly thing, a familiar thing, or a bad, mean thing. It doesn't seem very bad, if it is bad at all.

Vaclav decides to give a dishonest answer to the question, because the real thing that he would save in a fire is embarrassing to say. The real thing he would save in a fire is Lena.

"Collection of David Copperfield videos, I would save. Of course." Vaclav thinks that this is a safe answer, because all the other kids talk about videos. Immediately, he knows that he is right, because they all smile. "Or my favorite book, *Harry Houdini: Famous American.*"

"I thought he was gonna say some Polish thing or something," says Genesis.

"My family is not from Poland. My family is from Russia," says Vaclav. "You might be confuse because my name is Polish, because I am named for my great-grandfather, who was Polish and was called Vaclav. But I am Russian."

"Sorry. Russian, Polish. Whatever, same difference anyway, right?" says Genesis.

"No . . ." Vaclav begins, and trails off, because Nachalie is already interrupting to take his side.

"Genesis, it's like that time that boy said you were a Mexican and you cried because your dad is just from Mexico but you're Dominican like your mom, right? And plus, it's like everyone's American, right?" says Nachalie.

"Who's David Copperfield?" asks Ulysses.

"David Copperfield is most amazing living American magician since Harry Houdini," says Vaclav, with pride.

"I think David Blaine is cooler. Isn't David Copperfield like an old guy? David Blaine froze himself in ice. That's crazy. I could do that if I wanted to, I would just never want to," says Ulysses.

"Is that what you want to do? Freeze yourself in ice? That's disgusting, my mom said. Like, he just makes a scene and stuff," says Nachalie.

"No, I practice magic and the art of illusion." Vaclav looks at his tablemates, watching him so intently as he explains about the art of magic, the art of illusion, and he becomes excited and invigorated, and he decides to do something he has never done before; he decides to take a risk, in front of these, his first possible fans.

"This," says Vaclav, pulling open the zipper of his backpack, "is video of famous David Copperfield show of illusions and magic."

Vaclav places the case dramatically on the center of the table. He has it with him because its newness has not yet worn off; he continues to be excited by the sight of it in his backpack, though he's had it for months. He sometimes likes to slide his hand into his backpack during class and feel the plastic case.

Nachalie laughs. Genesis laughs, but she doesn't know why she's laughing. Ulysses picks up the case, opens it, and takes out the disk.

"This is so bootleg!" He laughs.

Vaclav grabs the disk from Ulysses's hand and reaches out to grab the case, but Ulysses pulls his hand out of reach. Ulysses gives him a look like *Whoa, man, patience!* Like there is no reason at all for Vaclav to be even just a little bit upset, which he is.

Holding the case away from Vaclav, Ulysses opens it and shows it to the girls. He points to the label.

"Look, this label is handwritten! This DVD is totally bootleg." He hands the case back to Vaclav.

"What is this bootleg?" Vaclav asks.

"Oh, you know, like when in the tunnel to the B train there's that man with a blanket out on the ground, and DVDs all over it . . ."

"Faw fuh fie dollah!" Genesis imitates the call of the man, the underground man, the video hawker.

Yes, thinks Vaclav, he has seen this man before, in the subway, on the way to Coney Island. Like all adults he meets on the subway or the bus, he behaves toward him as per his mother's instructions—he points his eyes at the ground and continues on his way, never staring but always keeping his wits about him, never, ever letting his wits get away.

"This is from that guy, or from some other guy like that guy," Ulysses says. Mr. Hunter clears his throat; class is starting. Ulysses lowers his voice to a whisper. "They just make a copy of the real thing, and then they sell it real cheap, like on the street or whatever."

"But my father bought this for me. . . ." Vaclav says.

"Yeah, he did," says Ulysses, "from the bootleg guy."

Vaclav decides to do much research, to get to the bottom of this, this bootleg issue, as he is not trusting Ulysses, and to find out why the great magician David Copperfield could be so taken advantage of.

In the meantime, Vaclav must get through the day. Vaclav must try to quiet his thoughts of Lena and her big *no,* thoughts of his mother and the terrifying conversation, and especially thoughts of his father, who tells on his son instead of talking about things or being fatherly and sharing adult secrets like fathers on American television.

But it is especially hard to stop thinking about how the video that his father gave him as a gift may not be a real video but may be even a video practically stolen from Mr. David Copperfield, which is not the way of the magician and is to Vaclav very disturbing, because he must go around the world earning everything so that one day he will earn the trust and the belief of the nation and his many fans, and also, this video, which might be a terrible thing, was, until now, the best thing his father had ever done for him in his whole entire life besides giving him the opportunity to come as a human being into the earth and into existence, which is not something that Vaclav feels he should be in particular thankful about, because what else was he going to do?

STINK-LUNCHERS

...

Vaclav is excited to see Lena during ESL class, to tell her about the bootleg DVD, because she will make him feel better, either by saying something smart about the DVD or just by listening to him. This is something Lena does for Vaclav; she makes everything better just by being there. This is something that Vaclav hopes he is also able to do for Lena.

On the door of the ESL room there is a poster that says WELCOME in many different languages, including some languages, like Russian and Japanese and Chinese and Korean and Arabic, that use their very own alphabets.

When Vaclav walks into the ESL class, he sees, written on the blackboard, *Welcome! Please take out your homework and compare your answers with a partner's.* Suddenly, Vaclav feels terrible. He has not completed his homework. This is unusual for Vaclav; he always finishes his homework. It is a half-truth, or a lie, to say that Vaclav has not completed his homework. The whole truth is that Vaclav has not even started his ESL homework *and* that he has not finished it. The truth is that Vaclav forgot about his ESL homework altogether. When his mother asked him if all his homework was finished, he fudged the truth a tiny bit, and said yes, even though he had just one more thing to do: an ESL worksheet. He had planned to do it later, but then so many things happened, and he forgot.

Now Vaclav's bad feeling of forgetting to do his homework is mixing in with the bad feeling about the bootleg video and the bad feeling of Lena's *no* and the bad feeling from the terrible conversation with his mother, and these feelings, all mixed together, are pushing hot tears into Vaclav's eyes.

"Seats! Everyone take your seats!" says Mrs. Bisbano.

This sentence, which Mrs. Bisbano uses frequently, is confusing to Vaclav, because he knows she means for all the students to sit in their seats and she does not mean that all the students should take their seats, and besides, where would they take them?

Now Vaclav does not have time to tell Lena about the bootleg video. Also, he would like to quietly and privately tell Mrs. Bisbano about forgetting, for the first time all year, to do his homework, and he would like to tell her that he will bring it in to be checked tomorrow, but it is too late now to do anything at all.

Lena walks into the classroom with Marina and Kristina, the only popular girls who are also in ESL. They have blond hair, and they both wear it exactly the same, in ponytails on the side of their heads that look as if they should make them tip over. Marina and Kristina are talking to Lena, and Lena is smiling. Vaclav waves at Lena so that she will see him and come over to him, because he wants so badly to tell her about the bootleg DVD before class starts. He would also like her to sit next to him, or in the seat in front of him or behind him, as she usually does.

Lena looks quickly at Vaclav, but it seems as if his calling her over is not strong enough, and the pulling of Marina and Kristina is stronger, because Lena follows along behind them and then sits with them. Vaclav is still watching Lena sitting across the room, far away from him, when Mrs. Bisbano comes up from behind.

"Vaclav, where is your homework?" She says this in a regular tone of voice, as if it is not the most frightening thing to say, ever, in the whole world.

"Uhhhh . . ." says Vaclav, which is really not a thing to say and is actually just a sound to make.

"Where is your homework, Vaclav?"

Vaclav tries to tell Mrs. Bisbano how sorry he is, and how he will make it up as soon as possible, how he will even stay inside during lunchtime just to make it up, but when he tries to open his mouth to say these words, only crying comes out.

Mrs. Bisbano leans closer to Vaclav and says, "It's okay. Go to the bathroom and blow your nose, and we can talk about this after class is over."

Vaclav tries to say that yes, that is okay, but his voice is interrupted by more crying trying to come up in his throat.

Vaclav looks over at Lena, and she is looking away. Everyone else is looking at him. Lena is looking away.

ESKIMOLOGY

...

After Vaclav came back to ESL from the bathroom, Mrs. Bisbano told him that he could get a free pass for his homework if he brought it in the next day, since he had never missed an assignment before, and Vaclav felt much better. He didn't get a chance to talk to Lena, since Lena wasn't in his group for projects, and after class, she left really quickly with Marina and Kristina, before Vaclav could even pack up his pencils and erasers.

The rest of the day goes by very slowly, and even though Vaclav tries to pay attention to the teacher, his eyes keep wandering to the clock. When school is finally over, Vaclav waits outside for Lena. He stands in a spot where he can see everyone coming out of both doors and they can all see him. He knows that from this spot he will see Lena when she comes out. Vaclav always waits for Lena outside her house in the morning, and outside the school in the afternoon, and this is how he makes sure, every day, that they will walk together. Vaclav wonders now for only a moment if Lena would wait for him if he did not wait for her, but he knows that this is silly, and that yes, of course she would.

Vaclav stands and waits and thinks about the playground. In the winter, when it is very cold outside, and all around is snow that is very dirty with rocks and is mixed up with the frozen ground underneath, this always reminds Vaclav of the first step when his mother bakes, when she mixes together sugar and vanilla and brown sugar and some butter and an egg. This makes the dirty snow look like something good and wonderful, and it makes Vaclav feel warm, even in the cold.

Vaclav thinks about how sometimes, even when it is cold outside, you might feel warm because you have people or thoughts of people that warm you up like a fire, or make you feel that you are an Eskimo who is not really bothered by extreme cold, even if you feel the extreme cold. Other times you might feel that everything in the whole world is cold for a reason, and that it is cold for only you, and you can see all the other people with fires to warm them up and you feel that you will be cold forever. Sometimes you can feel cold like that even in the summertime.

Right now it is fall, and there is a chilly breeze, but Vaclav is waiting for Lena, and he can feel the sun on his face, and he feels warm.

But then as he waits longer and longer he feels colder and colder, especially as he is watching all the other kids coming out of the school, and some of them are brothers and sisters hating and loving each other, and some of them are friends and they are giggling, and some of them are friends and they are running out to play ball on the macadam, and some of them are the Guatemalan kids whose mamas are already buying them warm churros rolled in crunchy sugar from the lady who sells them on the corner.

Then suddenly there is Lena with four girls from her class. She looks directly at Vaclav, right in the eyes, and then she opens her mouth and laughs loudly at something that one of the girls has said, and then they all turn together and walk toward the street as though Vaclav is not even there, waiting at the most central location where he can see everyone and everyone can see him.

Vaclav follows behind Lena and her new friends, watching only the sidewalk go by under his feet as he walks all the way from Avenue P to Avenue U and Seventh Street. When he gets to Lena's aunt's house, he sees Lena break off from the pack and toss her hair and run up the stairs to the front door and go and shut the door behind her without looking behind to see Vaclav, standing alone, feeling cold.

HAPPY FAMILY KEBAB HOUSE

...

Vaclav drops his backpack on the sidewalk and opens up the frontmost pocket to check that there is, in between all the crummy bits and pencils and old candy wrappers, one dollar in change, and there is, so he walks two blocks to Happy Family Kebab House to have a drink and think about his plan of what to do next.

Happy Family Kebab House is right next door to the Russian supermarket where his mother sometimes goes to buy treats, always pointing out what is a rip-off and what she could make better with one hand chopped off.

Happy Family Kebab House has wood paneling and a big glass case full of big trays of food, like lamb kebabs under a piece of Saran wrap and stuffed cabbages that are crispy on the top, and handmade sausages of lamb and onion that are bright pink because they fry those for you right when you order them. Vaclav opens the drink case and takes out one Dr Pepper and puts it on the counter.

"One dollar exactly," says Zev the owner, and Vaclav puts

one dollar exactly on the counter in change. Usually he likes to chat with Zev, especially when Zev tries out new English on Vaclav, but today Vaclav is not in the mood.

Zev takes the Dr Pepper can and slides it into a brown paper bag that is the exact perfect size for one can, and he hands it to Vaclav, who takes the Dr Pepper to the seat by the window. He sits there for a very long time, feeling very sad for himself, although he is at the same time very happy to feel cozy inside of his jacket, and to drink the Dr Pepper from the can with a straw, and to look out the window at the people walking outside on the sidewalk, and even though this soda is almost one-half the cost of a possible trip to Coney Island to see the Sideshow, he thinks sometimes you know that it is a very long road to become a famous magician, and sometimes you have to spend your last dollar on buying a soda so that you have something to be grateful for that day, even if it lasts just one small piece of time.

Vaclav takes a deep breath and reminds himself that these are, in the scheme of things, very small problems. Vaclav reminds himself that there are some things that are, in the universe, destiny. Sometimes a young magician must remind himself that his dreams are written in the stars. He takes the Dr Pepper out of the paper bag and smushes the bag flat on the table. Using a pencil from his bag, he begins an important list on the brown paper bag.

THINGS THAT *ARE:*

1. *One day being a famous magician*
2. *Lena being lovely assistant*
3. *Perseverance toward those goals in spite of any and every obstacle*

NO MATTER WHAT

. . .

Vaclav knows what he will do. He will wait for Lena every single day in front of her house to go to school, and he will wait for her after school, and walk with her, and talk to her and make her many offers to persuade her in some way to agree to work on the show, with or without permission from his parents. Vaclav bounds out of the Happy Family Kebab House, feeling again like an Eskimo who can walk many miles in the cold, and runs home four blocks, with his backpack flopping about on his back the whole way. Vaclav is determined to do his homework very fast in order to have time to think and plan. Just the thought of homework gives Vaclav the idea for the offer he will make to Lena, and he knows at once that it will work one hundred percent.

The very next morning Vaclav is waiting for Lena outside of her house to walk with her to school and to propose the offer he knows she will not refuse.

When Lena opens the door and sees Vaclav, she stops with one hand still on the doorknob, and stands and looks at him and rolls her big brown eyes. She is wearing her hair in a ponytail on the side of her head, which is not a way she has ever worn her hair before. She sighs out loud, and then stomps down the stairs to the sidewalk and begins walking toward school without stopping to talk to Vaclav.

Vaclav feels confident, and trots along after her, and begins to make his pitch.

"Lena, I have idea for you. We will continue to work on the

show. We will continue to try very hard to get permission to do the show without trouble." Lena keeps walking. Vaclav continues, "But if necessary, we will do our show without permission, in secret." But still, Lena does not slow down, or look behind, even to tell Vaclav no. She just keeps walking and pretending that he is not even there.

So that she will not be run over by cars, Lena stops at the corner of Eighth Street and Avenue R, because that is a very busy intersection. Because of this, she is forced to stand next to Vaclav, but she keeps her face hard and refuses to look at him.

"I will do your homework," says Vaclav, and he can see from the side that one of her eyebrows goes way up and is making small wrinkles by the fuzz of her hair.

"All of it," he says, and the eyebrow stays up. "Every day." Lena's eyebrow falls.

"ESL?" she asks.

"Even ESL," he says.

She takes a deep breath and looks him right in his eyes.

"*Da*," she says. "But secret only. My friends are not knowing, and we do no talk at school." She looks both ways, and when she is sure no one is around, she says, "We meet at your house after school. Not outside. And no walking to school at all."

"Okay! Is settled. Here. After school. We begin practice."

"First homework," Lena says. "Then begin. Bye-bye!"

Lena takes off, walking so quickly that Vaclav is left behind on the corner, watching the cars whiz by. He is so excited to have his assistant back, willing or unwilling, that it doesn't occur to him to feel hurt or sad. It doesn't occur to him that Lena, who has been his only friend since they were small, does not want to be seen with him. He thinks she will be his lovely assistant forever, and one day his wife. Vaclav doesn't feel sad on this day, the day he stops walking her to and from school, the day she tells him not to embarrass her in front of her new friends.

TO BE HER SOMEWHERE

...

After school, Vaclav does exactly as is required by Lena. Mostly. Yes, he does some things that are not what Lena wanted. He waits for her outside of the building after school, yes. He gets his backpack all ready before the class even ends so that he can rush outside as soon as the bell rings, yes. He sits and waits, his body electric with anticipation for the moment the bell will ring, yes. He rushes outside the moment the bell rings, yes. He runs in the hallway, ignoring previous no-running-in-the-hallway warnings, yes. He sprints outside and hides himself stealthily behind a tree, where he can see the door from which Lena will exit, yes. He follows her home at a short distance, close enough to hear her laughing with Marina and Kristina, yes. But, but! He stays behind the shrubs and mailboxes and cars so that Lena does not know that he is there, and does not even know that he can hear her.

No, he does not leave Lena totally alone until it is time to practice the act. No, he does not go directly home to wait for her at his house, which is what she has asked of him. Instead, he follows her all the way to the Aunt's house. Vaclav has done a nice thing, following her, so that she has never really been alone. Vaclav thinks that this is a nice thing, to always be there for someone, even if it is not exactly what Lena wants.

Vaclav watches from the street, but he does not understand exactly what Lena is doing. She is walking home with Marina and Kristina, saying goodbye to them on the sidewalk, laughing, and then she is skipping up the stairs to go inside the Aunt's house, putting her hand on the latch of the screen door to go inside the Aunt's house, but she is not going inside. Vaclav watches from behind a big blue mail-drop box across the street as Lena puts her hand on the door and as Lena watches Marina and Kristina turn the corner. As soon as they do, Lena skips down the stairs without going inside the Aunt's house at all. Vaclav pops out from behind the big blue mail-drop box and smiles and waves. Lena stops skipping.

Vaclav can see that Lena is angry, because she makes her face into a face of angriness, not her usual silly face of concentrating, and because she takes a deep breath and her eyes get big and she stares hard at Vaclav.

Vaclav knows that he did not do exactly as Lena has asked him to do. He is not sure, however, why Lena is angry at him. They always do everything together. He does not consider that Lena might want to be without him, might want to say and think and do things without him, might want to do these things with other people and not with him. He's thinking only that Lena is now having friends who are girls and this is girl time and is a natural thing, as he sees on television. He thinks that Lena will be excited that she is able to see him as soon as girl time is over, that he is there to meet her and walk with her from the Aunt's house back to his house, excited that they will waste no time and can start right away with practicing for the act.

Vaclav knows that Lena needs help doing her homework, but he does not know about Lena's feelings of having nowhere to go. He does not know the reasons that Lena would not go inside the

Aunt's house, not even for one single second to put down her knapsack and to drink a glass of water and to use the toilet. Vaclav knows only the letter, not the spirit of the laws in Lena's life, and sometimes he doesn't even know all the letters.

Vaclav does not know that to Lena, he is a place to go instead of nowhere. If he knew, he might be happy to be her somewhere, but he does not know.

TO BE NOWHERE

...

Right up until she found out that Vaclav was following her, Lena was having a good day. The popular girls, who had been ignoring her and leaving her out and not inviting her to their birthday parties since forever, asked her to sit with them at the lunch table, and they talked in really fast English about many things, and mostly she did not join with them, but she did laugh and agree. Lena, in general, does not talk, because her English is not good enough.

Marina and Kristina are in Lena's ESL class because they are also not good at English. They are, in fact, even worse than Lena. The difference is that Marina and Kristina do not have to feel ashamed like Lena, because they came from Russia only two years ago. When someone asks them how long they have been here, in America, and they say two years, everyone, parents and teachers and even other kids, is impressed and tells them what a good job they are doing, and to keep practicing, and that they are so smart.

Lena has been in America since she was a baby. When she

came she lived in her *babushka*'s apartment, and she knew only her *babushka*, and her *babushka* spoke to Lena in the only language she knew, which was Russian, and so it became the only language that Lena knew.

When Lena began kindergarten, she spoke only Russian, so for half the day she went to ESL class, which is for students who don't speak English well or at all. And Lena felt always shy and afraid to talk out loud and to practice the English that she was learning, and when she went home, no one in her house spoke any English, just Russian. At home, it felt so good to say what she wanted to and to go to the bathroom exactly when she wanted to and to not have to worry about raising her hand and remembering what it was she was supposed to say when she wanted to go to the bathroom or, worse, say the wrong thing when she was called on. The worst was when something Lena said made everyone laugh, and she did not know why.

When people ask Lena how long she has been here, in America, and she says, "Since I was a baby," they do not say anything like what a good job she is doing or "Keep practicing" or anything, because they think she has had plenty of time to learn to speak English, and they assume that she is probably more special-ed than ESL. So even though Lena is a very loud person on the inside, and very funny and smart, and sings songs and thinks big, loud thoughts, on the outside she seems quiet and shy.

No one knows how smart Lena is, because she doesn't answer questions in class, and the teachers always frown at her, and she is always the last to finish her worksheets. No one realizes that even though numbers are the same in every language, it is very hard to understand long division when the person telling you what is the quotient and what is the divisor and how to carry the one is speaking a language you don't understand. Everyone has the wrong idea of Lena, except Vaclav.

But today was different; today was new. Today Lena sat at the big lunch table with the cool girls instead of alone with Vaclav in the corner by the garbage cans. She didn't feel weird and left out because she was the only girl without any other girlfriends. Lena felt happy, because at the lunch table no one seemed to notice that she didn't speak. In fact, it seemed that the other girls were very happy that Lena was there, that she laughed and nodded at everything they said. It seemed to Lena that there were some girls at the table who were supposed to talk and some girls who were not. If the girls who were not supposed to talk were wanted at the table too, Lena was happy to be wanted. Lena learned that she was wanted because she was cute and quiet.

And then she saw Vaclav smiling and waving from across the street, hiding behind a mailbox, and it was all ruined. She didn't feel cute, and she didn't feel quiet. She felt angry and stupid. She felt like an ugly thing, like a person who has only one friend and is so ugly that they are mean to their only friend.

Lena wants only to find a space to be, between Vaclav and the cool girls, between what she wants and what she needs. Lena does not want to hurt anyone, and she thinks that maybe she has found a way.

FIGHTING AND BITING AND KICKING AND SCREAMING

. . .

"Hi, Lena! Surprise, I am waiting for you!" Vaclav says, and he sees that Lena is mad but thinks maybe if his mood is good enough, if he says enough cheering-up things, she will not be angry anymore, she will forget that she is angry, and she will just be happy to come over to practice the act with him.

Vaclav isn't afraid to have a fight with Lena. He has been friends with Lena since he was six years old, so of course they fight with each other. When there is someone who is your destiny, someone who you love more than any other person, sometimes you push on them and pull on them and feel like hurting them. Fighting is something that happens when there is someone who is your only other person in the world, someone you have no choice about, which is why brothers and sisters are always fighting and biting and kicking and screaming.

Lena stands on the steps of her aunt's house and glares at Vaclav. Vaclav stands on the sidewalk, at the bottom of the steps, and looks up at Lena, smiling. If someone were to walk by, they would think that the scene is very romantic, like Romeo and Juliet. This is exactly what Lena does not want to have happen; she wants no one to know about the time she spends with Vaclav, about the time she spends at his house working on silly and embarrassing things. She does not want anyone to know about how she and Vaclav talk about one day being husband and wife. She feels embarrassed about how she asked him to promise her, asked him over and over if those things would be true, over and over until she believed them and he believed them.

"Walk," says Lena.

"Where?" says Vaclav.

"Home," says Lena. "No look."

"No look where?" says Vaclav.

"Back," says Lena. "No look back."

And so Vaclav turns and walks toward his house, away from the front stairs of Lena's house, and he does not look back the entire way. Lena waits, and as soon as Vaclav turns the corner, she follows, one block behind, never on the same block, but still together. He knows, without asking and without looking, that she is there behind him. He knows it was Lena who asked, over and over and over again, if he would promise to be her husband one day, no matter what, so he's not worried.

When Vaclav arrives at his house, he goes inside without looking behind him, and of course, two minutes later, Lena comes right in without ringing the doorbell or knocking.

FIRST NOTHING THEN HOMEWORK

...

No one is home at Vaclav's house. Oleg is still at work, because he is a hack (which is a word that Vaclav likes better than *taxi driver*), and his shift most days goes from early in the morning until just before dinner. Rasia is still at work at the medical supply company on Kings Highway, where she answers the phone and makes calls and does all kinds of filing and inventory management and other things that are very boring for Vaclav to hear about.

Vaclav's house is the bottom half of a whole house. The house looks like one big house, but there are stairs that go up to Mrs. Ruvinova's front door, and there is also a door under the stairs, which is Vaclav's front door. Because Vaclav's house is underneath another house, sometimes he feels like he is hiding in a cozy place, like a fox's den, and sometimes he feels like he is on the underground subway because it is very bangy and cramped. He can hear all the people on the roof of his house, which is the floor of their house, and even though the houses are the same size, it feels like it would be better to be the people whose floor is someone else's roof than the people whose roof is someone else's floor. Also, it seems that it would feel better to be the people who look out their windows at a little bit of trees instead of at a little bit of underground and a little bit of dead leaves.

Vaclav and Lena walk through the living room, which is where later Oleg will snore while he watches Russian television programs, past the bathroom and the door to Vaclav's room and the door to Vaclav's parents' room, and into the kitchen, where they both slam their backpacks onto the ground with a bang.

Lena sits down at the table, and Vaclav walks to the fridge. Vaclav always holds on to the handle of the fridge and leans down to see what is in it, just like his father does, even though Vaclav is short and when he leans down he can't see half of the refrigerator.

"First snack. Okay, for drinks we have Brita, we have grapefruit juice, we have fruit punch. What would you like to drink, Lena?" Vaclav begins to take out the carton of fruit punch for himself, and he keeps standing at the fridge and waiting for Lena's answer, even though he knows that Lena will not want anything to eat or drink. Sometimes, though, when Vaclav's parents are not home yet, Lena will say that she has to use the bathroom, but then she will go into the kitchen and eat something out of the refrigerator secretly, and sometimes she will even put something from the pantry into her backpack and take it with her. Vaclav notices this, but he does not say anything about it.

"First nothing. Then homework. Finish homework. Then snack, then practicing," says Lena.

Vaclav knows that Lena will not have a snack after the homework is finished. He feels her urgency to do the homework as soon as possible. Vaclav feels a little bit of something not nice, a little bit of something angry at Lena, something that does not like for Lena to rush him, but he lets it go away, and he closes the fridge and pours the fruit punch into a glass that used to be a jelly jar, and he drinks a big sip from it and then fills the glass again.

When he sits down next to Lena and puts his glass on the table it looks like he is wearing fruit-punch lipstick and a fruit-punch mustache.

"What do you want to do first?" he asks Lena, pulling his binder from his bag and putting it on the table.

"Math," says Lena, and she pulls from the bottom of her bag a worksheet from her math class, which is the lowest math class. Vaclav's math class is the highest math class. The math classes are not called lowest or highest or dumbest or smartest or slowest or fastest, they are called yellow and purple and green, but everyone knows that in yellow there are more ESL kids and more pictures on the homework worksheets. The worksheet that Lena pulls out from her backpack is like a fancy fan at the bottom, because it has become smushed under all the books in Lena's bag.

The worksheet is about long division, which Vaclav studied in his math class last year, so he can explain it to Lena. Vaclav thinks he should tell Lena that her first problem is that she is not organized and that if she was more organized, if she had some folders and labels, then she might be more organized in her head, and that if she did not mash up and wrinkle every worksheet and homework assignment, she might care more about doing them and she might get better grades. But Vaclav is feeling that Lena does not want to hear this, that things between them are strange, because even though Vaclav is doing something nice for Lena, he is having to act extra-nicely to her, feeling like he should thank her or offer her a present, and this is making the angry feeling come again, but Vaclav ignores it.

"Here," Vaclav says, and points her eyes toward the first problem. "This is asking how many times two will go into six hundred twenty-seven."

"What is 'goes into'?" asks Lena.

"It is how many twos are in six hundred twenty-seven," says Vaclav.

"One," says Lena, pointing at the two in 627.

"No, it is like this. You are one. I am one. Together we are two, yes?"

"*Da*," says Lena.

"Together we are VacLena, one thing. But taking up two spaces—two chairs," Vaclav says, formulating in his mind, finally, how he will show her.

"If there were six hundred twenty-seven chairs, how many VacLenas could sit?"

"I don't know."

"Remember, each VacLena needs two chairs, and they cannot be split up."

"Why not?" asks Lena.

"Because," says Vaclav, "because then there is remainder, which is the next thing."

"What is 'remainder'?" asks Lena.

"Is when we split up VacLena, if there is maybe only one more spot—one more chair left. Then there is just Vaclav or just Lena."

"And this cannot be," says Lena.

"That was very good English, Lena," says Vaclav.

THE TIME PASSES QUICKLY AND SLOWLY

...

It takes a whole hour for Vaclav to teach Lena her mathematics, and then there is also a worksheet to do for ESL, and then there is also a writing assignment for Lena's regular daytime class. By the time they get to the writing assignment, Rasia is home, and it is dark out, and Vaclav's juice glass has been filled and emptied many times. When it is time to work on the writing assignment, Lena slumps her body down into the chair so that it seems to Vaclav that she has noodles instead of bones. Even Lena's head falls forward, and when Vaclav asks her to look directly at a sentence they have written or at the spelling of a word, she sighs and leans her arm on the table, and then leans her head on her arm, and then barely opens her eyes.

"You must use this pen, and you must write the sentence,

Lena! I can help you with it, but in my handwriting the teacher will smell cheating!" Vaclav says.

Lena sighs, loud and deep, releasing the sound from her entire body all at once.

Rasia is banging around in the kitchen, making it very hard for Vaclav to concentrate, and Lena is acting like a bag of noodles dripping all over her chair, and upstairs in Mrs. Ruvinova's house, people are watching a movie with a lot of yelling and screaming and gun noises and crash noises. The people watching the movie are probably not Mrs. Ruvinova but Mrs. Ruvinova's sons, who are big and have hair that always looks wet and who smell like magazines and who wear leather jackets that they never take off and that make a funny sound on Mrs. Ruvinova's leather sofas.

Vaclav has seen these sons on trips upstairs to Mrs. Ruvinova's for sugar or flour or vodka. He does not know how many of them there are, because they look very similar. They make him feel uncomfortable and unsafe, because when he goes upstairs and is waiting for Mrs. Ruvinova to give him a cup of sugar, the sons sit on the couch and do not say hello.

Vaclav is thinking of Mrs. Ruvinova's sons, and of the sounds and smells of his mother cooking, and what she is cooking, which so far is something that has onions and cabbage in it, something that makes a lot of smoke and steam. He is finding it very hard to think of what Lena should write next in her homework assignment about the American Revolution, especially while Lena is not helping at all, is just sitting like a Lena-shaped lump on the chair next to him.

"Get this homework off of the table and set for dinner or else," says Rasia. She says this in a sweet, warm voice, even though the words that she uses sound mean, because she learned a lot of her English by watching pirated episodes of *Law & Order* every night while she was still in Russia waiting for the paperwork and the stamps and the cards and the letters that would allow her to move her family to America.

Vaclav closes his binder and closes Lena's composition notebook, and clears all of the pencils and erasers and books off the table. Lena drags her noodle body out of her chair to go count the silverware, and Rasia asks, "Lena? You are staying?"

"*Da,*" says Lena.

"English!" says Rasia.

"Yee-us," growls Lena, as she does every night, because nothing has changed even though something has changed.

Vaclav has to pack up all the homework and put it away, and he feels terrible because he has not even started his own homework and already it is dinnertime, and it feels very late. He is beginning to understand that there will be no time to finish his own homework, and Lena's homework, and then to practice the magic act.

Vaclav brushes past Lena as he is reaching up for plates, and Lena whispers, "No finish homework, no practice nothing," in a voice like an old mean cat.

And Vaclav understands that every night from now on he will do Lena's homework for her, without teaching her anything. He will tell her what to write exactly in her essays, will not even ask her what she is thinking about the question—for example, if she would be a loyalist or a revolutionary if she was alive then and why—he will just do it for her without any help at all, because this is what is necessary, because this is what Lena wants. And what Vaclav wants is what Lena wants, because they are VacLena with no remainder.

EIGHT VACLENA, REMAINDER ONE LENA

...

The very next day Vaclav and Lena walk home from school exactly as planned. Vaclav walks home alone, while Lena walks with Marina and Kristina to the Aunt's house and pretends to go inside. They meet up at Vaclav's house, where Lena does not have to ring the doorbell; she just goes inside through the living room with the cushiony rug and the big, enormous TV straight to the kitchen, where Vaclav is already starting to work furiously on his homework so that there will be time to work on the act.

Lena puts her backpack down next to the kitchen table and goes to the fridge. Today Vaclav will do her homework, totally and completely. Today they will work on the act. She will not feel guilty, and she will not feel mean. She will feel finished with her homework, and she will feel friends with Marina and Kristina and with Vaclav, because they will work on the act. Vaclav is working on the homework, and he is not talking at all, not to offer snacks to Lena or to say hello. But this is okay. Today Lena wants to have a snack.

Lena opens the fridge, takes out a string cheese, and sits down at the kitchen table next to Vaclav and eats the string cheese one string at a time while Vaclav murmurs quickly over her math homework.

Vaclav does not hide from Lena how quickly he does the work that yesterday took her many hours. Lena feels bad that she doesn't understand math, but Lena is used to this kind of feeling bad, and watching how quickly he does what she cannot do feels good because it makes her feel sure of things without any questions, without any doubt.

LENA HAS A SNACK

. . .

Lena sits at the kitchen table until she finishes the whole string cheese, and then she throws away the wrapper, and then she takes down a big glass and fills it with milk from the fridge and drinks it all the way down and then puts it in the sink, and then she takes a loaf of Wonder bread from the bread box, and she takes out three slices, and she starts to eat one of the slices right away by making little bite-sized pieces with her fingers and looks into the refrigerator for something to make a sandwich with and then gives up and then puts mustard all over the two pieces of bread and then puts them together and then sits next to Vaclav at the kitchen table and then eats a mustard sandwich while Vaclav is doing her homework, and when she is done eating the mustard sandwich she gets up and goes to the refrigerator and takes out the peanut butter and takes a spoon from the silverware drawer and digs into the peanut butter and takes a big spoonful and then sits down at the kitchen table next to Vaclav and licks at it and then eats it and then goes back to the peanut butter jar and takes another big scoop and this time eats it standing up and eats another standing up and another until almost all the peanut butter is gone, and then she hears the sound of Rasia opening the front door, and then she quickly puts the lid back on the jar of peanut butter but does not even screw it down all the way and pushes it back farther in the fridge and then sits down next to Vaclav and pretends to be very interested in what he is doing and even nods.

RASIA IS NOT TRICKED

...

Rasia saw Lena scurry away from the refrigerator. Sometimes being a mother is like when you turn on the lights and all the roaches go running for cover, and if you are looking carefully at the floor, expecting to see all the scurrying, then you will see it, but if you are thinking about what snack to have or looking at the ceiling fan and thinking about how long it has been since you've dusted it, then you will not see the scurrying. When Rasia comes inside she always looks immediately toward the kitchen, and as with bugs, even if you did not see what the bugs were doing before the scurrying, you can see where they were and where they scurried to and what they scurried away from, and then you have some clues or ideas about what is going on.

Rasia also saw Lena pretend to be interested in the work that Vaclav was doing, so she walks right up to the kitchen table and sees that Vaclav is working on a worksheet that has Lena's name on the top of the page. Then Rasia opens the refrigerator and sees the peanut butter with the lid askew, and she looks inside and sees all the little spoon scoops, not the knife swirls you make when you put peanut butter on a sandwich.

Today Rasia is on high alert because of the strange behavior of the last few nights. She rehashes this strange behavior in her mind like a detective. First was Lena vomiting. Then was coming home to find Vaclav still in the kitchen, still doing work, with Lena slumped at the table beside him. This is evidence of something bad, because this is not normal. Normal is to come home and to find Vaclav and Lena working hard on a magic act in Vaclav's bedroom but with the lights on and the door open and feet on the floor because hers is a house with morals.

She noticed, last night at dinner, Vaclav's terrible mood, a mood like someone who has lost a long and hard game of *csyak svoi kozyi*. And now there is little Lena eating from the fridge and hiding it, and wanting Rasia to think that she is helping Vaclav with homework when she is not.

Rasia wants to know exactly what is going on and also exactly why.

THIS MUST BE PRACTICE TONIGHT

...

For dinner, Rasia has made *shchi*. She found, when she came to America, that for very little money she could fill the slow cooker with meat and cabbage in the morning and come home to a traditional Russian meal in the evening. Usually Lena just pushes the gray meat around in her bowl until it is time to clear the table, but tonight Lena eats all her *shchi* before Rasia even has a chance to sit down and pick up her fork. Meanwhile, Vaclav is using his fork to pull out the pieces that he does not feel like eating: pieces of cabbage that have become burned on the edge or the belly-button pieces of the tomato where the vine was attached.

Rasia looks at her husband, who keeps his hand on his vodka so that he can take a sip between bites.

Rasia watches Lena out of the corner of her eye; she is scraping her spoon around on the bottom of her bowl like the *shchi* is the last food on the planet earth.

"All homework is done?" she asks.

"All. All done, and so Lena and I will be preparing to practice our act as soon as we finish eating dinner, thank you."

"You are welcome," says Rasia, still looking at Lena, whose focus has not shifted from the *shchi,* not one tiny smidge.

"Lena, you eat so fast you will make yourself sick again. Slow down; you can have more." Lena looks up at Rasia, embarrassed.

"Vaclav—fill Lena's bowl," she says.

"Tonight you are practicing some tricks? Some magic? Some con-artist games?" Oleg says to Lena. Lena is afraid of Oleg, because his face is ugly to look at and covered with small holes, and because he smells and because a little piece of hairy belly always comes out from underneath his shirt, and because everything he says is yelling.

Vaclav doesn't feel like answering his father, or eating very much, and he doesn't feel like sitting anymore at the kitchen table. Vaclav doesn't even feel like practicing the act.

When Vaclav feels discouraged, he likes to read his Houdini book, and to remind himself that Houdini had many hard things to overcome before he became famous, and that he believed that perseverance and resilience were the most important qualities a person could have. Houdini worked very hard for many years with no money and no fame, and that is when he learned all of his important skills. Thinking about Houdini reminds Vaclav that to have struggles and perseverance is important to the forging of his character, and he reminds himself that one day in the future he may be thanking Lena for putting him through the troubles and difficulties of this time, for it will make him great and magnificent. This he tells to himself over and over in his mind, so that he will not forget it.

Still, Vaclav is feeling discouraged about all the time he is spending doing Lena's homework in addition to his own homework, that all this homework is taking time away from the magic that must be practiced for him to become the most successful and famous magician. Vaclav feels homesick, suddenly homesick, for a place that doesn't exist.

"May I be excused?" asks Vaclav, looking down at the table, at the half-eaten brown cabbage stew in his bowl.

"Sure," says his mother, while his father snorts in a laugh that might be a laugh that loves Vaclav, or might be a laugh that is mean.

Vaclav stands up from the table and puts his bowl of *shchi* in the sink, while Lena shovels into her mouth the last few bites of her second bowl and follows closely behind Vaclav, terrified at the idea of being left alone with his parents.

GLOVES

...

Vaclav sits down immediately at his desk and begins making a new, angry list.

"Act for practice first: box of disappearing. I think," says Lena. Vaclav does not respond to Lena but begins adding to his list:

COSTUMES

"No?" says Lena.

Vaclav does not respond to Lena but begins another list:

LIST OF THINGS NEEDED FOR COSTUMES
FOR SHOW AT CONEY ISLAND

"Or card. Cards trick," says Lena, looking over Vaclav's shoulder.

"Card tricks," he corrects.

"Okay!" says Lena. Lena is starting to feel worried that something is wrong, that her plan of making Vaclav feel happy, of making the balance between getting from and giving to, is not working.

"No, not yes to card tricks, just telling you it is not *cards trick,* with a letter *s* on the end of *card,* but it is *card tricks,* with a letter *s* on the end of *trick,*" says Vaclav.

"What it is wrong?" says Lena, even though she knows a little what's wrong. Vaclav does not answer but adds to his list as if he did not hear her:

LIST OF THINGS NEEDED FOR COSTUMES
FOR SHOW AT CONEY ISLAND

TOP HAT
CAPE
TUXEDO

Vaclav knows that there is more that belongs on his list, but he suddenly cannot think of the things that belong in the outfit of a magician, even though he has been picturing the outfit for many years. Vaclav knows that his thoughts and feelings about Lena are pushing around his memory. It is Lena's fault that he does not remember, and it is Lena's fault that they haven't been practicing the act enough.

"What do magicians wear? I can't think of what magicians are wearing!" says Vaclav, and he means it only as a question, but all his anger about Lena's fault comes out with it.

"Hat," says Lena, afraid.

"I have that already!" says Vaclav.

"Ummm, the long, on shoulders, the long . . ." Lena is looking for words, and this too is making Vaclav wait and making Vaclav angry.

"Cape? I have that one already too," Vaclav says, and he knows that his voice is making Lena afraid, is scaring her words away.

"Ummm . . ." says Lena.

"What?" says Vaclav. "I'm waiting."

"Ummm," says Lena, with her ummms getting more and more wobbly.

"Never mind!" says Vaclav, and he goes back to writing his lists.

"Ummm," says Lena, and her ummms now are like a violin that wiggles its notes.

"Forget it!" says Vaclav. And then Lena sits down on the floor, behind Vaclav's chair, where he can't see her, so she can hide the tears that are spilling from her eyes and down her face, and she says, "Gloves."

She says it too low, with the letter *l* too heavy, and the *o* too round to be an American *o*, but still, Vaclav hears her Russian *l* and *o*, and her rumbly *v*, and the *e* just the tiny bit of air exiting her mouth, with the *s* barely hanging on, and Vaclav understands, and he knows exactly the gloves she is talking about.

Vaclav does not notice that Lena is crying. He feels incredibly happy because the white magician's gloves complete the picture of what he wants to look like for the show on the boardwalk at Coney Island. He is happy because he can see himself looking like a professional magician.

He needs the white gloves, the brilliantly white gloves that will highlight his every movement and make his audience pay attention to his hands so that it is as if he has their eyeballs on fishing line attached to his fingertips. It is very important, in magic, to have the audience's eyeballs attached to your fingertips, because sometimes the magician is waving his hand and saying, look, the trick is over here, but actually the trick is somewhere else. Vaclav learned this from *The Magician's Almanac*, which said if you want to learn how a magician performs his illusions, when he says, "Watch carefully as I do this," you must watch carefully everywhere else, because he is trying to distract you.

"What do you want to wear for the show on Coney Island?" Vaclav asks, because the appearance of the lovely assistant is very important to the art of magic, just like the white gloves that make the audience's eyes attach to your fingertips as though with fishing line. The assistant is there so that while the magician creates an illusion everyone will look carefully somewhere else. Sometimes the assistant is the somewhere else.

"What do you think your costume should be?" Vaclav asks again.

Lena stops crying and takes deep breaths. She is starting to forget about being upset, because she is very excited. Lena will wear the golden fringed bikini of Heather Holliday.

The first time that Lena saw Heather Holliday she was just

five years old, and it was also the first time she saw the famous Coney Island Sideshow, and it was also the first time that she saw the ocean, and it was the first time that she saw a roller coaster, and it was the first time that she smelled a hot dog, and it was the first time that she went over to Vaclav's house, and it was the first time that she ever had a friend.

HOW IT HAPPENED: THE FIRST TIME THAT VACLAV MET LENA

...

Lena's aunt, Ekaterina, was always complaining about having to watch Lena, and about how she was always missing the good shifts, the shifts that made the most tips, because she had to pick up Lena or put Lena to bed, or feed Lena something for dinner. One of the people who the Aunt complained to was her boyfriend, who had a job picking up boxes and standing outside smoking in a T-shirt, and he did this job for the medical supply company on Kings Highway where Rasia was the receptionist. The Aunt's boyfriend knew Vaclav's mom, and he knew that she had a kid who looked to be about five, the same age as Lena.

The boyfriend was tired of the Aunt complaining, and was tired of the Aunt not making any money, and also of Lena always hanging around the apartment and getting in the way with her quietness, especially since school had let out for the summer and she was home all the time, and so he talked to Rasia and they set up a playdate.

HOW IT WAS FOR VACLAV

...

Rasia was happy to have someone for her son to play with who was also in his school, because he was the new kid there, and since he had just come from Russia, he didn't have so many friends. In fact, he hadn't had a friend come over to play since they moved from Russia, and she was so excited that she rushed home with her news to tell Vaclav.

"Vaclav. Turn off TV. I have something I can tell you." She was not yet used to speaking to her son only in English. The decision to switch, to speak strictly English at home, was easy, but speaking to her son in a language that was not her own, this was hard. Not always having words for the things she wanted to say, this was especially hard when she was trying to have a conversation about something for which she might not have the words even in Russian, or even if she also spoke Arabic, and the click language they speak in Africa on the National Geographic Channel. Even if she knew all the languages in the whole world perfectly, she might not be able to explain to her son the things she was feeling. What she was feeling was something close to, but not exactly:

> I'm so terribly sorry that you are lonely and that you do not have any friends and other kids think that you are strange, and it hurts me like someone tearing off my skin and pouring acid onto it, but we did something that for you would be the best thing in the end, and even if you

never, ever know it we will know it, and when you look at us and blame us for choosing for you a hard thing, we will know it, and when you look at us and blame us for being your parents, we will know it then too.

"Is video. I can pause," said Vaclav, rolling his eyes and pointing his remote up at the screen of the big TV and pausing David Copperfield in midair just as he was being lowered from the ceiling of a huge auditorium.

Rasia eased herself onto the big couch. Then she patted the seat next to her, and Vaclav stood up from the floor, where he had been watching the TV. Vaclav had been sitting about two feet away from the screen, so that he could see up close and be able to guess the secrets behind David Copperfield's tricks.

"I met a woman today who has a girl same age as you." Rasia paused and looked at Vaclav, who raised one eyebrow. Skeptical. *Okay,* thought Rasia, *at least he is not angry. He is interested.*

"This girl, she is coming from Russia when she is a baby, she is having not her mother or her father around for her, and she is very shy." Vaclav didn't stop her, so she continued.

"She does not have many friends, and her English is not so good, so I am hoping that you will have playdate with her, maybe help with English, maybe even make friend." Vaclav rolled his eyes in disgust, disinterest, and annoyance, all at the same time, and then asked, "What is her name?"

"Yelena. They call her Lena," said Rasia.

"Okay," said Vaclav. He knew who this girl was, the shy girl from ESL, but she had never spoken to him or to anyone else that he knew of.

"She is coming Saturday for playdate," said Rasia. "Maybe for activity, we go to Coney Island."

HOW IT WAS FOR LENA

...

Lena woke up on a Saturday morning and went into the kitchen. Ekaterina, her aunt, was sitting at the kitchen table in her robe, drinking coffee and smoking a cigarette and looking at the newspaper. Even though it was early in the morning, the Aunt had actually just come home from work and had not even gone to sleep yet. The Aunt looked at Lena but didn't say anything, and Lena didn't say anything either but reminded herself to be quiet. The Aunt didn't feel good in the morning; mornings gave her a headache, and she hated when Lena made any sounds.

Lena looked for things to eat for breakfast, but there was not very much there, not any cereal or any pancake mix or anything like that, and in the refrigerator there was no milk or orange juice or eggs or string cheese. The only thing in the fridge was Slim-Fast, and the only thing in the freezer was vodka, and the only things in the pantry were cans of things that are not really good for eating, especially if you aren't very good at using a can opener.

Lena closed the pantry lightly so that it didn't make any sound at all. She was planning to give up and go back to her room and maybe lie in the bed and try to sleep a little bit more to pass the time. She was waiting for the Aunt to go to bed so that she could take a dollar bill from the Aunt's purse to go buy a snack from the bodega on the corner, or so that she could drink one of the Slim-Fast cans from the fridge, if there were enough so that the Aunt wouldn't notice one missing and would not yell at her.

"Get dress. You are going to your friend's house," said Lena's aunt. Lena was confused, because she didn't have any friends.

Lena also felt that she had no choice, because the Aunt told her she was going in a no-questions way, which was the way she said almost everything. So Lena went to her room and put on clothes and shoes, and made sure she was dressed and ready to go to her friend's house.

SATURDAY MORNING

...

Vaclav woke up very early, and his mother was already awake, and Vaclav could smell furniture polish and lemons and bleach, and the house smelled like it did on mornings when there was company coming later, or the first time every year that it is nice enough outside to open all the windows and everything feels electric.

They had made a plan together. Rasia would take Vaclav and Lena to Coney Island on the subway, and they would ride the rides, and then come home and eat some sandwiches for lunch. Vaclav and his mother were very happy about this plan, both of them knowing that Vaclav would have a new friend, and both of them knowing that they were doing something nice for Lena. They could not know that many bad things would come from this day along with the good things. They did not know that the good things would happen and interact with the bad things like chemicals and make them worse, and the other way around as well. They did not know that Vaclav and Lena would wander past the famous Coney Island Sideshow and see magic tricks and Heather Holliday and her golden fringed bikini for the first time. They could not know that this would be the beginning of everything.

DING DONG HELLO

...

Ekaterina walked Lena right up to the front door of Vaclav's house, and Lena felt very bad and confused because she didn't want the Aunt to leave her there, but she also didn't want anyone to see the Aunt with her makeup still on for work. Unfortunately, there was nothing Lena could do. The Aunt held her wrist very tightly, and a little too high up in the air, so that Lena had to twist her body to keep her shoulder from hurting, and they stood and rang the bell. As soon as the bell chimed, Lena could hear movement behind the door.

On the other side of the door, Vaclav and his mother were both sitting on the big couch, with everything in the apartment clean and the TV off, not talking about how excited they were. When the doorbell rang, Vaclav and his mother both stood up, and Vaclav ran off to his room, pretending to suddenly need something, overcome with excitement and nervousness and not wanting to seem as if he was just sitting and waiting for Lena to come.

Rasia opened the door and stared at Ekaterina, who as the door was opening was pressing the doorbell a second time. Ekaterina had hair that started out dark brown at the scalp and became orange for a moment and then a glowing white-blond, stretched back tightly into a ponytail that started at the top of her head. She wore one of those fuzzy pink matching jumpsuits that all the young mothers were wearing, which made Rasia feel as though there was a club that she did not belong to, and on her feet she had big, high stiletto heels made out of clear plastic. Everything on her face was painted on as if she started with nothing there: big black eyebrows that did not match any of the hair that grew on her head, and thick, dark lines around her eyes, and thick pink lines around her lips, and even a thick line where her face ended at her jaw and did not blend into her neck.

Rasia looked at Ekaterina and then looked at Lena, who was gripping Ekaterina's hand and looking terrified, and her heart broke just a little bit at first because she had no daughter, and then a moment later because of what she had heard about the story of Lena's life and the rumors she had heard about Ekaterina's job, and she wanted to scoop up the little girl and feed her and hold her and make her safe.

"*Zdravstvuite,*" said the Aunt.

"*Zdravstvuite,* nice to meet you," said Rasia, switching to English. The Aunt glared at her.

"I have to go now. I pick her up in the evening," said the Aunt.

"Yes, of course," said Rasia, embarrassed to realize that she had been imagining that Ekaterina would sit down, that she would serve her the tea that was already steeping in the kitchen, that Lena would run off to play with Vaclav, and that she and Ekaterina would discuss Lena and Vaclav, and parenthood, and the neighborhood, and the challenges of finding good after-school child care and the challenges of being in this country, and become unlikely friends. Rasia was surprised and embarrassed to feel so very lonely. This had happened before, a few times: loneliness that snuck up on her at the grocery store or on the bus and caught her off guard.

"Do svidaniya," said Lena's aunt Ekaterina, turning to walk away on the crumbling, buckling sidewalk in her plastic high-heeled shoes without saying a word to Lena, like "Goodbye" or "Have a good time" or "I love you" or "Be good" or "I don't care if I ever see you again; I hate you" or "Have a good time on the Cyclone and have fun seeing the ocean for the first time." The Aunt just turned and left Lena there.

Rasia noticed that Lena still had tiny bits of sleep-crust in her eyes, and her heart broke a little bit more. She stood in the open doorway, watching, stunned, as the Aunt stomped away, lighting a cigarette as she walked.

"Do svidaniya," said Rasia, though Ekaterina was already too far away to hear.

VACLAV MAKES A GRAND ENTRANCE

...

"Lena, come inside, is very nice to have you . . . Take off shoes here, please," Rasia said, and pointed at the line of her family's shoes next to the door: her loafers, her husband's ugly work shoes, and Vaclav's special new shoes with the lights on the heels and the Velcro everywhere, because in America no one, not even small children, has time to tie his own shoes, and everything must have flashing lights.

Lena walked over to the line of shoes and stood so that her feet were in line with all the empty shoes. Lena was wearing white canvas sneakers, and without reaching down with her arms at all or changing the positioning of her torso one single bit, she used the toe of her left foot to slip the shoe off her right foot, and then used the toe of her right foot to slip the shoe off her left foot. In this way, she took off her shoes without moving very much, and without taking her eyes off Rasia.

Vaclav was spying from the hallway and saw what Lena had done, that she had taken off her shoes with the minimum of effort, stepping to the exact place where she wanted the shoes to be so that she did not have to move them once they were off her feet. He smiled a little bit on the inside and came forward to introduce himself.

"Hello. I am Vaclav. It is nice to meet you. Welcome to my house. Can I get you something to drink?" he said, and tried very hard not to sound rehearsed. Lena just looked down, embarrassed.

"Okay," said Vaclav. Vaclav started to feel embarrassed as he went over in his head why Lena maybe didn't answer him, why she looked down at the floor, embarrassed. He had said, "Nice to meet you," but, of course, it was not the first time he had ever met Lena, because they had been in school together and were in the same ESL class in kindergarten. Vaclav felt his face grow hot. He became worried, but he saw that Lena's face looked hot and worried too.

The three of them, the mother, the young magician, and the tiny girl, stood silently, looking at the floor between them.

"Does anyone need to use the bathroom before we leave?" said Rasia.

"No," said Vaclav. "I already went." He looked at Lena, but she said nothing.

"Okay, I pee and then we go," said Rasia, and she turned and walked to the bathroom, leaving Vaclav and Lena to stare at the floor together.

CHILDREN UNDER FORTY-FOUR INCHES

. . .

As they walked to the subway station together, Vaclav and his mother made strange efforts at having conversations that would be of interest to Lena, and that were in clear and simple English so that she could listen and feel included, but also in no way required Lena to respond or to answer questions. They talked about how they would be starting first grade at the end of the summer, about shows Vaclav liked on TV, and about how hot it was outside, but Lena did not join in.

All the way along East Sixteenth Street, onto Avenue U, all the way into the subway station and up the stairs to the platform, Vaclav and his mother did a dance around Lena, trying always to keep Lena between them, but Lena walked slowly, looking only down at the ground, and so Vaclav and his mother kept falling back to keep her between them, to keep up the illusion that they were enjoying the morning together.

Lena felt unsure of what to do. She had never been out with anyone besides her *babushka* and the Aunt. When her *babushka* was alive, they barely ever went out, because her *babushka* was weak and she had meals delivered for free from the nice volunteers at Meals on Wheels, and Lena and her *babushka* would share those. So mostly they went out only to the store on the corner for toilet paper or garbage bags, and that was only very rarely. The Aunt rarely took Lena anywhere.

Also, Lena had never taken the subway, and she felt very scared because she had no money. She didn't think the way that Vaclav did, which was with total trust that if he needed something his mother would give it to him, would know and prepare him. Often Lena needed money for things and the Aunt did not give her any. She had only asked the Aunt for money once, and then never did it ever again.

Lena was afraid as they got closer and closer to the subway that she would have to pay in some way, and that she would be embarrassed and would have to ask Vaclav or his mother for money, and also, even if she had money, she did not know at all what was supposed to happen at the subway, she did not know how to pay to board the train, and she was terrified.

When they approached the subway station, Lena hung back and would not walk any farther, because she did not know where to go in the strange tangle of gates that looked like cages, and she saw the people rubbing yellow cards through the machine, and she did not have one.

Vaclav stood next to Lena and waved through the big metal cages to the man who sat in the booth on the other side. Vaclav pointed to his own head and to Lena, and then held up two fingers. The spinning-cage gate made a buzzing sound, and Vaclav took her hand and said, "Come, we go through together!" and then, to make sure that Lena did not feel embarrassed, "It is more fun to go two together."

Lena was amazed that Vaclav knew the man in the booth, amazed that he knew the special hand signals to get the man to open the complicated gate to let them both in for free. She did not know yet, as Vaclav would later tell her, that up to three children forty-four inches tall and under ride for free on subways and local buses when accompanied by a fare-paying adult, and when he did tell her, the mystery of the subway went away and a new, amazing feeling of freedom took its place, but the safe feeling of Vaclav holding her hand never went away.

On the train, Vaclav showed Lena the best place to sit (in the back, facing backward, by a window), and Rasia sat across from them, with her purse in her lap, watching as Lena watched everything and Vaclav watched Lena.

RIDING ON THE Q TRAIN

...

On the train Lena saw: a white lady with a big leather purse and big leather boots and big, frizzy hair talking to a black man who talked to himself; a glass bottle half full of juice that rolled back and forth around the train, bumping into everyone's feet; a man in a business suit who picked up a newspaper from the ground and read it and tucked it under his arm to take it with him when he got off; a man with one arm; a lady who wore gloves like a doctor; a skinny lady eating chicken out of a paper tray; three girls putting makeup on one another's faces; two old ladies holding hands; a teenage boy with a tiny mustache and huge headphones; a lady with a plastic bag full of plastic bags; three men with big black hats and curls on the sides of their faces; three ladies with the same exact haircut pushing babies in strollers; a man sleeping on his own knees; a woman feeding a baby from under her shirt; a woman crying under sunglasses; and two girls wearing white shirts and red skirts, laughing and whispering.

Vaclav saw Lena looking at everything. Vaclav mostly

looked out the window when he rode the subway, and it took a very special thing, like a homeless person with no shoes dressed up as an alien or someone singing very, very loudly, to make him look.

When Lena had seen everything that was on the train, she looked out the window. Out of the window of the train, Lena saw: houses with tiny backyards filled with toys, clotheslines and more clotheslines, graffiti in bright colors, garbage that looked familiar and unfamiliar, the tops of buildings, billboards somebody forgot about, billboards with somebody's name written on them in black spray paint, the sky, pigeons in trees, the stop for Neck Road, the stop for Ocean Parkway, and then, finally, the sign for Coney Island/Stillwell Avenue, which was when it was time to get off the train.

THE WORLD, COLORED IN

...

Vaclav took Lena's hand again when it was time to get off the train, and he pointed to the gap between the train and the platform, to show Lena to be careful. They both walked along the platform to the stairs, with Rasia following closely behind. Vaclav knew the way to exit the subway station, because he had been to Coney Island before, but he glanced back just to make sure that his mother was still there.

A hot wind was blowing as they came down the stairs from the elevated train platform, and at the edges of the wind Lena could smell a smell like the back of the supermarket, where they keep the fish. As they crossed Surf Avenue, Lena and Vaclav could see the Cyclone snaking above the hot-dog stands and the tarot-card lady and the kids and the ladies in tight denim shorts. In the space between the streets, past the Cyclone and the hot dogs and the people, Lena could see the beach and, beyond that, the ocean.

To Lena, who had grown up in a tiny brownish-gray apartment, with her tiny brownish-gray *babushka,* and walked along cement streets to a big brick school, it looked as if the world had been colored in.

Together they snaked their way quickly through the games and the booths selling hats and T-shirts, and all the wild things and wild people and fried food. It seemed like everyone was in their way, and to Vaclav it felt as if they were already wasting time. Lena, holding tightly to his hand, did not look around her at all the people the way she had on the subway. She looked through everything, straight ahead of her, and not once did she take her eyes off the big, blue ocean.

They squeezed and excuse-me'd their way through everything and came out the other end, on the hot wooden boardwalk, where the boards squished a little bit with each step like piano keys. Rasia made her way to a bench and sat down.

"One minute," she said. "We take a rest." It was too hot out, Rasia was perspiring everywhere, and her sciatica was roaring up her leg.

"Come on, Mom, let's go to the rides," Vaclav said.

"One minute," Rasia said.

"One Mississippi, two Mississippi, three Mississippi, four Mississippi . . ." Vaclav began, counting off the seconds to a minute.

"Listen, Mr. Ants-in-pants, I didn't mean one minute exactly, I meant let's rest for a little while," she said. Vaclav looked like he would burst.

"Come on!" he said. "Time is running! We are missing the rides!" He could barely contain himself. She looked up at the gigantic Wonder Wheel looming over them. She could see, from where she sat, the baskets and the tops of the heads of the people inside. It didn't look very fast at all.

"Come on!" he said. "Come on come on come on!"

"Okay, listen," she said. "You go straight to the Wonder Wheel, you ride one time, and you come straight back here." And she handed Vaclav ten dollars in singles. She and Vaclav had talked at length about all the rules that would prevent all of the horrible things she saw each week on American television from happening to her son. He knew not to talk to strangers, how to ask a policeman for help, how to yell and shout if anyone bothered him, and to stay exactly where he was if he got lost. He would be fine for five minutes.

"Yes!" he said. "Lena, let's *go*!"

As she watched him walk out into the big American crowd, under the big American roller coasters, she felt the world spinning wildly away from her, and she sat and cried because she was happy and sad that he did not look back, because of how much she loved his little body and his awkward, cowlicky head and that tiny rib cage, and the way that he knew, already, to take a girl's hand if she was afraid.

CHILDREN LESS THAN FORTY-FOUR INCHES BUT GREATER THAN THIRTY-FIVE INCHES

...

Vaclav and Lena walked across the boardwalk, away from the ocean, Vaclav dragging Lena behind him by the hand, because Lena kept looking behind her at the ocean, always wanting to see if it was moving, because it seemed to come toward her, away and back, and it seemed like it might creep up, or rush at her suddenly and crush everything. She imagined the water flooding in through all the stalls and all the rides; she imagined everything being underwater; she imagined floating on top of the water, sitting on the top of the Ferris wheel.

"First we will ride the Wonder Wheel! There is no line!" Vaclav said, and he pulled Lena toward the entrance, rushing to beat the imaginary hordes.

Vaclav and Lena waited at the gate for the man to come take their money. The gate was painted blue, and where it was chipping you could see that it had also been painted green, and orange, and black, and all the way at the bottom, it was red and rusty.

The man said, "Hey, girlie, you're not tall enough to ride this ride," and he pointed at a clown made out of plywood, extending a plywood hand, palm down. On the belly of the clown were painted the words YOU MUST BE THIS TALL TO RIDE!

The man had talked to Lena loudly, and she did not know what he had said, and she looked to Vaclav, feeling afraid. Vaclav looked at the clown, and he looked at Lena, and he knew there was no chance that he could maybe make the man think that

Lena was tall enough, even by making her stand on her tippy-toes.

"It's okay. Is not so fun anyway," Vaclav said. Lena didn't understand what had happened, she didn't understand the clown or the words on the clown, she only understood that she had not been allowed to ride the ride but that Vaclav had forgiven her.

Vaclav and Lena walked back to Rasia's bench.

"We cannot ride that ride; it is not for us," Vaclav said. "We will go on a different ride. . . ." He turned behind him and pointed at the Cyclone.

"That one," he said.

"Okay, you ride this ride and then come right back," Rasia said, but at the entrance to the Cyclone, another clown told them that this time they were both not tall enough. Vaclav thought that his mother would not mind if they tried just one more ride. As Vaclav and Lena walked through all the stalls, they saw more and more rides, all of them guarded by the YOU MUST BE THIS TALL clown. When they thought that they might have spotted a ride that did not have a clown, suddenly someone would move aside to reveal that the clown had in fact been lurking there the entire time.

Vaclav did not give up, however, and he pulled Lena through the people and the rides and out the other end, so that they were almost back on Surf Avenue and Lena could not see the ocean at all. If they had only walked the other way, they would have found all the kiddie rides, but they didn't.

Vaclav and Lena stood on the corner, the rides behind them, the subway and all of Brooklyn and then all of Manhattan and the United States of America ahead of them. They did not know it yet, but they were standing right in front of the world-famous Coney Island Sideshow theater.

THE WORLD FAMOUS CONEY ISLAND SIDESHOW THEATER

...

"Only *five dollars*!" They turned around to see a man in a black hat and a tuxedo suit, standing on a tiny stage in front of a building painted in wild colors. There were signs all over the building that said FREAK SHOW and BEER, and these were things, in addition to the very dark entrance, that made Vaclav think that he and Lena were, again, too little to go in.

"Men, women, and children! Human beings of all ages, shapes, and sizes, step right up! Come on in!" the man hollered. The man had said "all ages, shapes, and sizes," but no matter what the man said, Vaclav thought that he and Lena should stay away, because he had a strange feeling about the place, which reminded him of the Video Palace where he was allowed to look at any video or DVD in the front of the store, but when he had accidentally gone behind a black curtain, not out of curiosity but by accident, the video clerk had yelled at him and he had felt embarrassed and afraid and hot and angry.

Vaclav wanted something good to happen so that Lena would be happy, but there were no more rides. So he decided to take a risk. He took out all of his dollar bills, and he handed them to the man who had yelled, "Come on in!" The man leaned back as he slid Vaclav's dollars into his back pocket, and then he reached out his hand to shake Vaclav's hand. Vaclav took it, afraid still that the man would turn them away, and that as punishment the man would keep his money. The man shook his hand up and down.

"That's a good choice, son! Show's starting, go ahead on in!" The man let go of Vaclav's hand, and in they went, into a dark hallway. At the end of the hallway there was a brightly painted sign that said FAMOUS CONEY ISLAND SIDESHOW THEATER with a big arrow beneath it, pointing to a door that was painted black and had dusty footprints on it.

Vaclav opened the door, and he and Lena stepped into the theater and a tingle went through their bodies from the tops of their heads all the way down to their toes inside of their socks and sneakers, and they both kept their sounds inside, sounds that were gasping or giggling or yelling, but the sounds pushed around inside of their heads and their eyeballs grew bigger and bigger with the pushing of the sounds, so that they could see more and more and more of what there was to see. They had to leave halfway through so that Vaclav's mother would not worry, but what they saw was enough to change everything.

After the sideshow, Vaclav and Lena went right back to Rasia. Without even talking about it, they knew that they were going to keep the sideshow a secret. Something can feel like it should be a secret if it is very close to your insides, so that if you tell it and someone else says a bad thing about it or, worse, laughs at it, then you will feel very hurt. Also, Vaclav knew that he had not exactly followed the rules, that the sideshow was not exactly the same as a ride, and that he might get in trouble if he told his mother. So it became a secret.

When Rasia asked them how the ride was, Vaclav told her that it was great but that he was ready to go home, because it was so hot out and because the rest of the rides were stupid and boring. When they got home, Vaclav and Lena went immediately into Vaclav's room to be alone with what they had seen.

The very first thing they did was make a list of the sideshow performers, and the tricks that they had performed, and all the things they had used.

FIVE YEARS LATER, SOMETHING ELSE THAT BECAME A SECRET

. . .

"The golden fringed bikini of Heather Holliday," says Lena. She says it quietly, like she is breathing it, not like she is saying it to Vaclav, just like she is saying it to the universe, like she is saying a prayer.

He looks down at Lena from his chair. Lena sees the concern on Vaclav's face, mostly in the eyebrows and a little bit around the nose.

"The golden fringed bikini of Heather Holliday," says Lena, "is perfect."

Vaclav knows that this is not a good thing for Lena to wear, and he also knows that Lena wants very badly to wear it.

"Okay," says Vaclav, "for you it shall be." Lena smiles and begins thinking about how to replicate the most amazing costume ever worn by any magician's assistant anywhere in the world, ever.

"We begin planning the act tonight. We begin with lists," Vaclav tells Lena, and Lena gets on her belly on the floor next to the bed and lengthens her body out at the hands and at the toes so that she can reach far under the bed and with her fingertips touch and pull at the magical box that holds all the lists and plans for their first-ever magic show together. Vaclav plops down on the floor in front of her with his legal pad and his pen, ready to make more lists. Lena lifts the lid off the box gently, ceremoniously, careful not to disturb any magic that may be brewing beneath.

They begin by un-wax-sealing the many folded lists, one at a time, reading each one carefully. They start with the lists that they made the very first day they met each other, when they came home from Coney Island and Vaclav wrote down everything they saw, and all the things the master of ceremonies said about the performers.

SPECIALTIES OF THE GREAT FREDINI

1. *World's worst magician* *
2. *Human blockhead*
3. *Sword swallower*
4. *Ventriloquist*
5. *Metamorphosis, illusion, and levitation* **

* *The Great Fredini is not the world's best living magician; that is David Copperfield. He is also not the greatest magician of all time; that is Harry Houdini, who is dead. He is most certainly, also, not the worst. This is a funny act with comedy, and the joke is that he is actually a good magician, and he performs many excellent tricks and illusions.*

** *This is Vaclav's favorite part.*

COSTUME AND PHYSICAL APPEARANCE
OF THE GREAT FREDINI

The Great Fredini is about seven feet tall and weighs about three hundred pounds, in Vaclav's estimation. He wears a wide range of costumes, including:

1. *Zebra-striped sequined tailcoat*
2. *Tuxedo*
3. *Aladdin-like outfit*

SPECIALTIES OF HEATHER HOLLIDAY

1. *Sword swallowing*
2. *Fire eating*

COSTUME AND PHYSICAL APPEARANCE
OF HEATHER HOLLIDAY*

Heather Holliday wears a few selected costumes, including:

1. *The golden fringed bikini*

* *Lena feels that important things to say about Heather Holliday are that she is the youngest sword swallower in the world, that she is lovely, and that she ran away from home because her family is Mormon, which sounds like a bad thing. Also, she has been struck by lightning. That is enough. Lena feels that it is of importance to know that Heather Holliday was struck by lightning, and it is obvious the lightning gave her some magic.***

** *This is a nice thing for Lena to know because she is waiting for* *her magic, but Vaclav is already magic because he was born with it. He has had indisputable magic powers since he was only a baby just born, and that is the truth.*

Vaclav looks over the lists, which are of great beauty in Vaclav's handwriting with pictures by Lena, and one day when Vaclav the Magnificent and his assistant, the Lovely Lena, are very famous magicians selling out more arenas than even David Copperfield, the lists will be sold by an auction like this: "Sold! For one billion American dollars!"

There are more lists.

LIST OF LISTS

Costumes
Supplies needed for costumes
Places to get supplies needed for costumes
Illusions
Supplies needed for illusions
Places to get supplies needed for illusions
The schedule
Things to make
Things to conjure
Things to levitate
Things to make disappear
Things to turn into doves
Doves to turn into things

These are the lists.

ILLUSIONS TO CONFOUND

...

To Vaclav it is clear that the first things to plan are the illusions, so he takes the list titled "Illusions" and begins reading it over. On the list are many possible illusions. There is the incredible shrinking girl, the dove-into-quarters trick, and finally, the amazing disappearing-audience trick.

"Lena, we will practice these three illusions first for the show on the boardwalk. We need, also, I am realize, a list of possible names for the show. I will add 'Possible Names for the Show on the Boardwalk' to the list of lists, and then begin a list. The first possible name will be 'The Coney Island Boardwalk Spectacular,' and then we will add more and more names. Once we have practice and perfected the three illusions, then I think we will add a disappearing trick and a levitating trick, maybe ending show with disappearing trick. I will make a list that is a list of the order of tricks in the show, and add that list to list of lists." As Vaclav updates his lists and his lists of lists, Lena creates her own new list.

GOLD BIKINI MAKE

Buy gold bikini
Take gold fabric secret
Glue
Fringes

Vaclav can read Lena's list over her shoulder, and he becomes more and more nervous, even more nervous than when

Lena first mentioned the golden fringed bikini, that something very bad might happen with Lena and her thinking so much all the time about it. Vaclav thinks again that this is not a thing for Lena to wear, a bikini that has two pieces and no middle piece, but Lena is in love with her idea.

"Lena, let us first be practicing, and then we will be worry with the costumes," says Vaclav, and Lena agrees, only because she has already finished her list and is happy with the plan. Vaclav and Lena begin by practicing the disappearing-coin trick, with Vaclav narrating and instructing the patient and fascinated audience to look here and pay close attention there, while Lena assists and plans and perfects the right way to angle her wrists to draw the attention to the right place and away from the wrong place.

The show is to be secret. They decide that they can probably build the disappearing box in Vaclav's room and hide it in Vaclav's closet. Then they will just have to carry it out of the house when Rasia is not looking. Lena agrees with this plan, because one of the things that Heather Holliday does at the Coney Island Sideshow is disappear into the disappearing box, and Lena wants in every way to be just like Heather Holliday.

Vaclav and Lena practice until very late, because luckily, Rasia falls asleep in front of the TV and does not stop them until it is almost ten o'clock.

"Lena, your aunt called and she ask me to walk you home," says Rasia.

BEDTIME FOR LENA

...

Vaclav knows his mother is lying, and Lena knows that she is lying, and of course Rasia knows, because she is the one who is telling the lie, but everyone pretends that Lena's aunt really did call, and they are good at pretending, because they pretend every night.

Lena packs up her bag, happy to put away her homework that is finished and one hundred percent correct for tomorrow, and ties her shoes, while Rasia puts on her loafers. Then Rasia and Lena leave for Lena's house. At the first intersection, Rasia takes hold of Lena's hand, only for safety to cross the street, but she does not let go of Lena's hand for the rest of the walk.

Each night that Ekaterina does not come for Lena, each time that Ekaterina shows that she is irresponsible, is untrustworthy, is unloving, Rasia is reassured that she has a right to love Lena as much as she does, which is very much.

Lena climbs the steps one at a time, slowly, to allow Rasia to keep up. She opens the screen door and holds it open for Rasia as she then opens the big heavy front door, and she steps inside the dark apartment. Rasia steps in behind her, mumbling about making sure Lena is safe, that there is no one in the house, that everything is okay. She mumbles this same thing every night she walks Lena home.

Tonight, Lena turns on the light in the front entrance, and all around Rasia can see that the mess is the same mess as yesterday.

Rasia waits a minute for Lena to go into the room where she sleeps, which Rasia will never, ever think of as a bedroom, only as a room where Lena sleeps, because it is not a proper bedroom for a little girl, not in the way that Rasia would have decorated a room if Vaclav had been a girl.

Rasia waits to hear the sounds of Lena getting ready, which are these:

> Sounds of Lena opening and closing drawers
> Sounds of Lena untilting the mattress from where it is tilted against the wall
> Sounds of air scooting out of the way of the mattress so that the mattress can plop to the floor

Once Rasia has heard all these sounds, she enters the room where Lena sleeps, and without saying anything, she goes to the corner and gets the worn-out felty blanket with silky edges that is peach with yellow blotches, while Lena sits, waiting, on the bed.

"All right," says Rasia. "Let's make this bed." She has said this every night since the very first night she walked Lena home, which was the day that Lena met Vaclav and saw the golden fringed bikini of Heather Holliday.

Rasia stands over the mattress and holds the blanket by two corners. Lifting her arms swiftly into the air, she billows the blanket out and over Lena, and then lets it fall softly over the whole bed, even over Lena's head.

The first time, she did this because it was the same thing she did to Vaclav every night; it was their bedtime routine. He would climb into bed and lie very still, and she would pretend to not see him, pretend to accidentally make the bed with him inside of it, pretend to be quite aggravated by a mystery lump, and then, finally, tell a bedtime story in the hopes that it might somehow make the stubborn lump go away.

The first night, Rasia did to Lena exactly what she did to Vaclav because she did not know what else to do, having waited for someone to pick the girl up; having decided, finally, to take the girl home; having waited too long for Ekaterina to answer the ringing doorbell; having taken too long to finally see the dread and shame on the girl's face; having paused too long in the entranceway, staring too long at the overflowing ashtrays, the sharp edges on the glass coffee table, the clothes flung over everything. She felt frozen, and she did not know what to do, and so she did the only thing she knew. Rasia told Lena to get into bed. Lena, following orders, marched straight into her bedroom. Rasia followed her. The room was empty except for a bare mattress on the floor. Rasia stood staring until she realized that Lena was waiting anxiously for her to leave the room so that she could undress and put on her pajamas.

Rasia waited in the hallway for a few minutes, and then she returned, saying, "Go lie on the bed," and Lena did, and then she pretended to not know Lena was there.

During the bedtime routine, Lena didn't giggle as Vaclav did when Rasia said, "Let's make this bed" or "Where in the *world* did this lump come from?" Lena seemed to submit to and welcome the ritual but did not ever smile. Still, Rasia had never considered altering or omitting one tiny word or gesture from the routine.

This night, Rasia played the game with Lena because it was what she had done each night for five years. So she went about her futile attempts to flatten the lump, pulling the blanket tighter, smoothing the blanket next to, over, and around the lump, and then said, "Okay, lump. You are winning. Let's have a story. If you can't get rid of something, or someone, you should always tell long, boring story, to make it go away."

THE LONG, BORING STORY

...

Rasia sits on the foot of Lena's bed, which is really just Lena's mattress on the floor.

"Okay, so here is the story." Rasia tells Lena her bedtime story in Russian, even though at all other times Russian is strictly forbidden. Rasia does this for Lena, so that she will not have to struggle to understand, but she does it for herself too.

"Once upon a time in the faraway land called Moscow, there lived a princess. Just so you know, in case you have heard things, Moscow today is very different from how it was then, once upon a time. The Moscow in this story is beautiful. The Moscow in this story is not full of breadlines, just people buying fresh bread from the baker down the street with real money, not money worth less than the paper it is printed on. In Moscow, once upon a time, you could walk down the street without going by a man sitting in the gutter, yelling at you as you walk by and showing you the fingers he lost in the gulag.

"Okay, so where are we? There is a princess, and this princess, she likes wandering around the markets, dressed in a ratty *shmata* and some ugly pants like a peasant, because like most princesses in a story, she sometimes hated to be a princess, and she didn't know how lucky she was. She liked to pretend that she was not a princess, because it made her feel like a normal girl.

"One nice sunny day, she was wandering around the market, and she bumped into a boy. Really, she was so busy staring at the blind old lady selling boiled eggs out of a bucket, because she was appalled that anyone would buy eggs that the old woman had touched with her dirty, knobby fingers, that she walked right into this boy. She fell, and there was a horse and cart coming by just at that moment, and it almost went right over her head and smashed it like a melon, but the boy, he grabbed her hand and pulled her to him and saved her life. Of course, she fainted in his arms.

"When the princess woke up, the boy was kneeling over her, with his face right almost touching her nose, and she was afraid of him for one second, and the next second she wondered what his name was, and the next second she wondered everything about him, and the next second she was terrified that he would go away forever and that she might lose him. She was in love with him, plus he had just saved her life. He was in love with her already, because she was a princess, even though he didn't know she was a princess. This is how it always is with princesses, boys love them for no reason.

"Next the princess and the boy did what everyone does when they fall in love: They sat in some crummy place, on some buckets turned over in a cold alley by the market, something like that, and they didn't care that they were hungry and that they were thirsty and that they were tired, and that their mothers were wondering where they were, and they told each other everything that they had ever known and everything they liked and everything they didn't like, and all of their favorite colors and books, and what kind of rain was their favorite, sprinkles or downpours.

"And then the princess told the boy that she was a princess, and he told her what she already knew from his raggy clothing: that he was a peasant.

"She told him, with tears coming out of her eyes, that she had to go back to the castle.

"She told him, with her stomach twisted into terrible knots, that they could not see each other, that her father, who was a nasty old king, would not allow it.

"He told her, 'Don't worry. We will run away together.'

"She was confused, because she loved him, but she also really, actually loved being a princess, and she loved her mother and her sisters, and she had never lived anywhere but the castle, and she was not sure if she could really run away forever.

"He told her she could have some time to think about it.

"He told her that every night for one hundred nights he would stand outside her window, at the foot of the castle, and wait for her, and that if she came out on one of those one hundred nights, they would run away together. If, after one hundred nights of waiting, she did not come out, he would have his answer, and he would leave her alone.

"She went back to the castle. That night, he waited at her window.

"She did not come.

"The next night, he waited at her window.

"She did not come.

"Every night, for ninety-nine nights, he waited, sitting like a bug outside her window, and she did not come.

"On the one-hundredth night, the last night, he did not wait outside her window, because he could not bear to know that the princess would never be his, that she did not love him enough, not as much as he loved her. He thought maybe it was better to not know.

"On that hundredth night, the night that he did not wait outside her window . . ."

Lena interrupts the story with a mighty snore from beneath the blankets. The snore startles Rasia, who has been so absorbed by her storytelling that she has failed to notice that Lena is already asleep.

LENA IS ASLEEP

. . .

Rasia sits for several minutes, watching Lena sleep, watching her back rise and fall, watching her mouth make the small baby movements that our mouths remember only when we are asleep. She feels a need to watch Vaclav when he is asleep, and she knows there is no one who feels the same about Lena.

After she has watched Lena sleep for several minutes, she stands up, walks carefully to the door, and turns out the light.

In the kitchen, flies are swarming around the dishes in the sink, little tiny fruit flies. She thinks of Lena, who might wake up in the middle of the night and want a drink of water, and who might find no clean cups and no way to fill up a clean glass of water. She finds, under the sink, a bottle of Ajax with a little yellow squirt left. She fills the sink with hot, soapy water and washes dishes until none are left.

She picks old cigarette butts out of the drain and throws them away, and wipes down the sink until it shines.

On the counter next to the sink there is a dish rack, and there are little spots of black mold in its joints and creases. Rasia cleans the dish rack until the mold is gone.

When the dishes are dry, there is nowhere to put them away, because the shelves in the cabinets are dusty and sticky and covered in spills, so with her wet sponge, Rasia wipes down all the cabinets.

The kitchen is clean (not as clean as her own, but much improved), but if Lena gets up in the middle of the night, she might trip over the clothes on the floor on the way to the kitchen. She might trip and bump her knees on the coffee table. She might knock over one of the ashtrays that is full of cigarette butts and matches and gum. She might step on one of the pizza boxes that are on the floor, full of bits of moldy pizza cheese.

Lena might, walking sleepily to the kitchen, step on one of the empty bottles of Stolichnaya that are lying about on the floor.

Rasia empties the ashtrays; she takes the bottles out to the blue recycling bin on the sidewalk; she takes the pizza boxes out to the trash. She washes the ashtrays. She throws away the fast-food drink cups that are crowding the table, the hamburger wrappers, the Diet Coke cans.

She collects in her arms a bundle of clothes belonging to Ekaterina, clothes that smell of perfume and smoke. She walks through the open door of Ekaterina's room, looking for a laundry basket. She turns on the light with one hand.

She is only looking for a laundry basket.

There is no laundry basket. She looks closer, just to be sure.

On the nightstand, next to the bare mattress, there are spoons and foil and straws but no laundry basket. There are tiny Ziploc bags but no laundry basket.

There is more of the same garbage that was in the living room, cans and bottles and trash, but no laundry basket.

There are cans of hairspray, wrappers of many kinds, but

Rasia will not clean this room, no way. This room is not on Lena's path to the kitchen to get a drink of water.

Walking home to her own house, to her own son and her own husband, Rasia thinks carefully about Lena, as she has so many times before. She thinks about the strange behavior of Lena and Vaclav; she thinks about Ekaterina.

Rasia is not an idiot; she knows what goes on in the world. She knows the story with those spoons and foil and straws.

She doesn't know what to do. Oleg says she should mind her own business. She doesn't know what to do.

THE ANCIENT EGYPTIAN SARCOPHAGUS OF MYSTERY

...

At school, Lena spends all her time with her new friends and ignores Vaclav. Behind closed doors, Vaclav and Lena practice the act each day after school in stolen hours between homework and bedtime. Vaclav does Lena's homework as fast as he can, whipping through long division, churning out paragraph after paragraph of perfectly Lena-accented English. He wants to make sure that they have time to practice over and over again. Both Vaclav and Lena think about the act all the time. They think about the act when they wake up in the morning, in the shower, while the teacher is taking attendance, during recess, during gym class, and at bedtime, when they both hear the same bedtime story told by the same mother.

In Vaclav's room, they consult *The Magician's Almanac* for directions to build a disappearing box.

"Read again," Lena says, pacing.

"The sarcophagus is, for all outward appearances, a sealed box with a hinged door on the front. Invisible to the audience, and essential to the illusion, is a false back concealing a small compartment in which the magician secrets himself," Vaclav reads.

"Hmm," says Lena.

"I don't understand," says Vaclav, "Where do I go when I disappear?"

"You go inside, you close door, like a closet. Then you sneak behind back wall, which is not really back wall, is another door, and then open the front door and the audience will see that you are gone, but really you are behind this second door. Easy," says Lena.

"Easy, but to build the box, look. . . ." Vaclav holds the book out to Lena. The instructions to build the Egyptian Sarcophagus of Mystery look wildly complicated; they are full of numbers and symbols.

"Hmm," says Lena.

"Where will we get all this stuff?" Vaclav says. Lena thinks.

"This is a thing takes long time to build. We find this piece of wood on the sidewalk, someone is throwing away, we take. Then later we find someone has extra wood at this house, we take. Then when we have enough, we will build." She sighs. "So this, it will not be on time. For the act."

Vaclav knows that she is right, that it will take them a long time to collect all the material to build this sarcophagus. He folds down the corner of the page so that he will remember to look and see what they need to collect, so that they can look in the piles on the sidewalk when it is time for people to throw away their couches and their old kitchen cabinets.

He flips through the almanac, looking for a new trick to add to their act. Lena practices her shimmy for the disappearing-coin trick.

When Vaclav and Lena are apart, Vaclav is excited to tell Lena what he is thinking about the act. He likes to tell her all about the problems that he is worrying about. He knows that when he tells her about a problem, she will look at him like he is a silly turtle, because in the same way that he saw the thing immediately as a problem she will see immediately its solution. He also likes, of course, to tell her all about his new ideas for tricks that will definitely work.

When Vaclav and Lena are apart, Lena too thinks excited thoughts about the act, but she also worries that her new friends would think the act is stupid, and she knows that the act is something that the Aunt would make fun of, even more than the kids at school might make fun of it, and in a worse way.

When Vaclav thinks about the act, and about how his magic is a secret he shares just with Lena, he feels excited. Lena feels ashamed, because she keeps her secret for different reasons.

THE DAY BEFORE THE SHOW

...

The day of the show is going to be Saturday. Vaclav knows that Saturday is the day that most people go to the boardwalk at Coney Island, because it is the day that most people have no work or school. The exceptions to this are his mother and father, who must sometimes work on the weekend, and also people who work in restaurants, people who drive the subway trains, and people who work in hospitals, because those things don't stop for the weekend. Also, of course, magicians. Magicians can do magic every day of the week. Even though it is fall, it is still warm outside, and the boardwalk will be crowded with people enjoying one last summer thing before it gets too cold.

On the day before the show, Friday, Vaclav wakes up early, and is unbearably excited. He brushes his teeth and feels that each moment is both slow and fast. There are butterflies in his stomach flapping their wings so furiously that they might burst into a puff of magical smoke.

Vaclav does not see Lena walking to school, on the sidewalk, as he usually does. He does not see Lena outside the school, talking to Marina and Kristina. Vaclav is worried that Lena might be late for school, and that she might get into trouble for being late.

All day Vaclav cannot concentrate on his classes, because he keeps thinking about his show, and it feels like he is holding candy in his mouth and trying not to eat it. It feels as exciting as getting to leave school early for a doctor's appointment, knowing the whole day that your mother will pick you up and will even bring snacks to eat in the waiting room. It feels like when it is your birthday and everything is special all day, and everyone you pass on the street and everyone in the pizza parlor and everyone in the world is part of your birthday, even if they don't know it.

Vaclav becomes more worried when he arrives at ESL, because Lena is not there, and she is usually there before him. Vaclav watches the door carefully, watches each kid coming in to see if he or she might be Lena, and even when the kid is clearly not Lena, he thinks he or she might be Lena just for one tiny part of a second. When Colin walks through the door, Vaclav thinks for a second that Colin might be Lena, even though Colin is a boy and is from a place in Africa where they speak French called Côte D'Ivoire, which you say like *koh-duh-vwah,* which means Ivory Coast, and does not look like Lena at all. Also, Colin is a little bit chubby, and Lena is skinny like a grasshopper. Even so, Vaclav's mind plays a trick and for a second Colin's dark arm is Lena's dark braid of hair, and then it is over and the person is Colin.

For every person who comes into the ESL classroom, Vaclav's heart makes his brain have a little bit of hope, until Marina and Kristina come in, and class starts without Lena, and then there is no more hope.

"Okay, let's get started. Everyone take their seats. . . . Who's missing? Lena's not here?" says Mrs. Bisbano, and then she says something that hurts Vaclav's feelings without meaning to.

"Marina . . . where's Lena?"

"She is sick, maybe," Marina says. Vaclav feels sadness because he was not the automatic person to ask about where Lena might be. This sadness becomes happiness immediately, because Vaclav thinks of how he and Lena are secretly more friends than Marina and Kristina and Mrs. Bisbano know. Vaclav smiles because he thinks of all the secrets he and Lena have that are secret from Marina and Kristina. Vaclav does not imagine secrets that Lena might have with Marina and Kristina, secrets that he might not know about. To Vaclav, this is impossible.

Vaclav is not worried at all about Lena, because she probably just has a cold or is just pretending to be sick and is not even sick. Sometimes Vaclav does this, he pretends to feel sick, and his mother pretends not to notice that he is faking, and she lets him stay home from school, and that is a wonderful thing.

Also, Vaclav is certain that Lena, even if she is sick, will still perform the act on the boardwalk at Coney Island, because she is his dedicated assistant and the show must go on. Even if Vaclav had one arm cut off and eaten by birds with no chance to ever sew it back on, he would still perform the act.

Probably Lena just didn't want to go to school. Probably she will meet him at his house after school for homework, snacks, and dress rehearsal. Most likely.

MOST LIKELY NOT

...

When Vaclav gets home, Lena is not there. Vaclav picks up the telephone and dials her house, listens for one ring, and hangs up. This is a secret code that Vaclav and Lena have, to call and let the phone ring once, and it means: Call me back if you are able! This way Lena can call Vaclav without having to talk to his parents, and Vaclav can call Lena without making the Aunt angry.

Vaclav waits by the phone for several minutes. The phone does not ring.

Vaclav is worried about Lena, but he knows that the show must go on, and he knows that Lena is knowing this too, and that they are thinking of each other always a little bit. The next thing to do, according to the list called "Schedule," is to have a dress rehearsal.

Vaclav puts on his costume, which is:

> David Copperfield T-shirt from David Copperfield performance at Madison Square Garden

Old blazer that no longer fits but can be squeezed into, decorated all over with glitter and puffy paint
Regular black pants
Shoes with aluminum foil on the top to look like silver shoes
Opaque white doctor's gloves from the company where his mother works, to imitate the white gloves of the magician
And yet to be obtained: one magician's magical top hat

Vaclav is planning to make the magician's magical top hat out of some materials that he has found around, including some shirt boxes from the department store and some tape and some black paint borrowed from school.

Vaclav hopes that at home, secretly, Lena is happily preparing the golden fringed bikini of Heather Holliday.

SHE IS SICK, MAYBE

...

Rasia walks into the house holding many bags from the grocery store as well as her purse, which is very heavy, and she has to pee. She drops everything on the floor, right in the entrance, and tears off her coat and runs to the bathroom. Every day she feels herself getting older, and every day she is surprised by things that leak when they used to hold tight. On her way into the bathroom, she sees that Vaclav's door is closed. While she is peeing, she decides that after she puts dinner on the stove to reheat, she will go into Vaclav's room and interrupt whatever is going on. She does not think that Vaclav and Lena are necessarily doing something bad, but she knows that they are doing something secret, and Rasia thinks that something secret might be on the way to something bad.

First, dinner. Rasia puts her bags from the grocery store in the kitchen and takes a stained and heavy Tupperware container from the freezer. She runs hot water over the Tupperware until the frozen borscht block is ready to slide out, and then shakes it loose until it bangs into the pot on the stove. She decides, as the icy block begins to melt and shift in the pan, and the first thawing dribbles sizzle on the hot metal, that she will knock on Vaclav's door to inquire if Lena is staying for dinner, and then will demand that Vaclav and Lena help her put away the groceries. This plan will get Vaclav and Lena out of the bedroom and away from whatever it is they are doing, and it will get her some help with the groceries, which is a relief, because she feels so exhausted, even inside of her bones and in her stomach and in the back of her throat.

Standing outside of the closed door to her son's room, Rasia hears tiny voices in a perfect rhythm, in a tiny little call and response, his voice high and scratchy, Lena's voice with its deep Russian full-mouthed color. Without knocking, Rasia opens her son's door and is very surprised at what she sees.

Vaclav is kneeling on the ground, completely absorbed in his project, surrounded by scraps of black electrical tape and cardboard. He does not notice that his mother has entered the room, and he continues to talk to himself, carrying on a conversation with an imaginary Lena. Rasia is so sure that she has heard

Lena's voice from outside of the room that it takes her a moment to really accept that he is playing both parts.

"Where is Lena?" she asks, breaking the spell of her son's concentration. Vaclav looks up, startled, and tries to hide behind his back the secret project he has been working on, wondering if his mother heard him practicing the act with invisible Lena.

"She is sick, maybe," Vaclav says.

"She was in school?"

"No," says Vaclav.

"No?" asks Rasia.

"Probably she is sick," says Vaclav.

"Probably she is sick," says Rasia, and she thinks for a moment. "I am going to go to check on her at her house. I'll be right back," she says, then she grabs her purse and rushes out the front door before she even puts on her coat.

Vaclav is relieved that his mother is going to check on Lena. He wishes for a second that he could go with her, but there is so much to do for the act.

Vaclav gets back to work on his top hat. His mother seemed not to have noticed at all the top-secret preparations for the act, which is lucky. He thought, for a moment, when she came in, that she would know what he was planning, and then the show would be ruined.

Half an hour later, when Vaclav investigates a terrible smell coming from the kitchen and finds the borscht burning on the stove, he realizes that his mother is still not home.

Oleg comes home, which means it is nearly time for dinner, but still Rasia is not home.

Vaclav calls Lena's house, but there is no answer.

Vaclav and his father wait an hour. Vaclav calls Lena's house again; still no answer. He is very worried.

"Where is Mom?" Vaclav asks.

"I don't know," Oleg says. "What did she say when she left?"

"She said she was going to check on Lena," Vaclav says.

"So she is going to check on Lena," Oleg says.

Later, Oleg brings matching mugs of cold burned borscht into the living room, and they eat dinner together while they watch Russian television.

It is dark outside, and nothing is the way it should be, and Vaclav is starting to feel that something is terribly wrong. Oleg does not tell Vaclav that he must go to bed. Maybe this means that Oleg cares a lot about him, and maybe this means that Oleg has forgotten about him. Either way, Vaclav feels that he could not possibly go to bed, with the circumstances being what they are, which is missing Lena, missing Mother, and the big day of the show on the Coney Island boardwalk only hours away.

The night before the big show, the young magician falls asleep very late, next to his father. His face, which is pressed to the black leather of the couch, is illuminated by the Russian sitcoms his father watches on satellite television, beamed in from across the world.

SECRETLY HE IS AWAKE

...

At a time late in the night, so late as to actually be the morning, Oleg wakes up, still on the couch, and knows because the TV is still on, and because he and his young son are both sleeping on the sofa, that his wife has still not returned home. If she had returned home, she would have clucked at him and taken their son to bed and turned off the TV, and he would have acted annoyed as he stumbled down the hallway to resume his snoring in bed. If she had returned home, he would have acted as if he minded the interruption, but really he would not have minded at all. He feels so lonely waking up on the couch to the TV and no wife clucking at him.

First he turns off the television, and then he does something he has not been able to do for several years, something he has not realized he has been missing.

He scoops his son into his arms and carries him, still sleeping, to his bedroom and tucks him in.

Secretly, Vaclav is awake. But he too has missed being carried to his bedroom, and so he pretends.

THE DAY OF THE SHOW

...

Rasia comes home from the police station at five in the morning, just as her husband is rushing off to work.

"Where have you been?" he asks. "I worried."

"You would not believe," she says.

"I am late already; we talk about it later." He kisses her once on the forehead and is about to head for the door, but then he stops and kisses her again.

"Everything will be okay," he says, and then he goes.

She checks on her sleeping son, just to remind herself that her family is okay. Later, when he wakes up, she will have to tell him about what has happened to Lena, and she doesn't know what she will say, what bad parts to take out, what good parts to put in. When Vaclav wakes up, she will make him pancakes and they will talk.

Rasia goes into her bedroom, takes off her shoes, and falls asleep on top of the covers in an instant.

When she wakes up, it is eleven o'clock, the latest she has slept in years. She expects to find Vaclav eating a bowl of cereal in front of the TV, or in his room, working on his tricks. But when she sits up in her bed, everything is quiet. Quickly she gets out of bed and runs through the house. Vaclav is not in the kitchen, not in the living room. She checks the bathroom, pulling back the shower curtain, and finally Vaclav's room, his closet, and under the bed, but he is gone.

Rasia knows that her son has kept secrets from her many times but that he has lied to her only once, and she thinks about this time now, and she knows exactly where he has gone.

LADIES AND GENTLEMEN

...

When Rasia buys a ticket for the famous Coney Island Sideshow, she is surprised at how familiar the little red ticket stub has become, how it looks to her, even as she sees the man tearing it off the big roll of hundreds of identical tickets, like a personal thing. She remembers the first day with Lena at Coney Island, the day when she knew her son had lied to her, the day when Lena became the most important person in his life. She remembers going through his tiny pockets that night by the washing machine, finding the red ticket stub, remembers reading the words. She remembers the sink of her stomach when, after he told her they had gone on a ride, she found, in his pocket, two ticket stubs to the sideshow. The sideshow!

Now, as she walks into the sideshow's theater, through the dark hallway, through the black door, she hopes that he will be there and that he will not be there, and she tries to breathe a little bit into the spaces around the awful thing she has to tell him.

HEATHER HOLLIDAY

...

Inside the sideshow's theater there is an audience of only one person, one boy magician. He is wearing his black electrical-tape-and-cardboard top hat, he has covered his sneakers in silver aluminum foil, and his hands, inside his white magician's gloves, are folded politely in his lap.

When he sees his mother come into the theater, he is surprised and confused about how she knew to find him here, and then afraid that he is in trouble, but mostly he is relieved. It has been very bad, very scary, to sit alone in the dark theater, knowing that something bad has happened to Lena, something terrible that would stop her from coming on the day of the show. He does not feel nervous for being in trouble with his mother for sneaking out. He guesses correctly that today is a day during which there is no getting in trouble for the normal things that usually get you in trouble.

Rasia comes and sits next to him, and she puts her arms around him, and he starts to cry. The lights go down; the show is about to start.

"Do you want to go home?" Rasia whispers.

"No," Vaclav whispers. "I want to stay."

Rasia is glad, because she is still unsure of what to tell Vaclav, and she is curious about the sideshow. Vaclav wants to stay to see the show because he is afraid of the day moving forward any more, and he knows that soon the day will move into a new time, and the time before, the time he spent sitting alone in the theater, not knowing anything, will be gone, and he will know something. There is no going back once you know something, because from then on, you always know it.

Together, they watch Insectavora climb the ladder of swords, then they watch the glass eater eat glass, and they watch the human blockhead hammer nails into his nose. Vaclav stays nestled under Rasia's arm, and even when the Great Fredini comes on and does a magic act that is both astounding and hilarious, Vaclav cannot keep the tears from coming into his eyes.

When the lights in the theater go down, just before the last act, Vaclav knows what is coming next.

Heather Holliday is very tan, not like she is tan from the sun but like she is a person who was born with skin that is already tan, and her hair is two different colors, light blond and black, and it is done in a hairstyle like a lady from black-and-white television. She has cheeks like a little girl's, and a silver loop through her nose. She smiles without showing any teeth, and her smile is like a wink.

She is wearing the golden bikini.

There are things about Heather's golden bikini that make Vaclav sad about Lena.

Heather Holliday's bikini is very small, and a lot of her skin is showing, but she does not look naked at all. The skin that is showing, the skin of her belly and the tops of her thighs, does not look like private skin. She is wearing black fishnet stockings on her legs, and her legs look strong, like the legs of a superhero, not like Lena's tiny legs. Also, Heather wears white high-heeled shoes, but she wears them like she could run in them, like she could do anything in them. Lena's feet look shy, always trying to hide behind each other, even in sneakers.

The best thing about Heather Holliday is the way that her arms are hanging casually at her sides, like she is holding someone's hand or holding a grocery bag with just a candy bar in it, when what she is holding are two big, long, shiny swords, like a knight in medieval times.

She takes the center of the stage, and she stands there, with her big winking smile and her feet in her white high heels slightly pigeon-toed.

At first Rasia is appalled: The girl can't be older than twenty-five, she's wearing almost nothing, and she has in her nose a ring like a bull—disgusting. But the way that she walks to the center of the stage and curtsies, and the way she smiles, is elegant. When she lifts her chin and tilts her head all the way back, Rasia wants to rush up on the stage and stop her from hurting her tender, exposed neck, to tell her that this is not something for such a nice girl to do, that she could easily find work as an administrative assistant; Rasia could help her. Heather opens her mouth wide, and Rasia is finding the whole performance terrifying, but she can't look away.

When Heather actually swallows the sword, she makes it look easy. Rasia is surprised to think that this sword swallowing is lovely, and that when Heather pulls the sword out, it doesn't look like it hurts at all. Rasia thought that it was going to be disgusting, but aside from a little bit of slobber on the sword after she pulls it out, it is actually pretty.

Heather swallows three more swords and then leaves the stage all of a sudden without taking her bows, but she returns a moment later with the man who hammered nails into his nose.

Heather pushes a box on wheels onto the stage. The man explains that she will contort herself to fit in the box, and that he will then drive swords through it from every angle. He announces that the audience must be quiet and to focus closely on this trick, because it is extremely dangerous. Vaclav has never seen this trick performed before, but he has read about it in *The Magician's Almanac*, so he is very interested. He thinks that this might be a perfect trick for the magic act, that Lena is the perfect assistant for this trick, because she is so small.

The nail-nose man helps Heather step into the box and watches as she folds her feet and legs under her, and then adjusts and readjusts and squishes down so that she is completely inside the box. Without warning, the man plunges Heather Holliday's long sword into the side of the box. Rasia gasps loudly, and Vaclav thinks he heard a tiny squeal from inside the box in Heather Holliday's voice. *She's been hurt,* thinks Vaclav. His mother grabs his hand and holds tightly.

The nose-nail man seems not to have noticed, and he plunges another long sword into the side of the box, perpendicular to the first. A small wheezing cough comes from inside the box. Rasia expects, at any moment, to see blood dripping to the stage from the bottom of the box, and as the man lifts yet another sword and prepares to stab it through the box, she again fights the urge to rush forward to the stage. She is sure at once that Heather Holliday is dying slowly, losing blood inside the tiny box, and sure just the same that it is all part of the trick.

Vaclav doesn't want to think anymore about doing this trick with Lena.

The man turns to the audience and announces that as an unprecedented treat, he will invite the audience to come to the stage and peer inside the box. He unlatches the lid and peers inside from above, and Vaclav and Rasia hold their breath, because they are sure that Heather Holliday is dead, impaled inside the box, but he only smiles and then beckons the audience to come to the stage.

Vaclav and Rasia get up from their seats in the theater slowly. They feel at once excited to go onto the stage and to peep inside and to see secrets, and they also feel bad for wanting to peep and to see. Vaclav feels nervous to be so close to Heather Holliday, and to look at her in the box.

Vaclav steps onto the stage first, one aluminum-foil-wrapped sneaker after the other, and turns to help Rasia up onto the stage. The stage is only a little more than a foot high, and for Vaclav it is easy, like taking stair steps two at a time, but for Rasia, who is older and thicker than other mothers, and is creaky from the changes in climates in her life, it is difficult to get on the stage.

Vaclav takes her hand firmly in two of his, and she concentrates on holding her purse and puts one foot on the stage, and they both heave a little bit so that she is on the stage, two feet and two ankles and thick-soled shoes. They both feel the hollow plywood shell of the stage beneath them; they both feel it is less solid than they would like, less solid than they had thought it would be.

They approach the box, still holding hands.

The nose-nail man tells them to get a close look.

They both inch closer.

The box is very small, and Heather is curled up inside just like a baby, except that her arms are over her head instead of at her sides. The swords are going in all directions all around her.

There is one sword that fits across her middle, where her stomach sinks away from her ribs before rising up again to meet her hips. There is one sword squeezed between her thighs. There is a sword just above her cheekbone, so that she is not able to turn her head.

Vaclav and Rasia are not able to focus on the swords and the incredible way that Heather Holliday has contorted around them. They are awkwardly trying to seem comfortable looking down at a live human being in a golden bikini stuffed into a box. Heather Holliday is not able to turn her head, but she looks at them out of the corner of her eye, and she still wears the smile that is like winking.

Vaclav can't stop staring at Heather Holliday's exposed left armpit. There is a diamond of tiny black stubble, and lines of white crusting the folds in her skin. Vaclav feels that this is the most private part of someone he has ever seen before. Even Heather Holliday cannot see this place on Heather Holliday's body.

They spend many seconds looking into the box while the nose-nail man looks at them, while Heather Holliday looks around, and up at the ceiling, like a person in a dentist's chair while the dentist's hand is in her mouth. Vaclav tries to find a good place to look, but among the golden bikini and the skin and the fishnet and the armpit, he does not know what to do.

"Is lovely," says Rasia, with her heavy, thick voice, surprising them all.

THE LIGHT OUTSIDE

. . .

After the show, Vaclav and Rasia leave the theater, and are blasted by the sunlight, the smell, and the rush of traffic outside. They walk toward the subway, holding hands, but they do not talk.

When they get home, Rasia tells him to change, and she goes to the kitchen, and she pours juice into two little glasses, and she sets them on the kitchen table, and then she sits. She hears the sounds of Vaclav changing into his regular clothes; she hears drawers opening and closing.

When Vaclav takes a seat across from her at the kitchen table and looks at her, so afraid and worried, she takes a deep breath and starts.

"Do you know this, what has been happening to Lena?" she says. Vaclav's face tells her that he doesn't know what she means. "Did you know that not-nice things were happening to Lena?" she asks.

"No," says Vaclav, thinking *Maybe*.

"Did you know that Lena's aunt was not taking care of her?" she asks.

"No," says Vaclav.

"I wasn't sure. I thought maybe. So I had to say something, because I was worry about Lena." Rasia feels the conversation settle into the reality of the kitchen, feels that it is getting easier to talk about these things.

"What did you have to say?" says Vaclav.

"I had to say somethings to the police," she says. This makes

Vaclav feel that his mother might be crazy for reporting something not nice to the police. Vaclav thinks of the not-nice things happening all the time at his school, like when the gym teacher yells at everyone to climb the rope faster, or when kids push one another in line for the water fountain. He thinks of large SWAT teams of police like they are on TV and on Russian news, rushing all the time up and down the corridors of his school, trying to stop all the not-niceness.

"Why did you do that?" says Vaclav.

"So that if things are happening, they are stopping them." This makes Vaclav feel that maybe the not-nice things are actually very serious, for the police to be interested.

"Right now, the police are also thinking that not-nice things are happening. So they are taking Lena away."

"What?"

"They are protecting her."

"Where is she?"

"I don't know. I am not her family. They will not tell me."

"How will we find out where she is?"

"I don't know. I can ask the police. I don't know. I don't know if they will be telling me. They say they are putting her somewhere safe."

"Who is with her?"

"Nobody."

"Nobody?"

"I cannot go because I am not her family."

"And . . ."

"And you cannot go because you are not her family."

"Is her aunt with her?"

"No."

"Why?"

"Her aunt, she was not taking care of Lena."

"She is alone!"

"Yes."

"Call her aunt and ask where she is!"

"Her aunt is not knowing either. No one is knowing where she is, so that she is safe."

"Lena will want me to know! Why can't I know?"

"No one can know."

"I am not no one."

"I know."

"Who will talk for her?"

"What?"

"Who will talk for her? Who will make sure that she is okay?"

"There are people."

"What people?"

"I don't know."

"Where is she? I have to go be with her. She's alone and she'll be afraid. You have to tell me!"

"I don't know, *I don't know*. I'm sorry! I'm sorry!" And now Rasia realizes that she was wrong about the parts of this conversation to be nervous about. She was as afraid as any mother is afraid both to embarrass her son and to embarrass herself, to not give him all the right information and to give him too much information, which would scare him. What she could not predict was that Vaclav would not focus on the bad things that happened to Lena at the hands of people bigger and more powerful than himself. He would focus on the very bad thing that Rasia did, which was to take away his only friend.

THE SAME BUT HORRIBLE

...

When Vaclav went to school on Monday, no one knew anything about what happened over the weekend. No one knew anything about Lena, or not-nice things, or the Aunt, or about Rasia ruining everything and calling the police. No one knew anything, and everything was the same but horrible.

Mrs. Bisbano asked Marina and Kristina again about where Lena was, and they didn't know, but they didn't seem too bothered.

Vaclav thought they might come by to talk to him, to ask him if anything had happened to Lena, but they didn't.

Sometimes some people just stop coming to school. Like Genesis's half-sister, who used to come but now lives in Puerto Rico most of the time and just comes for the summer.

Lena is gone, and it is because Rasia, who knows nothing about America and American police except for what she sees on *Law & Order*, and who has made a huge mistake and told some things to the police, probably not even the right things—probably they did not understand her, with her rumbling voice and her thick tongue—and she made them take Lena away because of her stupidity; she made them take Lena away.

Vaclav is like an empty person because he has nothing.

Vaclav has nothing, except for anger.

At his mother.

All day the anger is growing, and it is making new anger, and it is burning the back of his throat.

Every day he wakes up thinking that Lena might come back. All day at school, he waits for her to walk through the door.

After school, Vaclav comes home and goes into his room directly, and he does not come out for dinner and does not come out when he is called, and does not come out or respond when his mother sits outside the door, crying quietly and saying "Please, please."

APART:
VACLAV

A MAGICIAN, A MOTHER, AN AMERICAN GIRL

. . .

"Knock, knock. I am coming in," Rasia says loudly to the closed door of Vaclav's bedroom. Rasia has a new habit of both knocking and saying that she is knocking. This is a new habit that began when Vaclav became a person taller than she is, singing in the shower in a voice so low that on occasion Rasia hears this voice and thinks, *Oh, no, a man has broken into our home and is showering in our shower, a serial killer like the man on the* Special Victims Unit *television show who has a cleansing ritual that he must do before he brutally kills his victims, and this man is going to come out of the shower and kill me.*

She is amazed by him. When did he become seventeen? He was little forever, and now he's suddenly big like a man, and has a girlfriend. She worries, and this is the motive for Rasia's knocking, and this is also the motive for Rasia to enter the bedroom quite frequently.

"Mom! Come in! I want to show you something," Vaclav shouts. Rasia can hear in his man voice the softness and insistence of the little boy who is always needing to show her this, show her that. This needing is not going away, so far.

Rasia opens the door and feels relief because the bed is made and is totally unrumpled, and her little boy and the pretty American girl are not tangled together naked in the bed as she dreads. Her son is standing and holding many dollar bills. This is part of his newest trick, which is to make dollar bills disappear. Why this is a trick he is wanting to learn, why this is a trick anyone wants to see, Rasia does not understand.

The pretty American girl is sitting on the floor of the room, sitting with her legs out to both sides like a ballerina doing stretching. This American girl, with the name Rasia always forgets, is never sitting in a chair. She is always sitting on the floor with her legs all over the room, or twisted up like Indians from India, or on top of the desk, or she is lying on her belly on the floor, reading a book for homework. Who does schoolwork like this, on her belly on the floor like a snake or a potato farmer?

Why does Rasia always forget the name of this girl? Because it is a boy's name, something like Fred or Bob. It does not make any sense.

Another thing not making sense: Who are these parents who live in a fancy-shmancy brownstone house but don't teach their daughter to sit in a chair properly like a human being? Who are these parents who can't spend some money to buy their daughter some new blue jeans without holes all over the knees and just under the rear? Why not buy the girl a nice skirt and some pantyhose and teach her to sit in a chair?

Rasia looks at Vaclav, holding these dollar bills, smiling his goofy smile. Most people do not really mean their smiles, most of the time. For most people, their smiles are a lie, a trick, or a promise. Vaclav's smile is just a smile, and he always means it.

The girl is sitting on the floor, looking at Vaclav, and does not even seem to have a plan to stand up to say hello to Rasia.

"Maybe if you are not sitting in this way with legs out hilter-skilter you are not needing so many patches on your jeans? No?" Rasia tells the girl. The girl smiles big, with all her teeth out. This is not the way a girl should smile, without any modesty.

"Mom! Ryan likes the holes in her jeans," Vaclav says, and Ryan laughs, because to Ryan, everything can be a joke.

"Yeah! I do like them, actually." Ryan is still smiling at Rasia like a showgirl or a horse. Rasia just looks down at her. All around Ryan's long denim legs are tiny pieces of paper. In the V-shaped space Ryan has made with her legs are glue and tape and scissors and fat black markers. She is making a huge, enormous mess in Vaclav's room, and Rasia can give guarantees that the girl will not be the person who is picking anything up. Vaclav, the boy, will be picking up from the floor this mess that the girl has made. This is not the way.

Rasia is not happy to be picking up after Oleg, no, she is not, and many times she has thought, *If he does one dish, just one dish, I will not leave him,* but still she always stands there and washes all the dishes until there are not any dishes to do, and still he sits on the couch and lifts no fingers, and still she has not left him. Or else she has thought, *If he leaves his underpants on the floor of the bathroom again I will leave him,* but does she pick up the phone to call the lawyer to make a divorce? She does not. She picks up the damp underpants and brings them to the hamper, and still she is married to him because to divorce your husband over one soggy pair of underpants, this is not something that people do. This is a marriage, this picking up a little, putting away a little, forgiving a lot, and this is good enough. Why should it not be good enough for this girl who cannot sit in a chair? She should have a boy pick up after her? She should expect this? Why should this girl with the holes in the behind of her pants be waited on hands and feet?

The only thing that Rasia can understand is that all the pretty girls want to be the girlfriends of Vaclav, who is so tall and lanky (What a surprise! Look at the father! Look at the mother! Little Soviet tanks. Try to knock one over. Impossible.) and has such a head of hair, and the eyebrows that are the eyebrows of a movie star. He is so charming and handsome, who can blame the girl? This is something to like about the girl. Good taste.

Is it nice to see Vaclav with this American girl? This girl with freckles on her face and hair that is some of it blond and some of it red? This girl who wears shiny gloss on her lips all the time and smiles like a crazy person and laughs so loud? Is this nice? No, this is not nice. But what else had Rasia expected? Why else come here, to this crazy place of opportunity, but for her son to have a blond American girlfriend who is like an alien from Mars, she is so different. Why else? A Christmas tree in the window of the brownstone house and parents who do not introduce themselves. And what do the people do to live in such a shmancy place? Consulting. Vaclav says, "Mom, they do consulting." This is not working, giving advice to people who are rich and can pay for advice.

"What is this? Is project for school?" She points in a direct, strong way at the paper Ryan is working on. She always means to be more like the mothers on television, who are more gentle in their talk and more gentle in their bodies, but she is always too hard, she pushes too hard on the air around her with her arms, with her vocal cords, is always surprised when she crashes through this soft American air.

"No, it's not for school. I'm just making a flyer for my band. . . . We have a show next week at Ozzie's." Ryan holds her flyer up so that Rasia can see it. "You should come!" The flyer is covered all over with Xeroxed pictures of guitars and cassette tapes that are cut out and put on with Scotch tape, and it says, in very bad handwriting, PINK FLAMINGOS WEDNESDAY 7 P.M. OZZIE'S COFFEE SHOP FREE FREE FREE!

"Why are you not using Vaclav's computer and printer? You can make it nice with pictures and type the words so it is looking nicer. This way people will come to see the music, not think that you are some crazy people. Okay? You do it again on the computer," Rasia says. She is trying to make a suggestion, but her words rush out of her mouth, stomp, stomp, stomp, always sounding like a command.

"Oh, thanks. I know it looks kinda sloppy, but that's the thing. I mean, that's the cool thing. It's a whole movement, like an aesthetic, you know, the whole DIY thing, from the original DIY zines, I guess," Ryan says, and Vaclav smiles, because he knows that Ryan will have to explain, and re-explain, and further explain everything that she has just said, because Rasia will want to know what all these words mean, and Ryan will have to use more new words to explain these things, and to see Ryan try earnestly to make Rasia understand why her band poster looks homemade, for some reason this is one of his favorite things about Ryan, that she will do this.

"What is this DIY zine?" Rasia asks.

"DIY stands for *do it yourself*, and zine is from *magazine*—it's a small, independent magazine you make yourself—and since you make it yourself, it doesn't look like all the big, glossy magazines, it's cooler," Ryan says.

"Okay. You use the computer, is not do it by yourself?" Rasia asks.

"No, the computer would totally still be doing it yourself, it's just that it wouldn't look cool," Ryan says.

"The computer is the new cool thing. This everyone is saying. You should make the next one on the computer, show everyone how nice it can be; this is cooler," Rasia says.

"Well, yeah, exactly," Ryan begins explaining. "The whole thing is a reaction to the mass-produced slickness of—"

"Mom, I want to show you this new trick I'm working on," Vaclav says, in order to save Ryan from herself.

"Homework is done?" Rasia asks.

"Homework is done! We always do it as soon as we get home," Vaclav says.

"This I don't believe," Rasia says.

"No, really!" says Ryan. "I can't concentrate on anything else until I get my homework done and out of the way. I can't relax, I'll just be thinking, *I have homework to do*, you know?" Rasia smiles at her, says nothing, and then looks quickly back to Vaclav.

"All is done?"

"Okay, maybe I left some for later; it's not important," Vaclav admits.

"Ach! I knew it! I knew it! Magic happens after homework," Rasia says.

Rasia started her homework crusade when Vaclav was very young, because she did not come from Russia, leaving behind her mother and her grandmother Lidia, who she would never see again in this world, so that her son could be a street beggar, which is all that this magician thing might become for all anyone knows. She keeps him doing homework, every day of his life so far, believing that this will ensure that he has this magical thing, education, which is the key to being successful in the new country. He will go to college, get degrees, and have this education knitted into his life so that he will be good and successful.

Vaclav laughs, and hugs his mother and kisses her on the cheek. He has to lean down to do this now, and he knows that this makes his mother feel that he is a big full-grown man at the same time that she feels that he is still her little boy and that this is a feeling that fills her with joy. She pretends to be annoyed, but he knows that once he has hugged her in this way, she cannot be annoyed any longer. She is a warmed-up mushy mama now, and she cannot stay mad at him.

"Watch my trick? Please? Please? Please? Sit down on the bed, please?" He takes Rasia's hand and leads her to the bed, and sweeps his hand over the covers as if he is dusting her chair for her, and she is charmed by him as if she is just a girl.

When, she wonders, *did my son become so charming? When did he start to wear blue jeans in the way of American boys, so that they do not look like clothes that are covering the body but that they are part of the body? Even more so that they are part of the person? When did this happen? When did his hair become shaggy in the way of American boys, and when did he stop combing it? When did he get so tall, and how, with his mother and father so close to five feet, how did he grow to be nearly six feet tall, so that he looks like he is close to the ceiling? It must be this American food he is eating so much of; constantly he is eating.*

"Okay, okay. I am watching. What is this trick?" Rasia says.

Vaclav looks directly at Rasia, his eyes on her eyes, and his entire self pivots around this one point of contact, and he changes, and he becomes Vaclav the Magnificent.

Watching him, you would think that he changed his clothes, maybe into a tuxedo with tails, but you would look and be surprised that he is still wearing the same jeans and T-shirt. You would feel, irrationally, that he suddenly became taller. You would search for the physical transformation, and you would try in vain to put your finger on what is different. Nothing is different, and yet everything is different. He has become Vaclav the Magnificent and is no longer Vaclav, your son, your boyfriend, the kid down the block. He is a magician, and a magician needs a stage. His presence bursts into the air and takes up most of the bedroom, so that he seems confined, trapped, where just a moment ago he seemed right at home.

"Ahh, mother. This is absolutely the greatest trick yet. In front of your very eyes, I am going to levitate. Yes, I, Vaclav, in front of these two beautiful ladies"—Vaclav nods to Ryan and to Rasia—"will raise my body, all two hundred pounds of me"—Ryan and Rasia laugh out loud—"Correction. Correction. The audience is correct to laugh at such an exaggeration. All one hundred and sixty-seven pounds of human flesh I will raise off the ground, with no external aids, no wires, nothing, just the sheer strength of my will. I trust that an audience such as you, so obviously devoted to the truth, will aid me in verifying that there are indeed no wires or other apparatus at all in the room."

The audience agrees.

"Now I must kindly ask you for silence. I demand silence, for this feat requires absolute concentration," says Vaclav the Magnificent.

Rasia looks at Ryan, who is looking at Vaclav with wide eyes, with her thin, pink lips slightly parted, with total adoration. Rasia wants this for her son, for someone to adore him, for someone to look at him as if he is glowing. She wants all the heavy love to be on the other side.

Rasia decides that it does not matter if she likes Ryan or any other girl. What is it, for a woman who has lived for more than five decades to like some girl who is putting her little-girl hands all over her son? It is not necessary for Rasia to like this girlfriend of her son, but it is necessary for the girl to adore him.

Vaclav stands in the corner of the room, at an angle, so that his profile is facing Ryan and Rasia. Vaclav looks down at the floor, and he breathes in deeply, deeply, four deep breaths, and then suddenly he is breathing as if he has just run many miles or leaped up many flights of stairs. It looks like something is happening to him, like his heart will explode or his lungs will come apart in pieces under the strain. Rasia begins to feel worried about this trick. This worry is nothing new. She always worries about Vaclav's tricks. Of course she knows that it is only a trick, that it is not real, but she knows that he might fail at it, and to see someone fail at something they love is very hard when you love the person and all they ever wanted for their whole life since they could walk and talk is to be a great and famous magician. Also, Rasia is a little anxious because she feels that maybe the trick is really a little magic, and who knows what might happen to a person when they dabble in this magic; they could hurt themselves.

Vaclav looks terrified. His face is still looking at the ground, but his fists are clenched, and there are veins sticking out in his neck, veins that are working too hard, doing too many things. He raises his hands a little bit, and nothing happens. He lets his hands return to his sides, and his face, it looks like he is very upset. And then he breathes the deepest breath of all and lifts his hands only a little, only an inch from his sides, and suddenly he is moving slowly upward, his hands are moving up and his head is moving up, and his feet, yes, his feet are an inch off the ground.

Rasia gasps and throws her arm across Ryan's chest, because this is a reflex that she has had since she gave birth to Vaclav, that whenever she is surprised, like stopping short in the car, she throws out her arm to protect the child next to her. This scares Ryan, and Ryan yells a tiny little yell and then dissolves into giggles, laughing at herself, and then with an inelegant little plop, Vaclav is back with both feet on the floor, and he seems for a moment to be catching his balance, back on earth again after defying gravity and levitating, even if only two inches, up into the atmosphere.

"How are you doing that? What is that? What did you do?" Rasia sounds angry, but she is not angry, not at all. Ryan claps loudly, she is so impressed, so proud. Ryan knows exactly how this trick is done; she even helped Vaclav practice it, helped him to get the angle right, helped him to figure out how to obscure the anchor foot, the foot that stays on the ground behind the front foot, and she watched patiently as he did it over and over again until his body learned it.

What is so wonderful to Ryan about this trick, this trick she has seen so many times? It is Vaclav's performance, his very convincing performance, all the theatrics, the deep breathing, the concentration, which he had not practiced with her or discussed with her. He does these things instinctively, and he is so perfectly amazing that she is absolutely sure that he will one day be a very famous magician, of course.

Ryan sits on the bed and feels very proud of herself, to be the girlfriend of someone so smart and so handsome, someone who will one day be so successful at something so unique.

Vaclav, ignoring the questions, takes a deep bow.

"You have been a lovely audience—really, truly lovely—and I hardly ever say that. Thank you. Without you, I am nothing." Here he bows again, even more deeply, and to greater applause. "I do it all for you—for my fans."

He bows one final bow, and it is clear to Rasia and Ryan that the performance is over and that now the regular Vaclav, not Vaclav the Magnificent, is back.

"That was awesome! That was awesome. When are you going to perform that?" Ryan says.

"I might be ready for the world, but is the world ready for Vaclav the Magnificent?" Vaclav says, and Ryan beams.

Ryan smiles a flirty smile at Vaclav, and Rasia is starting again to think not-nice things about this girl who is too thin, as if her mother doesn't even feed her, this mother who has not bothered to pick up a telephone and call Rasia, and she starts to think that maybe this girl is every afternoon after school having sex or even just doing naked things on this very bed with her little boy.

Rasia is thinking that she wants so badly to be able to talk to Vaclav about things, private things, and she is feeling bad because she has planned to talk to him so many times in so many different ways, and she has not yet been able to get these things to come out of her mouth, out loud. Today, at her office, Pamela from accounting had said that she didn't need to go into detail about the "ins and outs." Pamela told Rasia that she just needed to set some rules so that Vaclav and she knew that they were on the same page. Pamela said that with her son, she had said just one thing: "Whether I'm home or not, you respect my house:

door open and feet on the ground. And when you're in the parking lot behind the supermarket, wrap it." Everyone had laughed at this, but Rasia had not gotten the joke, and she had felt too embarrassed to ask what this meant and what was funny.

Jessica from HR had said, "Kids these days are all having sex. The question is not whether they're going to do it or not but whether they're going to do it safely. You can't stop him, but you can give him all the information he needs." But what information did she have to give Vaclav? What would she tell him? What did she want him to know?

Ryan and Vaclav are still talking about Ryan's show and this Ozzie person.

"Who is this Ozzie?" Rasia asks. Rasia says this like she is sure that Ozzie is a drug dealer, or a person with earrings in his face, or a prostitute, or something like that. She is saying it like she is just wondering which of these things this mysterious Ozzie is, but she is sure absolutely that whatever Ozzie is, Ozzie's is a terrible place for children to be going.

"Mom, you would love Ozzie's. It's a coffee shop in Park Slope, an independent coffee shop, where they have a million different kinds of tea. And at night they have little performances, just in the coffee shop, there are just couches and whatever over there so people can just sit and listen or read or anything. They have really good cookies. And rugelach! They have really great rugelach." Rasia's son says *rugelach* like an American boy. Like this is a foreign thing. And she knows for sure that she would not like this place, this coffee shop full of mothers twenty years younger than her, with their fancy strollers, where she does not know what the rules are, where she will not know the right words, mocha this or venti that, where to order, where to pay, where to sit down, and she will feel like a buffalo walking into such a place, everyone looking at her and making her feel embarrassed while she pays four dollars for a drink she throws away, it tastes so awful.

"There is alcohol there?" she says.

"No, no. It's a coffee shop. They don't even have a liquor license."

"Okay. I don't know this place," she says.

Vaclav understands. When he was a little boy, they discovered places together. Maybe other kids had a mom who explained to them, here is where you buy your subway card, and here is where you give the prescription to the pharmacist, and here is where you pick it up, and here is where you stand on line to mail a package, but when they arrived in America, Vaclav and Rasia learned together.

Now that they do far fewer things together, he is always doing something where she doesn't know the place. This is something that can make a bruise on a mother, but Rasia tells herself that this is not so different from regular parents of regular American teenagers. But a little, she knows, it is very different.

"You know what, Mom? You should come. Come to Ozzie's and you can see Ryan's band, and you can see me do the trick," Vaclav says.

"Okay. We see. I don't know," Rasia says. Rasia doesn't want to feel this way, but she is scared of the idea of going to see Vaclav do a trick at Ozzie's, where she will feel so out of place.

A sad silence inflates in the room, because Rasia and Vaclav and Ryan all know that Rasia will not come. Ryan finds herself not knowing what to do with her hands, finds herself making excuses. Making an exit.

"Oh, I have to get home for dinner. Thank you so much for

having me over," she says. Ryan rarely stays for dinner at Vaclav's house. She tells Vaclav that her mother likes her to be home for dinner, which he understands to be the truth but not all of it.

Ryan doesn't mind the food at Vaclav's house. She minds the awareness, the very acute self-awareness she feels, the slow-motion awareness of her hands, her feet, the way she reaches for something on the table, the way she uses her fork and knife, the way she says "please" and "thank you." She minds the way Rasia serves everyone instead of letting everyone take from big bowls on the table; she minds the way this makes her too aware of how much Rasia gives her, and how much she can eat, and the enormous gap between the two amounts. She minds the difference in condiments. These are small things.

The big thing is that she is aware of every word that does and does not come out of her mouth when she talks with Rasia, and especially with Oleg. She feels hyperaware of her words, her slang, her tone of voice; she is so often unsure of what they understand; she is worried that she might be condescending to them, speaking too slowly or too fast.

What Ryan really likes is having Vaclav over at her house. She likes showing him off, how he performs magic tricks for her sisters and different magic tricks for her parents, how he charms them. She likes how her dad will say, "Now, that is something!" and then talk to Vaclav about physics, which is his favorite thing in the world besides magic, or about baseball, which Ryan's dad thinks Vaclav likes.

It is rare, though, that Vaclav can stay at her house for dinner. Rasia wants him home every night. And Vaclav never argues, he just goes home. This is irritating to Ryan, that he won't battle Rasia for her. So she excuses herself and refuses invitations to dinner, and has Vaclav walk her to the Q train, so she can take the subway two express stops to her house and have dinner with her family and not have to think about how she holds her knife.

Rasia thinks that Ryan will not stay because she doesn't like to eat strange food, and that to tell the truth, Ryan does not like to eat at all—just look at her, the evidence is in her wrists, she is so thin. On nights when Rasia is making something she feels with some level of confidence is totally normal and American, and healthy, she announces this loudly to Ryan.

"You are invited for staying here, if you like. Is grilled chicken. Healthy," Rasia says, but Ryan thanks her, says no, begins packing her backpack. This healthy American dinner is appearing on her table more and more frequently, since the doctor told her that she was too fat, that she needed to eat less meat and more things green, and lose many pounds. Rasia has much faith in doctors, especially these young American doctors, with their offices like space stations, so when the doctor told her that she needed to lose pounds (at least fifty!) she asked him directly to specify, to enumerate and write down exactly what she needed to do.

When the doctor chuckled and told her that replacing a few dinners a week with lean protein and vegetables, like grilled chicken with asparagus or spinach, or a salad with grilled chicken, would be fine, and to take a brisk twenty-minute walk each day, Rasia nodded seriously and asked how many is a few. The doctor told her that he had always thought a few meant three.

Three nights a week, Rasia prepared grilled chicken with asparagus and spinach, and every day, when she came home from work, she put on her sneakers and walked around the block for twenty minutes.

Oleg did not join her in this exercise, and he was not enthusiastic about the grilled chicken with asparagus and spinach, and he lived for the days, especially Friday nights, when there would be borscht and challah and big chunks of meat in the borscht and a big piece of meat on his plate and a big bowl of ice cream after dinner.

Vaclav walks with Ryan to the door, retrieves her coat, carries her backpack. Outside, it is not yet dark. The sun is gone, but the light is still clinging to the air and the evening is at the moment when the light is just about to slip away. It is fall, and it is still warm, even as the sun goes down. It is four weeks until Halloween, and a week until the air starts to smell each evening of burning leaves.

KISSOLOGY

...

Vaclav waits until they turn the corner to stop and kiss Ryan. Besides magic, French kissing is the greatest thing in the world to him, and these days during school he is thinking more about kissing Ryan and less about magic. No matter how many times he kisses Ryan, he feels nervous and good, like being at the top of the first big drop on the Cyclone.

Vaclav likes kissing Ryan on the corner, but he also thinks of everything else all the time, everything else that might be done between a boy and a girl, and how it would be and how many of these things they could discover together if only they had a bed and a room and a blanket and some pillows for an afternoon. To think of a whole night, of having a whole night, this to Vaclav is incredible, these ideas of the things he and Ryan might do. He feels all these things igniting inside of him when he kisses her, and so he loves this kissing more than anything. When he kisses Ryan he takes all his thoughts about the things that they could do if they had the time and the places to do them, and he puts them into the kiss. With the air from his nose he breathes them into her, with his tongue he shows her the wildness and wetness and intensity of these things. When he kisses Ryan, all of these things are inside the kiss.

Ryan is different. Ryan wants the kissing to be only a stop on the way to all the other things. Vaclav knows this, because she told him, and he also knows because when they kiss she doesn't seem happy, she seems desperate, and her body presses into him too hard, and she breathes too hard, and her fingers dig into his skin just a little bit, and she pulls him toward her with too much force. When she does this, Vaclav feels the same way he does when the subway train is too crowded and everyone stands too close to one another; he can't wait for the doors to open, to take a deep breath, to break out into his long, unhindered stride and swing his arms and walk wherever he wants.

They walk a block and stop and kiss, and walk a block and stop and kiss, and they rush a little bit because Rasia knows that it does not take thirty minutes to walk two blocks and that the rush-hour Q train arrives every eight minutes. When they get to the subway platform and have time to stand and wait for the Q train to come and take Ryan away, they kiss harder and harder because the clock is ticking, and any moment the lights of the train will come and ignite the tracks, and they will know the time is almost over.

Ryan steps forward and presses her body against Vaclav's body just a little bit, and Vaclav steps back just a little bit, but she steps forward again, and she pushes against him with surprising aggression, and then her breasts are squashing against him, and he steps back, and she steps forward, until his back is against the wall and there is no more backing up, and there on the subway platform Ryan pushes against him harder and harder, and he begins to feel a back-and-forth movement between them like a heart beating or waves going out and coming in, and he does not know really if they are moving at all or if together they are making the feeling of a movement, and then the train comes with a gust of cold air, breaking them apart.

Ryan hugs Vaclav and then steps onto her train and waves as the doors close. He watches the train leave, watches it snake away through the buildings and the billboards and the treetops. He stands on the subway platform, lifted just above the roofs of Brighton Beach, and he can see down into the backyards of houses that live against the scar of the subway tracks, and in these houses, families are loving one another in Russian and Czech and Spanish while they watch the news, and in these houses, on the stoves, the mothers are making stuffed cabbage and *pollo* and creamed spinach, and they have their ovens set to 375 degrees to turn frozen apple pies from the supermarket into the smell of a real American home in just thirty minutes, and the wind from the Atlantic ocean, which is the only thing between here and there, now and before, new and old, blows the clam-juice smell of Coney Island into the windows.

ASKING THE UNASKED QUESTION, OR THE TIP OF THE ICEBERG

...

As he walks down the stairs from the elevated subway platform back to the street, Vaclav admits to himself that he does not want anything more from Ryan. A little bit, he thinks, he is a little happy for her to leave. It is enough time together, and it is good for her to go home. Can he tell her this? No, he cannot. He does not want to spend more time with her. He does not want to involve himself with more of her body. She does want more, more time, more involvement, more knitting together of their selves. He walks faster. He shoves his hands deep into his pockets. *Do I want less Ryan because she wants more Vaclav? Perhaps she wants more because I want less? Whose feelings came first? Do the feelings have anything to do with each other? Maybe I would want what I want no matter what, and she the same.* This is a very frustrating game of ping-pong to play in his head, and he does not enjoy it.

Another thought is taking shape in his mind. Maybe this is how it always is. Maybe someone always wants more. Maybe everyone has a time when they realize that they've been accidentally lying when they say I love you, I miss you, you're pretty, you're the prettiest one, I never want you to leave. Maybe this time ends and it all becomes true again, as true as you ever thought it was. Maybe this time does not end. If this time ends, it would be a smart decision to wait it out. If it does not end, then perhaps you should not wait, and you should find another person to whom you can say these things without lying. But perhaps it always happens no matter which girl or boy you are trying to love, in which case you might as well stay where you are, because you would repeat the same process with anyone else.

He is walking on the block where he has lived since he moved to America thirteen years ago. The sidewalk is becoming craggier, more and more treacherous, every day, and Vaclav realizes that it has never been repaired in all the time he has lived here.

The light is just about gone from the street when Vaclav opens the front door to his house, and he smells dinner before his hand even leaves the doorknob.

"Vaclav?" Rasia is yelling. "Sit down! We are waiting! Dinner, it is getting cold."

"I thought it was salad," Vaclav yells back to his mother.

"It is salad. Is getting less cold. Whatever," she says. Rasia says "whatever" now, something she hated when she first heard it on the television, and hated more when she heard it coming out of her son's mouth, until she started saying it, and it wove itself into her vocabulary so easily and smoothly. This word, Rasia now thinks, it is very useful. It is saying the following things all in one word:

I don't care
&*#@ you
You are uptight
I am relaxed and free
I do not submit to your uptightness

Rasia likes to turn the tables and make it so that her son is the uptight one.

"Sorry, Mom," Vaclav says. He understands that the rush for dinner has nothing to do with the temperature of the food, hot or cold, but has to do only with the happiness his mom took from making food for him and the extraordinary unfairness of his making her wait to serve it to him. This is a slightly self-centered view of things, but time after time it has been proven that his mother exists only for him. Everything she does, in some way, is for him, and everything she wants is in some way for him. He decides that he can ask her the thing that he has wanted to ask all day.

Vaclav sits on his chair at the kitchen table. This table has always been their kitchen table, as long as Vaclav can remember, like the sidewalk has always been the sidewalk, the same, forever. The span of Vaclav's memory makes these things seem ancient, but thirteen years is not a long time for a sidewalk to go without repair, and thirteen years is not a long time to have a kitchen table. Thirteen years is not a long time to live in a country; it is a very short time to live in a country. But then again, thirteen years can be a long time in other ways. Thirteen years is a long time to be away from your old country, from your home. Even one year is a long time to be away from someone and to still think of them every day. Lena has been gone for seven years, and Vaclav still misses her, every day.

"Mom," Vaclav says, as Rasia serves wilted Caesar salad with grilled chicken to Oleg, "do you ever think about Lena?" His question hangs in the air, changing everything. There was one unasked question in their family, and this was it, and now it's been asked, and all the air has emptied out of the room. Rasia continues to drop the wilted chicken Caesar salad onto her husband's plate.

Vaclav has known for many years that he is not supposed to ask this question, which is really the tip of an iceberg: an iceberg that might be labeled LENA, or perhaps WHAT HAPPENED WITH

LENA, or perhaps WHAT HAPPENED TO LENA THEN, AND THEN AFTER THAT, or perhaps THE WHOLE LENA THING.

Twice since the night Lena went away, Vaclav has tried to ask. Once in the kitchen after Rasia found him at the sideshow, and once, two years later, when he was twelve. The second time, Vaclav asked Rasia, "Where is Lena now?" and she looked so upset that he knew immediately he should not have asked. She said, "How should I know?" and walked away, and though Vaclav was not sure why, it was obvious to him that he had made her angry. Even though he never asked again, and Rasia never spoke of it, the question was always with them. The iceberg was always there in the kitchen.

"No," says Rasia. This is a lie. Vaclav knows it, and Rasia knows it, and even Oleg knows it.

"I do," says Vaclav.

Vaclav has said good night to Lena every night since the night that she went away. Out loud. In a whisper. At sleepovers, if he has to, he says good night to Lena in the bathroom while he flushes the toilet so that no one will hear him. This is not because he is ashamed but because the words are only for Lena and not for anyone else; to waste his good night on anyone's ears but Lena's might usurp its power.

The power of saying good night each night to Lena is great. On the first night that Lena was gone, Vaclav said good night to her, put the good night out into the scary, lonely darkness, and meant each word in a very specific way. Good night. Good night. He wanted her to have a good night. Not a scary night. Not a dangerous night. Not a cold or lonely or nightmare-filled night. He filled the words with all his love and care and worry for Lena and launched them out to her, and like homing pigeons, he trusted them to find her, and he felt, that night, that his words would keep Lena safe, that if he thought about her and cared about her and showed this to the universe, then bad things would not happen to her. Vaclav was not asking an omnipotent god to grant him a wish. He was stirring in himself his own very true emotions, his pure feelings, and pushing them, birthing them into the universe, giving flight to a powerful energy that he trusted would do what as a child he was powerless to do.

Each night thereafter, he had carefully sent this good night into the universe for Lena, and each night after that, he had known if he did not take this precaution, that if he forgot or neglected or was insincere in his wish or in his mind or in his heart, that the good night might not come to Lena, and that would mean that Lena might have a bad night, and for Vaclav this meant that her life might be in danger.

"Do you know what happened to her?" Vaclav asks.

"No," says Rasia. This is true and not true. Rasia has an idea of what had happened to Lena, and what had been happening to Lena, but she does not know what has happened to Lena in the years that have passed. She knows that Lena was taken by Child Protective Services but not where. Rasia also has no idea of what being taken by Child Protective Services might mean beyond what she has seen on television.

"What happened that night?" Vaclav asks.

"I do not know this," Rasia says, and looks down at her Caesar salad with pieces of grilled chicken on top. She doesn't want to answer these questions. Rasia has always imagined a time when Vaclav would want to know what happened to Lena. She imagined herself sitting quietly in an old-age home. (Oleg? Dead, of course. She is not being mean, just honest. This is what men do, they die, long before women. This is how it is meant to be, so that women can finally rest.) Vaclav would come visit on a nice summer day, and bring the grandchildren, and they would look out on the beach, where the grandchildren were playing in the sand (the old-age home was the nice one on the beach by Coney Island, of course), and Vaclav would say, "Mom, I know it was a long time ago, but do you think that you could tell me what happened with that little girl that I used to play with?" And she would say that she was surprised that he remembered that, it was so long ago, so long ago; could you imagine she is a grandmother now, and the little girl, she would remind him, her name was Lena, and she could tell him the story with misty, teary-eyed sweetness because it would have happened in such a long-ago faraway place.

But this, this is too real. This is the same place, the same neighborhood, nothing has happened since, nothing has healed, this is still bad, and to talk about bad things is not good.

"Mom, you don't want to tell me what happened that night?" Vaclav says.

"I don't remember this night," she says.

"Okay, I wish you would remember," Vaclav says, in the nicest voice possible.

"Listen," she says.

"It's okay," he says.

"You are just thinking this because it is her birthday today, in three days you are not thinking of it anymore," she says, and takes a big sip of water. Vaclav smiles, because this statement is an affirmation and a promise. Of course Rasia remembers.

"Yeah. Okay," Vaclav says. And waits, three bites. "How was work today?"

"Och," says Rasia. "Och." And she shakes her head as if to say, "Today has been the most horrible day that anyone ever working in any office has ever experienced, the atrocities that I have seen you cannot imagine, but I will tell you just one short piece of my day to demonstrate to you how awful, and you will know that I am not sharing with you the very worst parts, and this is to spare you the pain that I know all too well."

"Barbara, you know Barbara, who is always taking this day and that day as a sick day and coming back to work the next day with a box of tissues and her hair frosted with a new permanent? She comes in today and she was supposed to do a whole pile of orders yesterday, but all day yesterday I hear her on the phone, chatting, chatting, who knows with who but probably with men from the online thing she is always talking about to find dates with Jewish men, not a bad thing, but on the Internet, everyone knows there are too many perverteds. Why a woman would want to throw herself into that pit with snakes I do not know. Anyway, she doesn't do a single thing with this pile of orders. . . ." As Rasia talks and talks, Oleg falls asleep a little bit, snoring through his nose at the table, the air sneaks slowly and silently back into the room, and things seem normal, except there is a new tenderness that Vaclav and Rasia feel for each other, because she told him, although it was hard for her and she did not want to, that she still thinks of Lena, remembers her birthday, and so has promised her son that not only does she remember Lena, that she thinks of her, has thought of her that very day, and at a good time, at a right time, she will tell him.

Also, Vaclav feels a new closeness with Rasia, because he has found out that something that is big in his heart is big in her heart too.

AN AFTER-DINNER LIST

...

After dinner, Rasia and Oleg watch Russian satellite television in the TV room on the big black leather couch. Vaclav sits on the floor with his legs stretched in front of him and his school binder on his lap. He is studying for an exam in physics, but he knows already that he is solidly grounded in this subject, so he is going over the formulas he needs to know but only to fine-tune, to make sure. Vaclav has a perfect average in physics; it is his favorite subject.

On a piece of lined paper, Vaclav tests himself, copying the formulas he has memorized for the test. As Vaclav does this work, his mind wanders, over and over again, back to Lena. Vaclav needs to go into his room, and be alone, and think of Lena, and this feels for him like a fantastic thing—like having a mystery novel you are reading and you cannot focus on any of your routine daily activities, you want only to go back to your book, want only to spend time in the world of that book and to see what happens next.

In his room, Vaclav lies down on his bed, with all his clothes still on, on top of the covers, which Vaclav realizes feels special, as it is something he rarely does. This feels indulgent, perfect, to lie on his bed on top of the covers, and to think of Lena.

He thinks about what she must look like. This is difficult, because he cannot really even remember what Lena looked like when he knew her.

He thinks about what Lena sounds like, but it is difficult for him to remember Lena's voice. He thinks that this might be because Lena rarely spoke when he knew her. He remembers her saying things, but he cannot hear her voice.

Lena is turning seventeen today. She must be taller. Vaclav wonders whether she is a short person or a tall person; she was a short person when he knew her, much smaller than other kids their age. She might still be a short person. Vaclav wonders how she wears her hair. She might wear her hair in a ponytail, or short, or might have bangs. Vaclav realizes that she might have piercings in her nose or she might bleach her hair to be blond and then dye it pink. She might be fat or wear big, heavy boots, or she might dress in tank tops that say "princess," and now Vaclav realizes that there are many years between them, that they might have become different types of people.

She might be the kind of girl he would never want to talk to, a girl who listens to bad music, a girl who talks only to football players, or a girl who smokes outside during lunchtime.

He's tried to find her on Facebook, but the last time he checked there were 193,000 girls named Lena, and none with her last name. Once he realized that she might have a new last name he gave up; he would be looking for a girl with a first name, no last name, living anywhere.

Lena could have a driver's license. Lena could have a boyfriend. Lena probably speaks much better English. Lena probably has boobs. Vaclav realizes that for the last seven years he has kept Lena little, he has kept her the same age, and that now, on her seventeenth birthday, he is finally letting her grow up, and she is getting away from him. The only Lena that Vaclav has is the Lena from his memory; the real Lena is someone he does not know, someone he may not like. He feels, lying in bed, that Lena is escaping him, and he thinks, for the first time, that he may not say his good night to Lena tonight. This feels suddenly frightening and satisfying and liberating.

Vaclav tries to think about what it might mean to not say good night to Lena. He writes a list:

NOT SAYING GOOD NIGHT TO LENA: THOUGHTS

I have been saying good night to Lena for
seven years
This means that I should continue
This can also mean that I should stop
What will happen if I stop
Maybe nothing
Maybe Lena will die

This last line in the list is surprising to Vaclav, because he has never wanted to admit to himself or to anyone else that he thinks Lena will die if he does not wish her good night.

It is a silly thing to think, but Vaclav wonders if Lena actually will die if he doesn't say good night to her. He is not sure.

Vaclav then realizes that he will never know if saying good night to Lena has ever had any effect, because in all likelihood he will never see her again, and even if he does, he will never have proof that his good nights ever kept her safe.

LENA IS UNKNOWABLE

. . .

Vaclav is still trying to decide what to do about the good night, and he feels that if he says good night tonight, it will mean that he has to say good night for the rest of his life, because if he decides to say it tonight, then he will never be able to stop, because stopping means he will be responsible for something bad happening to Lena. If he doesn't say it tonight, he is taking a very great chance, but he will not say it ever again. Also, he is afraid that not saying it tonight is letting go of Lena, but he also knows from his thinking about Lena that Lena is gone from him already.

Vaclav changes out of his clothes and into a pair of sweatpants. He folds his jeans and puts them back in his drawer, and he looks at himself in the mirror.

He decides that he will get into bed and he will not say good night to Lena. His bed is cold, and he is aware of his body slowly warming the bed, the comforter and the pillow beneath his head.

He wonders when it will become the first night that he has not said good night to Lena, because right now he could still say it. Will it count when he falls asleep, or will it count only when he wakes up in the morning and has not said it? He fears for a moment that he will say it by accident; just by thinking it, he will think the good night, and that might count.

Vaclav's eyes go all over the walls of his room like it is a new room he has never been in before. He closes his eyes though he is not at all sleepy in this new room, where everything looks different.

Vaclav does not say good night to Lena, but he wonders. He wonders and wonders at something that seems as unknowable to him as the edges of outer space or the face of God. No, not even the face of God, which a person might try to imagine. Lena now is as unknowable to Vaclav as the feeling of the skin on the backs of God's knees, if God even has knees, which of course is something no one can know. Lena, to Vaclav, is an inconceivable concept. Lena is infinity. Lena is the universe expanding. Lena is the deepest part of the ocean, where no light has ever been.

APART:

LENA

LENA IS IN A BATHROOM STALL

...

Lena doesn't feel like it is her seventeenth birthday. She does have a nice happy-birthday feeling, though, a feeling like the day smells a little bit different than the other regular stale days. This day smells sunnier, brighter, sharper, lighter, but Lena doesn't feel seventeen, doesn't feel the way she sees her friends feel on their seventeenth birthdays. Lena is not excited about the seventeen things, the driving, being one year away from buying cigarettes, from lottery tickets, from being a guest at a live taping of the David Letterman show, from voting, from high school graduation and adulthood. The last birthday that really felt like a birthday was her ninth, and she's been on a wild spinning carousel since then, barely holding on, and though she has memories of going around and around, of one year and another and another and another passing, she feels that she is still nine and has not caught up to where she is supposed to be.

Today she has already received many presents, including the following:

New journals from Em
Gift certificates to the movies from grandparents and a Hallmark card covered in glitter
New socks from Em
Collection of ten "necessary" albums to improve her musical character from Em
Bracelets from the store that sells Tibetan stuff from Olivia
Card signed by the student council
Birthday shirt decorated with puffy paint from Perri and Faye
Copy of *Franny and Zooey* by J. D. Salinger, old and used-looking, with an inscription, "To my very own real-life Franny, on the occasion of her seventeenth birthday," from Em's boyfriend, Allen
Stack of twenty birthday cards from fictional characters, really from Em
Box of fun art supplies, including kneaded erasers and pens with tiny points from the members of the art club

In addition to these presents, Lena's birthday has included much birthday festivity, balloons tied to her locker, a cake with candles at lunch, and a birthday announcement over the loudspeaker during homeroom.

Lena does not feel like today is her birthday, because Lena does not feel like a person today. This is not a new feeling, it is a feeling that is always there, though it surfaces and subsides like her wisdom teeth. On bad days Lena finds it difficult to talk to other people. This is especially difficult when she must lead a meeting of the student council or the art club, or rally her teammates at soccer practice, but she gets through it, one minute at a time, by pretending.

Sometimes these feelings are just bothersome, like being at a party where you don't know anyone very well, and you have to think of what to say all the time. Sometimes these days hurt a lot. Today hurts a lot. All day there have been people who want to wish her happy birthday, and she has felt all day that speaking to each of them was like rubbing a small spot on the inside of her skull that had a lingering bruise. These little conversations in the hallway all day, they were going down the wrong pipe, they were getting up her nose, they felt like landing badly on an ankle on a trampoline, over and over and over again.

The final bell of the day rings, the end of Friday, the end of the week, and although Lena is supposed to go out for a birthday dinner with lots of friends who begged enough money from their parents to go out for sushi and to pay for her, she slips into a bathroom that is known to be a gross bathroom, a bathroom in the old hallway of the school, in the part that has not been renovated yet, a bathroom Lena and her friends usually avoid using.

In the hallway everyone is rushing toward the weekend, toward a night that is still warm like a nighttime in summer. It is a Friday, and the weekend still seems completely expansive, like a big ocean stretching out endlessly.

In this bathroom there are only two stalls. The handicapped stall at the back of the room is already occupied, so Lena takes the smaller stall, and she dumps her heavy backpack on the floor and sits down on the toilet. The embroidered script LENA on her backpack looks foreign and completely arbitrary. Her name, her identity, in white embroidery on a navy-blue background. *How could it be as simple as script embroidered on a backpack? This is me?*

She can count four feet in the stall next to hers, and she can tell that the two girls are smoking from the smell, and from the hush that fell over them when she entered.

Lena holds her head in her hands, looks straight down at the floor. She feels a momentary consolation at a new discovery: No matter what, there will always be bathrooms, and these will always be private places where she can go away and be safe. She tells herself that she can stay in the bathroom stall forever. Inside her head, she says, *Lena, you never have to leave this stall ever.* Lena has two selves. There is a self who is consoled by hearing that she never has to leave this bathroom stall, and there is a second self who did the consoling, who said, *You never have to leave this stall ever.* Lena decides to converse directly with self number two. Does this consoling self believe that once consoled, her first self will soon be ready to leave the bathroom? Yes. Once calmed, her first self will be ready to face the world outside the bathroom. Her second self must therefore remain separate from the first, who never wants to leave the bathroom. Then there is a third self, a Lena number three, who is able to interrogate the other two selves and draw conclusions, and then yet another, who is able to make this observation. Lena feels her many selves multiply, like looking into parallel mirrors and seeing the back of your head, surprisingly unfamiliar, spiral into infinity.

Lena looks at a spot on the bathroom floor between her shoes. She likes this spot. This spot is ambiguous, and she feels a kinship with this spot. The spot is either dirt on the tile or part of the speckled design of the tile that was intended to hide dirt. It does not hide dirt; it makes dirt ambiguous. Is this spot dirt or a spot? The tile has not tricked Lena into thinking the floor is clean, not at all. The floor looks both dirty and ugly. Lena wonders if she will remember this spot forever. It looks to her like the most important spot she has ever seen. She marvels at the spot. She closes her eyes and tries to picture the spot. She wonders what it is about the spot that makes it so marvelous, that has attracted her eye, what has made this spot stand out among all the other spots. She thinks she might perhaps be the first person to ever notice this spot, to acknowledge this spot, to perceive of this spot in all its spotty specificity.

Does the spot conceive of itself as a spot? No, certainly it does not. What Lena likes, she decides, is the unknowing specificity of the spot. She has the urge to write this phrase down; it seems so brilliant to her, seems to express something she has been wanting to express. The unknowing specificity of the spot. Although the phrase strikes her so cleanly between her eyes, lights up new and exciting spaces in her brain, she is not certain that she will remember it. She wonders why she does not trust her own memory at sixteen. Seventeen. She's seventeen. She decides that she does trust her own memory. She remembers all the trigonometric functions, the difference between mitosis and meiosis, all the prepositions in the English language. Aboard, above, across, after, against, along, and so on. This is not a problem of memory. The problem is the enormous gaps between her multiplying selves. She worries that she will lose the self who has observed the spot. When she speaks again, leaves the stall (no, don't think of it, shhhh), she will lose this self, and with it the spot. Certainly there have been other moments like this, other spots, grander and far less grand. She can remember vaguely having thoughts about being in a moment, about connecting with specific scenery. She even has fuzzy memories of telling herself to remember. She does not, however, remember the specific spots. She decides to start remembering all the specific spots in her life, starting with this one specific spot. She decides that the spots are the keys to living a life as a complete person, not as a disjointed puzzle person made up of many different people trying to masquerade as one person. She unzips her backpack to find a piece of paper to write down this plan.

"Lena?" One of the girls in the handicapped stall is saying her name.

"Lena?" A response is required, and now the stall has become unsafe. She has to answer, because that's part of pretending to be a person and not many selves looking at a spot. Not answering would give away her state. One of Lena's selves is asking some of the other selves, "What is your state?" The conglomerate of selves is unsure of its state but is sure that its inability to produce an answer is a sign that the selves are not functioning as one, not enough to pretend. At least one of Lena's selves is concerned that if she does not answer, she will give the smoking girls cause to worry about her. Another of Lena's selves thinks that allowing them to worry about the state of Lena might be a good move. Yet another of Lena's selves panics at this idea, rallies a strong contingent of pro-answering, pro-pretending selves. Other selves watch the commotion.

"Lena?"

Lena is sure that other people don't have many selves. She is terrified that she doesn't have a core self, an essential Lena. She feels that she used to but that she lost it along the way, that at some point it became buried, suffocated, and died, because when she looks beneath the chattering of the selves, nothing is there. Maybe the fractured feeling is taking hold because something is dead inside her, or missing.

"Lena?"

Again, the voice. Lena starts talking quietly to herself: "If we have the capacity to make decisions about whether or not to reveal our state, then now is not the time to debate what the state is, in particular. What I'm saying is that if we have the capacity to decide, then we are in control, still, and should exercise that control."

"Lena? Is that you? Are you okay?"

Lena again feels the mirror behind the back of her head and sees the infinite multiplying of her selves, and this feeling is unpleasant. *This mirror behind my head,* she thinks, *is fuzzing my thoughts.* Does everyone have so many selves? Do they just artificially align the selves? If you stand straight and look straight forward, you will not see the endless reflections of yourself in the mirror, because your own head will obscure them. Is this the solution, or are the many selves the solution?

"Lena?" This time the word *Lena* (Her name? How odd to have a name! To be Lena!) is being spoken by lips, lips on a face, and this face is floating on a floating head attached to no body, which has appeared upside down under the divider between Lena's stall and the next.

"Hi, Serena," some of the selves answer, and the other selves line up behind these selves, and things begin to settle a bit. Serena is bending over to look into Lena's stall. Serena stands up and becomes feet again.

Lena waits.

"Yeah, it's her," Serena says to the other set of feet in her stall. Then her head reappears under the divider.

"Are you okay?"

Lena looks at Serena's face. Serena's head is much lower than her heart. The way she is bending over and looking up at Lena is making her face do strange things. A big vein is sticking out on her forehead, and she is wearing dark eyeliner all around her eyes. Some people wear eyeliner to do something, to make their eyes look nice or something, to look sexy, but Serena seems to be wearing eyeliner just to wear a lot of eyeliner. Maybe she just wants to look more grown-up.

"Are you okay?" Serena asks again. Lena is admiring the bravery of wearing a lot of eyeliner just for the fuck of it. Lena realizes that she doesn't do anything for the fuck of it, and she is disappointed in herself. Lena rarely even says the word *fuck* out loud.

"I'm worried about the vein on your forehead," Lena says. This is so true that Lena hadn't realized she was feeling it, the feeling emerged and was articulated instantly.

"You're worried about my vein?" Serena asks.

"Are you guys smoking cigarettes in here?" She is not embarrassed by the stiff way she says *cigarettes,* which she usually feels uncomfortable saying. Maybe right now she could even say *period* and *vagina* and *puberty* and *navel.*

"Yeah. Sorry. Do you want one?"

"Yes. Thank you." Again, she has answered honestly without thinking, without conniving. Lena is not used to saying exactly what she means without calibrating, and she has never smoked a cigarette.

"Do you want to come in here? There's a ton of room. It's the handicapped stall."

"No," says Lena. Serena passes her a cigarette under the stall divider, and then she passes her a lighter.

"I don't know how to do this," says Lena, unashamed, though she feels aware that this is not cool.

"Unlock your thing," says Serena. Lena reaches up and feels

for the lock but keeps her eyes focused on her spot. Serena's feet come into her peripheral vision, and then they cross, and Serena's butt is on the floor, and now Serena's whole body is in her peripheral vision. Lena locks the coordinates of the spot into her memory. There it is. In the corner of that linoleum tile. Not the one that is part of this stall and part of the next stall. The first tile from the left that belongs to this stall only.

Lena shifts her focus from the spot and onto Serena's face. Serena takes the cigarette out of Lena's hand and lights it, then hands it back to her.

"Just breathe in a tiny little bit, not a lot," Serena says.

"I'm not going to smoke it. I just want to hold it and do the flicking thing," Lena tells her.

"Okay," says Serena. Lena looks at Serena's face. It has a lot of things going on all over it. There is the eyeliner, which is black, and there is makeup on her face that makes her seem a lot paler than she really is. Her hair is in pigtails, but it also has a lot of little braids in it, and it has a lot of little clips all over it too. Also, her eyebrows are really thin on purpose. Other than that, she has exactly the same face that she had when Lena first came to school, when they were nine, when Serena wore stupid trendy jeans just like everyone else before everyone became a kind of person, when they were all just trying to learn math and not pee in their pants.

Lena wants to tell Serena about this, how her face is the same, because it is interesting, but she is afraid that Serena might feel upset about it, that she might take it the wrong way, because she seems to want to look grown-up. Suddenly Lena is not being honest; she is not saying each thing she is thinking. Lena feels a sudden and extraordinary sadness about this space between them, between all people. Everyone is worried, and everyone is wearing something on purpose, but no one wants anyone to know about it, and no one wants anyone else to say anything at all about it. Everyone wants to go about as if they were a fantastic superhero, born into the world complete; no one wants to acknowledge that they are self-consciously creating themselves, but everyone is. *Everyone is,* Lena thinks.

"So why are you freaking out?" Serena asks.

"I think it is because I found this spot on the floor. It is unknowing and specific."

"Yeah," says Serena, nodding. Lena is surprised that Serena seems to understand. Then Lena thinks that Serena might just be agreeing to be nice, and there is maybe a fifty-fifty shot that Serena understands, and then Lena thinks that she herself is not one hundred percent sure about understanding the spot, but that she likes the way that Serena just nods and says "Yeah." Then again, maybe the unknowing specificity was obvious to everyone and Serena had always known about it and Lena was just now discovering it. It wouldn't be the first time that Lena would be surprised to discover something that everyone else had known all along.

"Also," says Lena, not realizing until the word is vibrating all about in the bathroom air that there is an also, "it's my birthday and I don't know anything about when I was born."

Lena realizes that she has to explain, that she should just go on and tell Serena her biggest thing, this thing that encapsulates so many other things but that generally could be called "I am not like everyone else, and the first part of my life is a wild, spiky ball of mess."

"I was adopted when I was nine—" Lena starts.

"I know," Serena interrupts. "Sorry, go ahead," she says.

"Does everyone know that?" asks Lena. She knows that all

her friends know it, but she is surprised that Serena, who is sort of peripheral, socially, and with whom Lena has never had a significant conversation until this very moment, knows. But now Lena thinks, *Oh, of course,* that she knew these strange tidbits about everyone, things a mom might tell another mom; these things just got around. Kids who had an autistic brother, or whose dad cheated once, or whose mom used to be a model, or who had an uncle who committed suicide, everyone knows.

"Yeah, I think everyone knows it. I mean, it sounds kinda cool, you know? It makes you seem interesting, or mysterious." While Serena is talking, Lena starts thinking about the mysteries in her life, which seem inextricably linked to her missing self. Maybe having so many things missing from her story, things she has been afraid to know, maybe this is the key to finding the part of her that seems to have gone missing, numb, dead, or worse.

"Yeah, I guess it is mysterious. The whole first part of my life is a mystery," she says, "and I don't think I want it to be a mystery anymore."

THE PARENTS WHO DISAPPEARED, AND THE GIRL WHO WOULD NOT

...

Lena does not know where she was born. In a squat in Moscow? In a concrete apartment building in Brighton Beach? Someone knows—certainly Lena's parents, wherever they might be, know—but Lena does not know. All Lena knows is that she turned up in Brooklyn, a tiny, parentless child. How she ended up in Brighton Beach is a mystery.

Lena tries to imagine what happened. Her parents came from Russia, and she was born in Brooklyn, or she was born in Russia and they brought her here. Then either they went back to Russia and left her, or they're still in America somewhere. Either way, they leave Lena in Brighton Beach, and they disappear. Lena does not disappear. Lena is the girl who will not disappear but stays behind pitifully, like a dull stain. Lena's parents go and leave Lena behind. With a babysitter? Here, watch the kid for a few hours, will ya? *Da?* On a doorstep? In a lobby? With a doorman? Perhaps they meant to take her, packed everything, all the tiny, torturous baby things, diapers and nipples and formula and tiny clothes and books for bedtime, and realized only too late, as their plane soared over the great stinky Atlantic, with comic slaps on the forehead, "The baby! We forgot the baby!"

Lena tries to put together a picture; she tries to imagine how she wound up where she did. Maybe something happened to her parents, new immigrants, and they tried desperately to get someone to care for her. She imagines that distant relatives were all around. Maybe her grandparents were still in Russia. The relatives, so happy to share vodka and news, to tighten relations (Third cousins, twice removed, but we grew up like brothers!), began to distance themselves (Fourth cousins. By marriage only, and that didn't last. Not really technically even related, otherwise I would take the girl, absolutely, but with things as tight as they are, the price of everything, and to raise a kid and not even family, and where is her family? They should take responsibility!), and no one wanted her. Lena was passed, from here to there back to here and away again, and learned that she was a burden, and got quieter, and stayed in the background, watching, not to be a bother, and this was not appealing, and the people feel her quietness like a sound, and her shadowy small presence and her serious face like a heavy rock in their stomachs, and they did not want her around.

Lena does not know how it happened that she was placed in the care of a woman to whom she had no relation, but in the gel of Lena's earliest memories, she is living with Radoslava Dvorakovskaya, whom she calls Grandmother but who is not her grandmother.

LENA IS A STAIN ON THE LIFE OF RADOSLAVA DVORAKOVSKAYA

...

The summer before Lena would turn five years old, she had been living with Radoslava for as long as she could remember. Lena was trapped alone in a little apartment building full of little apartments full of little old ladies in the Russian neighborhood called Brighton Beach, which was full of Russians, which was in Brooklyn, which was full of immigrants. The old ladies all looked the same; they were variations on a theme, with their head coverings and their medical-supply apparatus for walking slowly, painfully, to the grocery store to collect the many shopping bags necessary. Necessary for what? Necessary to give purpose to a day. Necessary to buy onions from the stand on the corner at Ocean Avenue, the ones at the supermarket, two pennies more per pound. A crime when down the street there are perfectly good onions, two pennies less. Who do they think they are, these supermarket people? The old ladies cannot be fooled.

The old ladies go to the stand to get the good onions, and come back. The next day they go to the butcher. All the ladies get dressed for the butcher in their something special. They sponge foundation on their faces in a color matching nothing, or matching perhaps the skin tone of a photograph from 1934. Then they dab rouge on top of that, and smear lipstick in the approximate area of their lips, lipstick that always seems to escape the lips and advance onto the face through deep trenches around the mouth. For the butcher, some women even take their hair out of their curlers. For the butcher, they are dressed and polished and smelling of perfume that says, "I am wearing perfume; it is from a bottle; I put it on this morning, both before and after I pulled on my support hose."

Radoslava always told Lena that the butcher was like all the other men, everywhere. The butcher, she said, has what you need, knows that you will pay. He knows that you are hungry, but that you will pretend you are not hungry. He smiles at you, calls you gently by your name, and it sounds so nice in his tough, sweet, manly mouth, but he will steal from you and give what is yours to another woman if you are not careful, so you must be careful. Like all men! But if you want what is yours, then smile at him, show him that you know about meat, that you are not pushy, that you trust him (but never trust him). Ask yourself, Radoslava would tell Lena, is he giving maybe an extra quarter-pound, no charge? Is he giving the leanest part? Is he using the freshest or the scraps from yesterday, dried out? If he is not giving the best to you, who is getting it?

Radoslava was like a million other old ladies in their *shmatas* puttering around the sidewalks of Brighton Beach, doing errands, waiting to die in the new world, where their daughters took advantage of a healthy flourishing capitalist market and had their acrylic nails adorned with plastic gems.

Radoslava Dvorakovskaya liked to feel that she was special,

because she suffered more than most. She made a point of leaving her apartment as infrequently as possible. She told her friends, the other ladies who puttered over for tea and cookies, that she was terrified that a black person would mug her. Or one of their own sons, who were so disrespectful and committing so many crimes so you didn't know who to trust. Or she was terrified that she would fall down and break her hip just like Mrs. Galipova, who could no longer do for herself so that her sons and daughters put her in that godforsaken nursing home, which was worse than hell. Or that she would get run over and killed by one of these crazy taxi drivers. These were the reasons.

The real reason that Radoslava Dvorakovskaya did not leave the apartment was that she was lazy and fat and did not like to walk. She had always been this way; she had always been an unkind and unhelpful person; as a child she was lazy and spiteful, and age had given her beautiful excuses to do exactly what she had always wanted. She complained with vigor that being old was awful, a shame, and she moaned about how horrible it was, but really, truthfully, old age was Radoslava's dream come true.

And then there was Lena. Lena ruined everything. This was no secret. Radoslava Dvorakovskaya would yell to the girl in Russian, "Yelena! I am old and I am dying, and you have ruined my last years of peace." There were usually other people around, as Radoslava Dvorakovskaya often had visitors. Lena was always around. Lena was shy and quiet, and she did not make friends with the other children in the big apartment building and on the street. She was terrified of these children, who knew one another already, and ran around, and yelled, and made a lot of loud noise. She could not imagine interacting with them. When she and Radoslava Dvorakovskaya would venture outside of the building for groceries, or to do the laundry, or to send and receive mail, Lena would cling to Radoslava's legs, grabbing fistfuls of her dress, staying close to her wide, soft flanks. Radoslava Dvorakovskaya would swat at her like a cow swats flies with its tail.

The day that Lena most remembers hearing about her mother, she was playing in the shag carpeting. She would lie on her belly in this carpeting, which was green, and imagine that it was a lush forest, or a jungle, and she would walk her fingers through the jungle of the pile, tiny, pale, round explorers in a noodle wilderness. Her fingers had conversations with one another, or they simply explored, avoiding the dangers that lurked. Surely there were tigers about! Even lions! Or those black panther cats!

While Lena played with the rug, Radoslava Dvorakovskaya would sit several feet away, at the kitchen table, with the friends who had come by to sit with her and commiserate. They smoked and they drank tea, and picked at the pile of dry pastries that sat in the middle of the table, and gossiped and kvetched in Russian.

"Why not give her to someone else? Why should you have this burden?" This from Mrs. Yablokov, who sat with Radoslava Dvorakovskaya at the table on this day, whose husband was alive, and whose sons were in high school and were handsome, and were, according to Mrs. Yablokov, studying to be doctors. Mrs. Yablokov did not work, which was rare, but went about to every apartment to tell sad stories of other people and to become upset about them. Her life was very difficult, and she felt everyone's pain so much that she always had to share it with everyone else, and then she would take a bit of everyone else's pain, and she would talk and talk and make sure that everyone was always aware of everyone else's suffering.

If you had fallen down and bruised your ankle, she would tell you about the neighbor woman who died in her sleep.

"You think that's bad? You should see Malka. In so much pain she can't move! Bruised ankle, you should be so lucky. This is pain. This is life. Isn't it terrible? It is terrible. Oh, I can't stand it anymore, it is terrible. So are you able to dress yourself? I should think not. Just terrible, oh, I feel so terrible for you. The shame."

Mrs. Yablokov made you feel worse. She made you feel worse about this new country, its dangers and mysteries, and she made you feel worse about the old country you left behind, the country you missed like an abusive spouse, because at least you knew each night what was coming.

"Look at her there. What is she doing in the carpet? She might be retarded," said Mrs. Yablokov, and so Lena began to listen, because they were talking about her.

"Who knows. Who knows what drugs the mother was on. Or the father! Who knows." Lena did not know what drugs were. She was incredibly confused about drugs, in fact, because she had seen the posters in Russian saying not to take drugs, and showing the pictures of people out-of-their-minds crazy, or very sick, or stealing things. You could tell they were bad people from the way they were drawn. So drugs were for bad people.

And yet she and Radoslava Dvorakovskaya would often go to the drugstore, and Radoslava Dvorakovskaya would buy drugs, and the man there would sell to her the drugs, and this did not seem like the thing on the poster, that this man was bad, or that Radoslava Dvorakovskaya was bad. Perhaps it was okay to do drugs when you were an old person but not when you were young like Lena. This made sense. Lena's mother had taken drugs, which was wrong, because she was young.

"So young!" Radoslava Dvorakovskaya would moan. "Babies giving birth to babies! It's terrible. And not married. No wonder." And so Lena became terribly confused about her mother, who was a baby who did drugs, who was not married, and who was now gone. Was she dead? Lena did not know. She was afraid to ask.

"Lena! Our tea, it is cold. You make new tea. And not so strong this time. I'm weak, and I can't have my heart spinning along."

"Yes, *Babushka,*" Lena said. Lena had always called Radoslava Dvorakovskaya *Babushka,* Grandmother. This was the only name Lena had for her, though she did not believe that Radoslava was the actual mother of her own mother. If Radoslava were the mother of Lena's mother, she would not talk about Lena's mother the way she did.

"Like a stray dog, she was raised like a stray dog. So who would be surprised that she squats and gives birth to this mutt in this mutt country and then scampers off? Yelena! My tea is becoming cold. It's the very least that you can do, don't you think?" Lena would get the tea and think, *Oh, I am the mutt. I wonder what a mutt is. My mother is the stray dog who scampered off. How is this a mutt country? What is a mutt? This woman,* Lena thought, *is not the mother of my mother, or she would not say that my mother was raised like a stray dog.*

Lena, at four, was very good at making tea for her *babushka.* She would pull a chair from the table and push it against the stove, where she would retrieve the teakettle, fill it with water, replace it on the crusted burner, light the fire, sit in the chair, and wait for the whistle. The hard part was the pouring, because the kettle was heavy, and often the first water to escape the tipping spout would miss the cup and splash against her shins or sprinkle onto her toes.

Lena brought the ladies their tea, and this reminded them of her.

"Where is the mother? Where is the father? Is there no other family? Surely someone else should watch her, with you unable to even walk three blocks to the grocer. . . . A shame."

Mrs. Yablokov seemed exquisitely pleased that Radoslava Dvorakovskaya could not walk the three blocks to the grocer.

"The mother and father are gone. They are either dead or they have gone back. If they were here, they would be banging down my door, asking for money, asking for using the telephone, to take a bath, to sleep on my couch, as if I live in excess and have so much to give!" Mrs. Yablokov accepted this explanation, as it offered further evidence of the disrespect, the irresponsibility, of the young.

"There is no one else?" she asked.

"There is the sister of her mother, the one who first left her here," said Radoslava, and Mrs. Yablokov's eyes became electric.

"And why will she not take the girl?"

"She refuses. I have asked her, begged her, to take this burden off my hands, for the sake of Lena. She hangs up the phone, and later the number is no longer her. I see her on the street and I yell for her; she runs away from me, an old woman." Mrs. Yablokov shook her head at this. Too terrible. Too terrible.

And meanwhile, Lena, on the floor, was listening to every word. Because she was silent, adults forgot themselves in front of her, and Lena acquired a superpower that most kids wished they had; she became invisible. She knew everything that went on, and everything that was said, just by being very still and very quiet. She had always thought that adults were like animals, that if you held still they forgot you were there. It was hard for a little girl like Lena to hold still for so long. But she held herself still now, because she was a collector of this information, about her parents, about other people who might want her, about her life.

"Can I tell you something? And this must remain a secret between us," said Radoslava, lowering her voice.

"Of course, Rada. Your confidences are safe with me. Go on."

"The sister, she works at the club." Mrs. Yablokov's eyes widened, for this was better than not being able to dress yourself. To work at the club was a nebulous idea for the women, but it had something to do with dancing, or taking off one's clothes, or serving alcohol to men, or taking naked photographs, or having sex for money. To work in the club was to do all this and more.

To Lena, the club sounded wonderful, like she had seen clubs on television, where you might have a hat with your name on it and a group of friends and secret passwords and a secret key to a secret clubhouse. Lena wanted to work at the club too, and she wanted to be with this woman who seemed to be the opposite of Radoslava.

MRS. YABLOKOV'S DREAM COME TRUE: RADOSLAVA DVORAKOVSKAYA DROPS DEAD

...

Two weeks after Radoslava Dvorakovskaya sat with Mrs. Yablokov and spoke about Lena's parents, and her aunt, and the club, and Lena being retarded, Lena woke up while Radoslava Dvorakovskaya was in the shower. Lena could hear the water running in the bathroom. Lena quickly folded her blankets and put them away in the linen closet, and rearranged the pillows on the couch where she slept, and then she sat in front of the television and turned it on and watched a cartoon goat on *Sesame Street*. Lena liked *Sesame Street* because she could tell what was happening even though she didn't understand any English, and she liked the funny sound the goat made when the dog pulled on his beard.

When *Sesame Street* was over, Radoslava Dvorakovskaya was still in the shower, and Lena had to pee. She walked to the bathroom door and listened. She went back to the TV and watched the cartoon shows that were on after *Sesame Street*. Lena liked to watch these but became bored easily because she did not understand the words the cartoon characters said. She could put on the Russian channel, but it was for grown-ups and did not have fun pictures.

Lena still had to pee, and now it was very hard to sit still, even sitting on the floor and rocking back and forth with her ankle wedged into her crotch. Now Lena could not watch the television or concentrate on it; she could concentrate only on needing to pee and trying not to pee in her pajamas. Radoslava

Dvorakovskaya would be very angry if she peed in her pajamas, because this would make work for her (which Lena would do), and Radoslava Dvorakovskaya would be sure to tell all of her visitors that Lena was still wetting her pants.

Lena wiggle-waddled back to the bathroom and listened. The shower was still going. This was strange, because usually the hot water would run out, and when Lena bathed, Radoslava Dvorakovskaya would stand outside, yelling at her not to use it all up. Hearing the water was too much for Lena, and so she wiggle-waddled to the kitchen, little drops starting to sneak out, and she took down a bowl and she put it onto the linoleum floor under the kitchen table so that if Radoslava Dvorakovskaya came out of the bathroom, she would not see Lena right away.

Lena squatted over the bowl and peed, and even though it was a large mixing bowl, some pee danced out onto the floor, and when Lena tried to move, to better her aim, it only got worse.

When Lena was done, she did not feel too much better, because of the warm bowl full of pee and the pee on the floor, and the possibility that she would be caught and embarrassed. What would Radoslava say if she found that Lena had peed in a mixing bowl? She would tell everyone how strange and off and bad Lena was. Quickly Lena pulled a chair up to the sink, and she picked up the bowl, which was fuller than she thought it would be, and she tried to climb the chair without sloshing out any of the pee.

Lena got one leg up on the chair, and then another, but as she was standing up, she wobbled a bit, just a bit, and pee from the bowl, so cold now, sloshed onto the front of her pajamas, above her belly, which was unexplainable too. How do you explain a pee stain on your belly, where pee does not come out?

The rest of the pee she dumped into the sink and rinsed away with water. Lena then wet a sponge with dish soap and cleaned up all the other little drips everywhere, and then dabbed at the front of her pajamas. She realized that this was better; she could tell Radoslava Dvorakovskaya that she spilled water. She could even say that she spilled water while trying to make tea. Lena decided to clean everything up, and to then make the tea so that there would be less lying. The shower was still going in the bathroom. Even if it stopped right now, there would be plenty of time, since Radoslava took so long in the bathroom to get out of the shower and to powder herself, and replace her teeth.

Why was Radoslava Dvorakovskaya still in the shower? Lena was afraid to knock.

Everything was clean. Lena's pajamas were only slightly wet on the belly. The teakettle was on the stove, getting hot and ready to boil. Lena changed into her daytime clothes from a little pile next to the couch where she slept. Dressed, she sat down again in front of the television and surveyed the apartment. Everything was clean, and dried, so that there was no evidence that the pee bowl had even been used at all, no evidence even that the kitchen rags had been used to wipe anything up. No evidence at all. Why was Radoslava Dvorakovskaya in the shower, still?

There was another episode of *Sesame Street* on the television. Lena tried to learn the letters of the alphabet, the numbers from the Count. Three bats flying. Ah, ah, ah, ah, ah. What were these sounds the Count made? This was his laughing. What are these things flying, black things? These Lena could not figure out.

When *Sesame Street* was over, it was too long for Radoslava to have been in the shower. Lena figured that four shows had gone by since she had woken up, and that was a very long time for Radoslava to be in the shower. Lena was hungry, and that was a sign too. Too long. Lena thought of what should be done. She could knock on the door, in case something was wrong. This was a bad plan, because if Lena interrupted her shower, Radoslava would be very angry. Lena watched a commercial about a doll as big as a real live girl, whose hands you could hold, and who would cuddle with you while you took a nap together.

Lena got up and walked to the bathroom, and she pressed her face to the door, careful not to make the door bang around in its frame, because this would make Radoslava know that she was listening, and Radoslava would be angry. Lena did not hear any noises, except for the shower water. Lena lifted her fist and knocked three times.

There was no answer. Lena's knock was too soft; it was like she had not knocked at all. She could go back to watching television and pretend she had never made the knocking plan. She walked two steps away. She turned around quickly and took two quick steps, the second one almost a hop, and she banged on the door very loudly. And stopped. And listened. Nothing. Bang, bang, bang, again. Nothing. *One, two, three bangs,* thought Lena. Ah, ah, ah, ah, ah.

She is dead in the bathtub, thought Lena. This did not make Lena very upset, because she was not quite sure of what it meant. She thought of it because Radoslava had said it over and over again. "One of these days they are going to find me dead in bathtub." Lena had not understood the part about one of these days, but now she understood a new part. Lena was the "they" who would find her dead in the bathtub. She had thought before, *Who are these people, this team of people who walk around, finding people dead or finding people and sending them away, or running about robbing people? Who are "they"?*

Since Radoslava was dead, Lena thought, she could not be mad. So Lena opened the door to the bathroom. The water was running. It was cold in the bathroom, when usually it was very warm from the warm water. There was a shower curtain the color of peaches, only with brown mold growing up from the bottom, so Lena could not see into the shower. There was no fog on the mirror. *Fog must be from hot water*, Lena thought. Lena closed the bathroom door behind her.

Lena got down on her hands and knees next to the edge of the bathtub. She took one finger and very, very carefully, without making any rustling at all, pulled the curtain, making a very tiny gap that she could see through. Slowly Lena moved her head toward the tiny gap in the curtain. Lena was being very careful in case Radoslava was not dead in the shower, in case she was alive; Lena did not want Radoslava knowing that Lena looked in at her in her shower.

The first thing that Lena saw was Radoslava's hair, which was gray, and straight, and missing in patches. At first Lena thought that she was looking at the back of Radoslava's head, that Radoslava was looking down at the tub floor, but then Lena saw that this was the face of Radoslava, with her hair all pressed against it with wetness. Her eyes were open, but they were not looking at Lena, and there was hair covering them, so Lena felt certain that Radoslava could not see her.

Lena looked at Radoslava for a very long time. Radoslava did not blink or breathe. After a long time, Lena made a little noise in her throat. Radoslava did not seem to hear this. Lena pulled back the curtain more, and then she knew that Radoslava could not see or hear anything that Lena did.

Lena looked down at Radoslava. She was not supposed to look at her. Lena knew this, because Radoslava was naked, and she was dead. Lena's *babushka* lay in the tub with her legs splayed, and Lena could see between the dark hair that spread from her thighs to her belly, and the folds of skin between her legs, and this skin was purplish, or brownish. It was the ugliest thing that Lena had ever seen.

Lena looked again at Radoslava's face, which had not changed. The water was coming down on Radoslava, and it was hitting her in the belly, in the chest, where her breasts started before they sloped off, one to each side, nipples wide and purple, like the eyes of the characters on *Sesame Street*, looking two places at once when they were being silly.

There was a bathroom smell coming from the shower, and Lena saw that there had been poop but that it had mostly been taken down the drain by the water, except for some big pieces that did not fit.

There was no blood anywhere, which was how people on television died, and so Lena was unsure about the whole thing. She thought she should turn the water off, but she thought that somehow that would wake up Radoslava, and then somehow she would know about Lena looking at the hair from between her legs to her belly. She would tell the neighbors, and Lena felt that this was embarrassing. Lena left the bathroom and closed the door.

When Mrs. Yablokov came by for tea at four o'clock, Lena was in front of the television again, watching from too close. Mrs. Yablokov came in without knocking, and saw Lena, and she said, "Where is Radoslava?"

"Ona miortvaia v dushe," said Lena.

"She's dead in the shower."

THESE PEOPLE MIGHT BE THE THEM

...

What happened next was that Mrs. Yablokov screamed and ran to the bathroom and screamed a lot in the bathroom and turned off the water (what a waste!) and called 911 on Radoslava's telephone, and then called everyone else she knew. Lena stayed watching the television while Mrs. Yablokov cried and called. Finally, Mrs. Yablokov came out and knelt on the floor next to Lena and said, "You poor thing," and then put her arms around Lena, and hugged her, and cried in Russian, "Your *babushka*, she's dead! She's dead, forever! You have no one. You have no one!"

Pressed to Mrs. Yablokov's perfumed bosom, Lena felt trapped. She wanted Mrs. Yablokov to let go of her so that she could watch the television.

"Where are you going to go? What are they going to do with you?" Mrs. Yablokov wailed.

Lena kept watching the television, in a language she did not understand, trying to ignore Mrs. Yablokov.

Mrs. Yablokov seemed to think that the paramedics would come right away, and while she called and cried on the phone to all the neighbors, she watched out the peephole to see if the paramedics were there yet, and occasionally she would open the door and peer out into the hallway, to see if the paramedics were there. She also spent a lot of time telling the people who had gathered in the hallway what was going on, and how she had been the first to find Radoslava, since she was Radoslava's closest friend.

After fifteen minutes, Mrs. Yablokov became nervous. She began a second round of phone calls.

"Can I tell you? They have not arrived yet to take the body away. She is rotting in there in that bathtub. Fifteen minutes ago. It is horrible. What a disgrace."

After thirty minutes no one had arrived.

"No, just me and the little girl in the apartment with the body, just lying there. No. I don't think she really understands what is happening. No, she's sitting watching television. I think there might be something wrong with the girl. Trapped in here with the dead woman, it can't be good, just to have her rotting in there. Rotting! It's too much." Mrs. Yablokov said this in Russian, in full earshot of Lena. After two hours, Mrs. Yablokov became too nervous about being in the apartment with the body. She told the telephone that there could be diseases in the air. She told the telephone that she could smell the decay. Lena noticed no smell. Mrs. Yablokov told the telephone that she was having a nervous breakdown, that the day had been too traumatic. Then she left.

After three hours, when the paramedics arrived, Lena answered the door and pointed them to the bathroom. Then she went to Radoslava's bedroom and took the envelope out of the top drawer of her bedside table. This envelope contained Radoslava's will. Radoslava had told Lena, over and over again, "Give it to them when I finally pass on, when my suffering is over." Lena thought that these people might be the "them," might be the people who come and find you dead. She thought that perhaps she was not meant to find Radoslava, because these men knew what to do, they talked very much, and they had equipment.

When Lena handed the envelope to one of the men, he was talking on the phone, and he said into the phone, "Hold on."

"What is your name, hon?" He said this in English, so Lena stared at him, and then at the floor, because she did not understand. The man went back to his phone.

"She's not talking. I want to say around five, maybe four. She's little. No. Alone in the apartment. Okay. We'll stay here until then? Okay." And then he hung up the phone and smiled at Lena.

"Someone's gonna be here real soon to talk to you, hon," he said, smiling. Then he went back into the crowded bathroom with the other two men, and Lena sat down in front of the television.

Lena could hear the noises of the men in the bathroom. She wondered how they would take Radoslava Dvorakovskaya out of the tub, not because she was large, and dead, and wet, but because she was naked. Lena could not imagine anyone touching another person who was naked.

For a long time the men talked, and Lena could hear their voices coming out of the bathroom. There were three men, and sometimes one would come out and get something from a big red bag that they had left in the hallway. After a little while, the three men came out of the bathroom, and the man who had talked to Lena before talked to her again.

"We'll be right back, okay? So don't worry. Right back." He said this slowly, and then the three men walked out of the apartment and closed the door behind them. Lena wondered what he had said. She could see when the door was open that there were a lot of people in the hallway, and that these people were watching the paramedics, and that they looked very excited. No one came inside the apartment, and no one knocked.

Lena went back to the bathroom to see what they had done. Radoslava Dvorakovskaya was still in the bathtub, exactly the same, but she looked different. Her skin was the wrong color, and some little things had changed. The men had closed her eyes, so she was not looking up at the ceiling anymore. Also, her lips seemed to be going away, and more of her teeth were showing. Lena looked down at Radoslava and still could not think of how the men would get her out. She heard a knocking on the door and then the door opening, and a man's voice saying, "Paramedics," and Lena ran out of the bathroom, because she did not want the men to know that she had been in there. She felt that she was not supposed to want to look at her *babushka* dead and naked and wet, and with her eyes closed and her teeth showing.

The men did not see her coming out of the bathroom—they did not see where she had come from because they were struggling to bring a metal bed into the apartment. They brought the bed into the living room, they pushed it, and it rolled along on wheels, making deep marks in the carpet jungle.

On the top of the bed was a board with red cushions on it, and they took that off the bed and took just the board into the bathroom.

Even from the living room, even with the television on, Lena could hear the sounds of Radoslava's wet skin moving against the bathtub. She could hear the men and their grunting noises, and their breathing. She could hear the wooden board banging on the tile bathroom floor, and then banging against the bathtub, and then a squeak, which must have been Radoslava's skin moving a little bit harder against the bathtub. Lena had made this sound herself, with her body in the bathtub, when she moved herself against the bottom, so she knew what this squeak was.

The sounds coming from the bathroom were wet sounds and hard sounds. Lena wanted to see. This day was different, Lena could feel it, and the rules of other days did not apply. Her *babushka* could not see her. Lena could look at her naked in the tub and she would not know, and Lena wanted to see what the men were doing, and what the noises were.

Lena walked very slowly with her tiny feet in socks against the linoleum floor in the hallway, and she did not let the floor make any sounds. The bathroom door was open, and Lena looked just a little bit to see if the men were looking, if the men could see her. They all had their backs to the door.

Lena leaned farther, looked more, and then stepped into the doorway. Still, they did not see her. She could watch.

The men had turned Radoslava Dvorakovskaya on her side, so that now she lay on her side facing the men. Two of the men held her up that way: One of the men held her shoulders, and one of the men held her legs right below her bottom.

Lying on her side like this, she looked worse and scarier to Lena. Her belly lay in front of her like it was not attached enough, and there were lines all over it, and her belly button was an ugly dark thing. Her breasts were the same, covered in lines.

The third man, the one who had talked to Lena, then put the board behind Radoslava, and the two men then leaned her back against the board. Lena saw that now they could pick up the board to get Radoslava out of the tub instead of picking up her squishy body. They used some black straps to attach her to the board, and then one of the men said, "One, two, three."

As they picked up the board, Lena could see that it was difficult to keep it straight, because the men's arms were shaking a lot and they had to lean over the bathtub and squat down a little bit. All the men were very strong.

When they had Radoslava on the board and they were carrying it, they moved toward the door, and one of the two men who had not talked to Lena saw Lena now, standing in the doorway, and he was not expecting to see Lena there, and he sucked in his breath.

"Holy *Christ*!" he said.

"Shit," said the man who had talked to Lena. "Honey, you shouldn't be here. Why don't you go watch some TV?" The man's voice was nice; he was not angry. Lena did not understand the suggestion to go watch television, did not understand that the man wanted her to go away from where they were doing this difficult work. She did not think that she should walk away, especially since this man was talking to her, and so nicely.

Lena moved aside so that the men could get her *babushka* out of the bathroom, and she followed them into the living room, where they moved Radoslava onto the bed with wheels, and they covered her with a white sheet, her whole body, even her head and her face. This looked very nice to Lena. The talking man held open the front door for the other two men, and they wheeled Radoslava out into the hallway and past all the people who had been waiting just for this moment—to be so close to Radoslava Dvorakovskaya, who dropped dead in her bathtub, and to see, on the stretcher, a real dead person.

The talking man stayed behind with Lena, and closed the door, and looked at Lena and sighed as though he was very tired.

"I'm going to wait with you until the social worker can get here, and it might be a while. Do you need anything?" His voice was still so nice, and he seemed not to be frustrated with Lena for not answering.

"You've had a tough day, huh. Do you need a snack? Do you need a drink?" Lena wished she could understand, because she liked this man and hoped he would continue talking.

"Well, I'm going to have a glass of water, and I'll get you one too. We might as well get comfortable, right?" Lena watched the man walk over to the kitchen, and she watched him reach up with his strong arms to open the cabinets, one after the other, looking for something. He found two water glasses, and he filled them at the sink, and he handed one to Lena, and then he sat on the couch. Lena took her glass and sat on the couch as well. The man picked up the remote control, and he turned on the television.

"I love this show," he said. It was *Sesame Street*. "Watch it with my kids all the time." He smiled, and he looked at the television. Lena loved *Sesame Street*, and she could see that this man loved it too, because he showed her with his smile.

Lena sat next to this man and thought, *Maybe he is here to take care of me*. He had come into the house when Radoslava Dvorakovskaya went away. He had walked right in and looked for water glasses as if the cabinets were his own cabinets in his own house. *He is acting like he lives here*, she thought. *Maybe he lives here now*.

Lena felt very excited to sit on the couch with the nice man with the nice voice who laughed at *Sesame Street*. Bert and Ernie introduced a cartoon that showed a boy and a girl and a plant. The plant looked very sad. Lena liked this cartoon because she understood it. There were English words in it, but she still understood what was happening.

First the boy called the girl over and pointed to his plant, which was sad. You could tell that it was sad because its big, green leaves drooped to the floor. Then the girl looked at the plant, and she said something, and the boy came back with an alarm clock. And the alarm clock made an alarm-clock noise. And then they said some things to each other, and then the boy went away and came back with a dog. The dog slobbered and barked at the plant. Then the boy and girl said some more things to each other, and the boy ran off, and he came back with a watering can, and he watered the plant, and the plant got happy, and its leaves sprung up and the music told you that the plant was happy and that the boy and the girl were happy.

The man liked this cartoon too, and they both laughed together at the end, Lena and the nice man.

The nice man received several phone calls on a phone he kept in his pocket, and each time he sounded a little bit sad to Lena, but when he hung up the phone he smiled and spoke to Lena in a tender voice.

The man even made them a plate of cookies, with cookies that were in the pantry. He poured a glass of milk for himself, and a glass of milk for Lena, and he showed Lena how to dunk her cookie in the milk and then eat it. Lena had never put a cookie in a glass of milk before, and she thought it was the most wonderful thing, and that the nice man must know so many of these wonderful things. She felt warm, and nice, and she fell asleep.

KNOCK KNOCK BYE BYE

...

Lena did not wake up because there was a knock at the door, she woke up because the nice man got up from the couch.

The nice man stood up from the couch and walked to the door, and opened it, and Lena opened her eyes and wanted him to come back. She liked sleeping while the man sat next to her, awake. She liked this nap in the warm evening, curled on the couch with the television on, even when the man switched it to the news. When he switched the TV to the news it woke her, just a little bit, but she pretended to still be asleep so that their time together would never end.

The woman at the door spoke to the man for a few minutes, and then she came in and she sat down next to Lena on the couch. The nice man stood above them.

"Do you speak English?" The woman's voice was as nice as the man's. Lena did not understand, so she did not answer.

"Do you speak Russian?" the woman asked, in Russian. Lena understood. *"Da."*

"What is your name?"

"Yelena," she said, giving her full name, as she always did with adults.

"Yelena, my name is Anna, and I'm going to ask you some questions, but there are no wrong answers." The nice man was putting on his coat.

"Do you live here?" she asked. Lena did not understand why she asked this question. Where else would she live? Lena did not like that the man had his coat on. She watched him carefully, worrying. She wanted Anna to stop talking so that the man would stay.

"Where do you sleep?" Anna asked.

"Here," said Lena, and she pointed to the couch. Anna nodded and then looked up at the nice man.

"Mark, thank you so much. I can take it from here." Mark smiled and nodded, and then he leaned down and talked to Lena.

"You're gonna be okay, kiddo. Okay?" He patted her on the head, and then he turned and walked to the door, and opened it, and left. Lena wondered when he was going to come back. She hoped it was soon.

Anna asked Lena a couple other questions, and then helped Lena pack her clothes into a bag, and then they held hands and walked out the door and into the empty hallway, to the elevator, and they took the elevator down to the garage, where her car was parked, and then she took Lena away from that place and brought her to a new place.

Lena didn't want to leave, because she wasn't sure that the nice man would be able to find her, and she began to worry that he would come back to watch *Sesame Street* and she wouldn't be there.

GOOD MORNING, SUNSHINE

...

Lena fell asleep in Anna's car, and when she woke up, they were parked in front of a big house. Anna brought her inside, where it was dark and quiet, because it was the middle of the night, and put Lena to bed in her very own room, and Lena fell asleep right away.

Lena woke up early to the sounds of the house, busy morning sounds, sleepy children sounds, excited children sounds. There were children running up and down the hallway; there were children yelling. She had never been around so many other children before. In the room next to hers, someone was playing a radio and singing along to it, and then there was someone singing along to the singing along.

Lena had to pee, but she did not want to leave her room, and she could not imagine what, but she was sure that she was doing something dumb, that there was something she should have known to do or not do, and she was sure that the other kids would make fun of her, and she did not want to talk to them or see them.

Lena waited until the noises all went downstairs before she left her room, slowly, quietly, and ran to the bathroom to pee. The bathroom was closer to the staircase, and smells were coming up the stairs from the kitchen. The smell was familiar to Lena—it was toast—and Lena was hungry, but she was not brave enough to go downstairs.

She went back into her room and sat on the bed that she had slept in, the one with the blue flowers, and waited, quietly. She became afraid that when someone came in, they would wonder why she was waiting quietly, or they would know that she was too shy to come and talk to everyone and have everyone see her, and Lena did not want that, because she was ashamed of being shy, and she was ashamed of not understanding what everyone was saying and of not being able to talk.

Lena lay down again on the bed, and she pretended to be asleep. She heard footsteps in the hall and made sure that her eyes were closed and that she was very, very still.

The footsteps stopped outside her door, and the door creaked open.

"Here's some toast in case you're hungry." Lena heard words but did not understand, and kept her eyes closed, thinking that maybe the person would think that they did not wake Lena up because Lena was so tired she was sleeping like a princess in a fairy tale, and this person would go away.

"Anna told me to bring you this toast in case you were hungry, so you should wake up and eat it," the person said, louder. Lena was starting to hate the person.

The footsteps and the smell of the toast—it had butter on it!—entered the room and came closer and closer to Lena.

The plate of toast was set down on the wood floor, and it made a nice clunking sound, and then the hand of the person shook Lena by the shoulder. Now Lena could not pretend to be asleep anymore. Lena rolled over and looked at the person. The person was a girl, older than Lena, and much taller than Lena. She was black, and she had braids in her hair and clips at the ends of those braids. The clips were shaped like butterflies, all different colors.

"You wasn't really asleep," she said. "You don't talk?" Lena was embarrassed that she did not understand, and she wished the girl would stop talking to her.

"*¿Habla español?*" she said. Lena said nothing.

"Okay, fine, you don't talk. Whatever. Eat the toast or not. You gonna come downstairs ever? Your lady is here." Lena said nothing; she did not understand. This girl seemed not as happy as Anna or the nice man to talk to her without getting any answers, and this girl certainly was not as nice.

The girl left, and Lena ate the toast. Lena decided that the plate from the toast was a good reason to go downstairs. She couldn't just keep the dirty plate in her room, and she knew that it was more polite, that it was the right thing to do, to return the plate and to bring it to the sink and to wash it. This she knew how to do.

Lena walked out of the room and into the long hallway. Some of the kids were back in their rooms, and all the doors were open. All the rooms had one or two beds. Some of the rooms had a lot of stuff in them, stuffed animals and posters, and some had nothing, like Lena's room.

Inside the rooms, some of the kids were folding their clothes, or reading, or talking to one another, or playing a game.

Some of the kids were just lying on their beds, facing the wall, like Lena had been.

As Lena walked down the long staircase, she heard Anna's voice. She was talking to another lady, and they were using the same serious voices that they had been using the day before, when Anna dropped Lena off. Lena followed their voices.

They were sitting at the kitchen table, and Anna was talking on her cellphone. There were papers in front of them, and Anna was writing a lot of things down on her piece of paper.

Anna saw Lena walk into the kitchen. She popped up out of her seat.

"Hey! Good morning!" She took the plate out of Lena's hands and put it on a pile of dishes by the sink. Two kids were standing at the sink, washing dishes together, and they were talking and bumping each other with their butts, making each other splash water or soap on themselves. They were laughing. They weren't laughing at each other, they were laughing at the fun they were making together.

Anna took Lena into a room off of the living room.

"This is the art room, craft room, general playroom," she said in Russian. "You can do anything you like in here." Lena looked around the room. There were shelves on every wall with toys and books, and there were tables in the room that had boxes of crayons on them, and big, huge pieces of white paper. There were clear plastic tubs everywhere with toys in them. There were kids Lena's age on the floor, playing with cars on a rug that had streets and houses drawn right into it.

"Do you like to color?" said Anna. "Come on, we'll color." Anna pulled out a chair for Lena at a table where there was one other little girl coloring. This girl looked older to Lena, but not as old as Toast. The girl did not look up when Lena and Anna sat down. She was coloring an ocean of blue around a tiny pink fish, trying to make the ocean come closer and closer to the fish without going onto the fish.

"Janelle, this is Lena." Janelle said nothing. Anna pulled a big piece of paper in front of Lena, and then she pulled a big piece of paper in front of herself. Then she put a big box of crayons between them. She took out a brown crayon, and she started to draw a big flower in the center of her paper. It had perfect tapered petals, and once they were outlined in brown, she began filling them in with orange.

Then Anna reached into the crayon box and took out a pink crayon, and handed it to Lena.

Lena slowly, carefully, introduced the tip of the crayon to the paper, as if to do so would spark a chemical reaction. Then, staring at the crayon, not at the paper, she pushed the crayon along, barely making a mark on the paper. She was focused on gliding the crayon across the paper. Then she laid the crayon on its side and glided it across the paper that way. She wiggled it back and forth and moved it along in her best approximation of an earthworm. She thought about how she had seen earthworms move, how they scrunched their bodies together and expanded, and she tried to capture this back-and-forth forward movement with her crayon. She thought about her fingers in the carpet, and she thought about the new carpet at this house, and how fantastic it would be to be alone with it, to walk her fingers along its roads, to drive her hands on its highways.

Lena liked this activity—it required no talking—and she liked sitting at the table and quietly concentrating while other people were quietly concentrating. She wanted to make marks on the paper like the other people—that seemed good—but she also liked the way that she was coloring. Lena's way, she could color forever without using up any paper or any crayons.

HOW LENA BECAME A STAIN ON THE LIFE OF THE AUNT

...

The people who took care of Lena for those strange hours after Radoslava Dvorakovskaya died, with their caring faces and their protocol and paperwork and best intentions, these people examined the will that Radoslava Dvorakovskaya had left by her bedside table. Radoslava Dvorakovskaya had clearly wished that custody of Lena be granted to Lena's aunt, Ekaterina. Radoslava, however, was not Lena's legal guardian and had no authority to will Lena to Ekaterina or anyone else. To complicate matters, there was no paper trail suggesting who should have custody of Lena. Lena had been off the kid grid since her parents had disappeared. In fact, it was unclear whether Lena had ever been on the grid: Lack of an American birth certificate suggested she had been born in Russia; lack of immigration paperwork suggested that she had been born in America.

Radoslava Dvorakovskaya's will, which identified Ekaterina as Lena's aunt, was the only paperwork that even acknowledged the existence of Lena. After much searching and discussing,

Ekaterina was determined to be the best legal guardian for Lena. The relation was close; Lena's parents were nowhere, disappeared by all accounts; and Ekaterina was willing. Eventually.

"She is how old?" Ekaterina asked.

"That is old enough for free school?"

"My job is not making me wealthy; how am I to pay for all of the things? Schoolbooks and food and clothes and things?"

"Stipend? What is this?"

"How much is this?"

"When will the first check come?"

So Lena goes to live with the Aunt. This Lena remembers. Too clearly and not clearly enough, as that is how memory is.

It was several days of coloring with Anna before the Aunt came to take Lena home. Lena remembers these days as days of coloring, because they were filled with coloring, as much as she wanted, as much paper as she wanted, as many crayons as she wanted, and she fell into the hours of coloring, and meals came, and snacks came, and some of these she put into her mouth and some of these she did not, depending on who was looking at her and how brave she felt. Mostly she was allowed to go on coloring all day, and when it was time for bed on the second night, she knew the room she was going to, and she knew that no one would disturb her and that she could sleep under the covers, and go to use the bathroom whenever she wanted, and when she woke up, she could color again.

By the third day she was starting to feel really good, starting to look forward to the next day, to coloring, to getting lost in it so that her eyes hurt and her hands hurt. Everything about the house that had been frightening she now understood. She knew where the food was and where to put your cup when you were done with it. Also, someone new had come, a boy who was younger than her but taller, and who had a head that was very round, rounder than any other head she had seen, so that she was not the newest person anymore, she was a girl who knew things about the place and was comfortable and was there, and she was aware that when the new boy saw her, he would be feeling unsure and afraid, and he would be thinking that she must know everything, which she did.

Then the Aunt came. Lena had never seen her before, but she had heard of her, from Radoslava, and she thought, for the first time since she found Radoslava Dvorakovskaya dead in the shower, about Radoslava being gone and dead, and she thought about how nice the days had been since Radoslava Dvorakovskaya died, with the coloring and the food and everyone being nice and playing and leaving her alone, and she thought she was happy that her *babushka* was dead, and she thought that things were going to be even better with her aunt, who she had heard about.

From Radoslava, Lena knew that the Aunt danced, and wore makeup, and liked to go out late and have good times.

When the Aunt came, Lena felt so shy, she wanted to say something so that the Aunt would like her, but she could not say anything, because she did not know what to say. Lena was coloring when the Aunt came, and the way the Aunt looked at the coloring made Lena feel embarrassed of coloring; it made her want to stop and cover the little pale circles she had made so that no one could see them.

The Aunt didn't act the way Lena thought she would act. She didn't act excited; she didn't smile at Lena; she didn't really say hi to Lena or do anything nice.

Lena thought that she had messed something up; she wondered how she had made the Aunt upset, how she had made her angry. She thought it could have been really good, to live with the Aunt, but now she had messed it up. She had a lot of questions for the Aunt, but now she felt like she wasn't supposed to ask them. She wanted to know what the Aunt was to her, how you became someone's aunt. Lena thought, from things Radoslava had said, that the Aunt might know things about her mother.

The Aunt and Anna did some talking together; the Aunt filled out a lot of paperwork, and signed things; and Anna talked and nodded, and smiled even when the Aunt did not smile back.

Then the Aunt came over to Lena and spoke to her in Russian, which was a relief, because Lena had been worried that maybe the Aunt spoke English.

"You are ready to go? You have any things with you?"

Lena nodded.

The Aunt took her hand, and they walked to the front door of the house, and Anna smiled at them, and Lena felt that Anna was maybe a little bit nervous, or something, and that made Lena feel a little bit nervous.

The Aunt had a car, and it was parked in front of the house. Radoslava Dvorakovskaya had never had a car, and this car looked shiny and new (It was silver! And tiny! For two people only!), and it looked so fancy, and Lena thought that the Aunt must be rich and have many nice things just like this car.

Lena did not understand yet about cars and leasing and boyfriends and insurance fraud.

The Aunt went to the front seat of the car, and Lena went to the other side, and she opened the door, and inside the car was not what she expected, because there were things and garbage all over. There were clothes everywhere, and there were soda cans on the floor, and it smelled bad, and there were cigarettes coming out of the ashtray and CDs on the floor, all sorts of things on the floor and on the seats and everywhere. There was a tiny backseat, which Lena did not understand. (There were only two doors? How did anyone get back there?) And this backseat was also full of clothes and other things.

The seat that Lena was supposed to sit on was covered in things too, and Lena did not know what to do. She sat at the edge of the seat, not wanting to sit on or disturb any of the Aunt's things. Lena knew she was supposed to buckle her seat belt, but she was afraid to move, afraid to move from her perch on the edge of the seat. She sat at the very edge of the seat for the whole bumpy, bumpy ride, and there was a lot of swerving, and very loud music, and Lena was getting hungry but feeling very sick and not good at the same time. Lena was starting to feel afraid about going to the Aunt's house, and Lena was starting to miss Anna, and even Toast.

What is there for a Lena-type person to do in this situation? What is there to do when you are a person who is young and small? When you own only the clothes you are wearing and the one barrette clipped into your hair, which is always sliding out of place and getting stuck in the knots behind your ears? When you do not have a phone or any phone numbers to call? Even if you thought that someone, like Anna, might be able to help you and make you feel better, even if that might be true, how would you call her? How would you even begin to think about how to make a plan to get out of the situation you are in, which is making you feel very, very, very bad? Even if you start to feel, in your aunt's car, that you would like to be anywhere else in the world, that you do not want to go where you are going, what can you do?

WELCOME HOME, LENA

. . .

The Aunt parked the car on a street that was very pretty. The street had many trees with their leaves all in colors, and there was a sidewalk and a little grass next to the sidewalk and cars parked all around. The Aunt's house was a house split in two pieces, up and down, and the Aunt (and now Lena) lived in the up part, so you walked up stairs, up, up, up to the door of the apartment.

The Aunt looked for a long time for keys in her purse, standing wedged between the open screen door and the real door, rumbling around, rumbling around, and she took out a square pack of cigarettes. Lena knew what these were because some of Radoslava's friends had smoked them when they came over, and Lena knew that these were bad and not for kids, because Radoslava Dvorakovskaya had forbidden her to touch them, or to handle the little burned dirty pieces of them that people left behind in their teacups and in glass dishes that Radoslava Dvorakovskaya had set out on the table.

"Hold this," the Aunt said, and handed the pack of cigarettes to Lena. Lena felt strange, because she was not supposed to hold cigarettes, but she liked that the Aunt asked her to do something and that the Aunt had talked to her—that was good—and that the Aunt trusted her to hold them and not do anything bad.

The Aunt found the keys, and she pushed open the door. The Aunt stepped inside, and Lena followed her.

Lena took two steps and stopped. Ekaterina took many steps,

dropped her purse on the couch, went into a room, and shut the door.

Lena stood still and looked all around her because she didn't know what to do. Everything looked exactly the same as it had in the Aunt's car. There were things all around. There were too many of some things and not enough of other things. There was a carpet, which was white and very squishy, and covered all of the floor. There were a lot of spots on the carpet, spills and stains and little hard gray-black holes. There was a big leather couch that was black with some places where a rip let some of the white insides come out. There was a table in front of the couch, and it had glass on top, but it was covered all over mostly with garbage, with cans and glasses and ashtrays and some white boxes that used to hold food.

There was a kitchen that was separated from this main room by only half a wall, not a whole wall, and inside the kitchen also there were things everywhere, boxes and cans and wrappers everywhere, but one of the cabinet doors was missing, and Lena could see that at least one of the cabinets was totally empty.

Then the Aunt came out of the room, and she was wearing a bathing suit, in two pieces. Her body was orange, or mostly orange, and she had an earring coming out of her belly button. She picked up a pair of jeans from the floor and pulled them up and buttoned them fast, and she did this as though she was angry at her own two legs.

Lena was still standing there, just two steps inside the front door, and the Aunt was acting like Lena was not there at all. The next thing that the Aunt did was the strangest thing of all. The Aunt rubbed shiny pink gloss from a little pot all over her lips, and then she pulled aside one of the triangles of her bikini top and rubbed the same shiny pink gloss all over her nipple, and then she pinched it, three times, and then she put the triangle back on it, and then she did the same to the other one. Finally she picked up a sweatshirt from the floor, and she put that on.

"I am going to work," she said, and then she picked up her purse, and then slam-slam, the doors closed behind her, and she was gone.

Lena was relieved that she was gone. Lena was also very hungry. She looked in the kitchen, and there wasn't anything really that looked like food. She ate some rice out of a container in the refrigerator. The rice was cold and white and grainy, but Lena ate all of it.

She went to the couch and made a spot between some clothes and some magazines, and she fell asleep.

When Lena woke up, it was dark out, and she didn't know what time it was, and she didn't know how to turn on the television to make things less scary, and she didn't know where the light switches were, so she stayed on the couch, and she tried not to cry, because she was afraid to start.

THE BATHROOM STALL IS STILL A BATHROOM STALL

...

Lena thinks about the days she spent alone in the Aunt's apartment, and the day she met Vaclav. Lena doesn't want to tell Serena anything about Vaclav. Vaclav she keeps packed away inside her chest, in her rib cage, tucked between her delicate ribs and her pumping heart, so special, so sacred, is he to her, she cannot even bear to speak his name out loud to anyone; he is a secret she will keep with her forever; like a child's sacred talisman blanket, she cannot stand for anyone else to touch him, even with their ears.

She is afraid to touch the perfect memory she has of Vaclav. She has wondered about him, especially in the last few years, but she has been terrified to take him from her memory and risk losing him to real life.

Lena thinks about the bedtime story Vaclav's mom told her. She remembers it, almost word for word. She thinks about the ending, about how the boy can't stand to go to the castle window on the last night, that he would rather forfeit his chance, to continue to not know. As terrified as she is of ruining her perfect memory, she doesn't want to lose Vaclav to the safety of not knowing. She wants, now, to call Vaclav, and she wants to find her parents.

"I mean, being adopted at nine, it's just fascinating," Serena interrupts her thoughts. "What was that like, suddenly having, like, a brand-new mom?" Serena asks.

"Yeah, it was kind of scary, kind of really happy," Lena says.

Lena remembers the first days she spent with Emily as the best in her whole life. She remembers Emily showing her the house, telling her that it was her house too. She remembers Emily telling her that this was going to be her home, forever, that she was never going to have to move or leave ever again. She remembers the first time she saw her room, with her very own bed, a big four-poster bed with blankets and lots of pillows. She remembers that there was a big closet, filled with empty hangers, and that Emily said that they were going to go buy

Lena any clothes she wanted to put on the hangers. For Lena, it was perfect, it was a dream come true.

Emily remembers things differently.

WHAT EMILY REMEMBERS

...

Emily was terrified. She took Lena through the house, showed her how to use the microwave, how to use the stopper in the bathtub, and how to turn the TV on and off, because she didn't know what else to do. Lena said nothing, and her face was blank. Emily had been worried that Lena would be frightened, or shy, or very moody, but she seemed to be completely gone, totally noncommunicative. She had read about parents who adopted neglected children from Romanian orphanages, how the children wouldn't attach, would never be normal, perhaps would even become sociopaths. She'd read about parents who, after years of struggle, decided finally that their children needed more than they could give, that they had to send their children away, to institutions.

Days went by, and Lena didn't speak. Emily took her to see a therapist, a lovely woman in an office with toys everywhere, who, after an hour-long session alone with Lena, called Emily in and told her that Lena would need hours of testing and extensive therapy. Emily looked at Lena, sitting in her little chair, appearing more terrified than ever.

The therapist told Emily to bring Lena back the next week, that they would start testing, and that Lena needed to be seen three to four times a week. Emily took Lena home, and Lena watched from the kitchen table as Emily made grilled cheese sandwiches.

"We'll never go back there again, and you never have to speak again if you don't want to," Emily said, "but I've made you this grilled cheese sandwich, which is hands-down the best sandwich in the tristate area, and it would be really great if you said thank you." Emily put the sandwich in front of Lena.

"Thank you," said Lena.

"You're welcome," said Emily, stunned.

Over the next few days, Lena started talking, asking questions, even smiling at TV shows. She didn't talk at all about her aunt, about what happened before. It was like she was born nine years old, like she had no memory. She cared about what was right in front of her; she asked Emily if pigeons had names, what sidewalks were made of, and where the colors in paint came from. Mostly Emily made up the best answers she could, and Lena seemed satisfied.

Going back to school was a different story. Every time Emily mentioned school, Lena became agitated. On a shopping trip for school supplies, Lena threw a tantrum, knocking down a display of dry-erase boards when Emily did not understand what kind of pencils she wanted. They left the store without buying anything.

Nothing Emily did to prepare Lena seemed to help. They took walks to the school, met Lena's teachers, and took a tour of the hallways, the library, the gym. Still, the morning of her first day of school, Lena's hands shook while she tried to eat her cereal. Emily spent the entire day sitting on a bench around the corner, trying to read. At the end of the day, Emily walked Lena home. Lena refused to talk; she answered none of Emily's questions about her teachers, the other children, the books they were reading in class.

After the third day of school, Emily was called in for a meeting.

"She's throwing tantrums every day," said Miss Rhys. Emily sat uncomfortably in a small classroom chair, holding her purse in her lap.

"That's surprising," Emily said.

"Really," said Miss Rhys, raising an eyebrow.

"At home, well, she's talking, she's expressive . . ." Emily said.

"Is she angry at home?" asked Miss Rhys.

"She gets frustrated," said Emily, unwilling to admit that when they sat down to do homework, Lena was full of rage.

"Well, in class, she's disruptive; she bangs on her desk and—it's hard to describe—she makes this sound. She screeches." Emily knew exactly the sound Miss Rhys was referring to, a stifled raw scream that Lena produced in the back of her throat. "The other children seem afraid of her."

Somehow this was a relief to Emily; she had been afraid that Lena would be made fun of or bullied.

"Listen," Emily said, "she needs time to adjust. . . ." Emily was terrified that Lena's teacher would have her removed from this school.

"I'm sure you understand, I can't allow a student to threaten the safety of the learning environment—"

Emily cut her off; she didn't want to hear the end of this sentence. "I understand. It will improve, it will. I thank you for being so compassionate." Emily left the room enraged, she felt so upset at having to defend Lena to this woman who was threatening to have Lena expelled within the first week at a new school. As Emily walked back home, where Lena was with her new babysitter, the daughter of one of Emily's best friends, she thought about how disappointed she was in this woman, in the school. Everyone had sworn up and down that the school was a safe, loving environment, supportive of difference, that they would be Emily's allies on the path to Lena's success. But Miss Rhys had suggested nothing to help Emily, to help Lena, and now Emily would have to go to the principal; she would have to describe the subtle ways in which this conversation made it clear that Lena was not accepted or supported.

Emily was furious, but when she arrived at her house, she took a deep breath. She did not want Lena to know she was upset. As she dropped her keys in the bowl by the door, she could hear Lena in the kitchen screeching at her homework.

In the kitchen, Lena was holding her head in both hands, pulling at her hair. Amy the babysitter sat patiently next to Lena, looking overwhelmed. When she saw Emily, she made an apologetic face, and Emily instantly said, "Amy, it's okay. I'm so sorry, let me pay you so you can go home." Emily handed Amy twenty dollars, far more than she was owed.

When Amy had gone, Emily sat at the table with Lena.

"Lena, stop pulling your hair," she said, and Lena seemed not to hear her.

"Lena, stop. Stop." She felt anger building in her, anger that she had tried to leave at the door but could not, anger at Lena for hurting herself, and at the teacher, at everything.

"Stop!" she yelled. "You're frustrated, you're angry, you have a right to be angry, of course you're angry. You are smart. You're smarter than anyone in your whole class; you're smarter

than your teacher. You just don't have enough words, and that's not your fault. It's not your fault; it's not your fault."

Lena cried.

"No more tantrums at school. That's the rule. No yelling. No screaming. That's the rule." She didn't know what else to say, but she suspected that Lena liked rules. "You can yell at home; you can do whatever you want here. Not at school."

Lena nodded and wiped her eyes, her lip still trembling. Emily sat down at the table, and they started her homework.

The next day, while Emily knew the students were at recess, she called the school and asked to speak to Miss Rhys. She paced her kitchen while she waited on hold.

"Hello?" Miss Rhys was clearly annoyed at being interrupted during her lunch.

"Hello, it's Lena's mom, Emily—I'm sorry if I've caught you at a bad time. I just want to make sure everything is going more smoothly with Lena today, so far." It was only eleven-thirty.

"She sat quietly at her desk all morning," said Miss Rhys.

"Fantastic. Just what I wanted to hear."

"Is there anything else?" Miss Rhys asked.

"Certainly not," Emily said. She knew that Lena was following her rule, and her hunch was confirmed. Lena was terrified of breaking rules.

Lena continued to go to school and came home every day looking wounded. Emily sat her down and they went through her homework, word by word. Lena cried when it was time to do homework, and sometimes she cried the entire time they worked on it. It took hours. Lena's math was terrible; it seemed that she had never learned even the most basic skills. Lena told Emily that she felt like an idiot, that she sounded stupid, that everyone was making fun of her behind her back. Emily knew, from frequent calls to Miss Rhys, that this was not true.

Slowly, it got better. Lena started to understand more and more of her homework, of her classes. She was calmer. One day they finished her homework while it was still light out, and then they went for a walk, and they found a robin's egg that had fallen out of a tree in Prospect Park. Lena took it home and put it on her night table. The next day was a little better. Eventually, they spent less time doing homework and more time taking walks, collecting things that they found.

By middle school, her teachers were thrilled with her improvement, and her grades were perfect. Lena read voraciously, and her vocabulary expanded. One day when she was twelve she came home and told Emily that a group of girls was going into Manhattan, alone, on the train, for a birthday dinner.

"Absolutely not, no," Emily said.

"What?" said Lena, seemingly incredulous, though she must have known that Emily would never have allowed this trip.

"You can't go, Lena, no way."

"Why?" Lena asked calmly.

"Because you're too young, and it's dangerous."

"You don't trust me?" Lena asked.

"Of course I trust you. It has nothing to do with you, I just don't trust the rest of the world, Lena."

"So why does it matter that I'm young?" Lena asked. "If it has nothing to do with me, and the world is just dangerous, then I should never go anywhere by myself, right? I should stay home forever."

"No," Emily said. "Someday you'll be old enough."

"But you said that it had nothing to do with me," Lena said.

"You're not allowed," Emily said. "End of discussion." It

was the first time that Emily realized that Lena could argue her into a corner, and it wasn't the last. Lena was discovering the power of her intellect, the power of her words, and Emily often had to remind herself that she was dealing with a teenager.

Lena had quickly made friends once she began talking in school. It seemed to Emily that it was easy for Lena to become a popular girl, because all the other children were already afraid of her. She was smart, and bossy, and fun, and had a gaggle of girls sleeping over every weekend.

By the time she was seventeen, Lena had joined the student council, and her teachers said she lead class discussions, but she was still obsessing, still fragile. Homework time was like a minefield of a different kind. Lena sat for hours, sometimes until late at night, writing and rewriting, checking and rechecking. Lena had mastered English, it seemed, through sheer force of will, meticulously memorizing grammar rules and idioms. She was driven by her terror of seeming unintelligent and of her classmates' laughing at errors in her speech. Even after her English was seamless, she couldn't let go of this severe diligence and control. She was calm when she started her work but easily became irritable and obsessive about small glitches. Anything could set her off: an equation she couldn't solve right away, a mildly critical comment from a teacher on a paper Lena had spent hours editing. Lena looked like a perfect teenager, but Emily felt like she was in the eye of a storm.

BYE BYE SPOT

...

"But you don't know anything about your real parents?" Serena asks. "Who did you live with until you got adopted and came here?"

"No, I don't know anything about my parents," Lena says, choosing not to answer the second part of Serena's question. Lena is getting tired of talking to Serena, she's tired of all the things she has to patch together and hide, and she doesn't want to try to explain anything else—Lena doesn't like these many shades of fuzz in her life story, where everyone else's are sharp and colorful and happy like a postcard. Lena does not like editing out the rotten spots; she doesn't like the times she only barely remembers, or things about which she has been given sketchy information, handed down from person to person, and she especially does not like having enormous gaps missing in between, so that to think about all of the days leading up to today feels dangerous.

She told Em about this feeling once, about not liking to think about the past for fear that she'd come upon some black ice or puddle or dead spot, and Em said that that was how a lot of grown-ups felt, all the time. Lena asked Em if anyone felt this way when they were young, and Em said no, that most people have nice childhoods behind them that they like to look back at, and it's only when they get older and start having mistakes and regrets and unhappiness that they stop liking to remember, to think back. Most, Em said, not all. You get to look forward to your happiness, said Em, instead of back, that's all.

Lena doesn't want to look only forward and not back. She wants to fill in the holes.

"I just want to fill in the holes," she tells Serena.

"You go for it, man," says Serena, meaning it.

Lena decides that she will fill in the holes. She's going to find Vaclav. He's going to help her find her parents. She's thought before about asking Em about finding her parents, and then immediately dismissed the idea. It's not that her relationship with Em is delicate, or that Em wouldn't let her; she can't explain it, it's just that she can't bear to see Em worried, or hurt, or disappointed. She doesn't even want to think about it.

"Thank you," she says to Serena.

"No way. My pleasure," says Serena, and suddenly Lena is ready (all of her selves are ready) to go out into the hallway and back into the day. It isn't until Lena is in the hallway, on her way to meet her friends and have her birthday dinner, that she remembers the spot with its unknowing specificity, that she forgot to say goodbye to it, to fix it in her mind and remember it, and now she is sure that it will fade like all the others.

TOGETHER AGAIN

AT THE VERY SAME MOMENT

...

At dinner with friends everything is nothing, and in the cab ride home everything is nothing, and at home with Em everything is nothing. Lena is so excited, so nervous, so jammed with adrenaline that every moment seems like an hour and every hour swells in an impossible way, and time does not pass at all. But of course the time passes; it is one of the truths of the universe: No matter how much pain, how much joy, how much nervousness, how much anxiousness, how much love, how much fear, how much itching, how much scratching, how much fever, how much falling, time passes. So the impossible event is suddenly upon her, and then those hours, even the hours that at the time seemed to be made of millennia, seem, in retrospect, to collapse upon themselves, so that the arrival of the event seems, actually, sudden, and the waiting seems to have passed impossibly quickly, and those hours seem to have never existed. That's how Lena feels when she is finally alone in her room at ten-thirty on the night of her seventeenth birthday, picking up the phone to call Vaclav.

Does Lena know that at the very same moment Vaclav is thinking of her (actually, thinking of *not* thinking of her)?

She locks her door and sits down next to her phone. She dials Vaclav's number without hesitation. A seven-digit number buried since the year she was nine, dialed by a powerful but quiet part of her mind, like balance, like breathing, like the squish, squish, churn of your stomach, something your body knows. Her fingers just know what to do. That's how it is with the phone number of a boy you love. Loved. Will love. Whatever.

While the phone rings, Lena considers the possibility that someone who is not Vaclav may answer the phone. It is ten-thirty. It is a slightly inappropriate time to call someone. And then she calmly lets it ring, because she knows who will answer. She knows, somehow, that he is waiting for her call.

Vaclav has just fallen asleep for the very first time without saying good night to Lena when the phone by his bed rings. He grabs it, and even before he says hello his heart is tumbling about in his chest.

"Hello?" he says, but they both know without saying who it is on the other end of the telephone wires.

"This is Lena," she says. What else to say?

"This is Vaclav," he says. What else?

"How are you?" She is smiling big, big, big.

"I'm good! How are you?" It seems that the conversation is moving forward on tracks neither of them can see; it is saying itself.

"I'm good too. It's my birthday," she says.

"I know," he says. "I know."

"You do?" she says.

"Yeah. Of course. Yes."

Vaclav and Lena have now communicated the ultimate thing,

the thing that they both want to know but couldn't ask: *Did you remember me? Was I as important to you as you were to me? Was I alone in my remembering? Or were you with me the whole time?*

Of course they were with each other the whole time. Even when they weren't looking, they never had to check. She was always there; he was always there. Outside her bedroom, somewhere in the darkness, like the moon.

"Where are you?" Vaclav says. It seems like a strange question to Lena.

"Home." She realizes he does not know anything at all, where she lives, anything. "Park Slope," she says. She knows where he lives.

"You still live in Brooklyn?" he says, astounded that she could be so close.

"Yeah," she says.

"Where do you go to school?" he says.

"The Berkeley Carroll School? It's tiny," she says, apologizing in advance for his not knowing it, not wanting to make any gaps, any bubbles in the skin of this conversation. Vaclav, however, knows this school. Lots of his friends live in the neighborhood, and he walks by it all the time, to go to the coffee shops nearby.

"I know it. I go by there all the time—Ozzie's is right around the corner. I can't believe I haven't run into you," he says, feeling incredulous that he has been within blocks of Lena, that he's been on the sidewalk outside of her school while she sat inside reading, going to gym class, learning calculus. She was right there the whole time.

"I go to Ozzie's all the time," she says, wondering if she's seen him without knowing it, but it seems impossible. "Where do you go?"

"I go to Brooklyn Tech," he says.

"Oh, wow. Good job," she says, because Brooklyn Tech is a magnet school, and it's so hard to get into. It's a public school for super-genius science-whiz kids, and when she thinks about it, she's not surprised that he goes there.

"Oh, thanks. It's a little far from my house, but I like it."

"Do you want to get together?" she says.

"Yes," he says.

"Monday after school," she says. "Three-thirty?"

"Yes," he says.

"I'll meet you by your school. Across the street at Fort Greene Park," she says.

"Okay," he says.

"Okay," she says.

"Lena," he says, and saying her name feels like a somersault.

"Vaclav," she says, and saying his name feels like singing in public.

"I'm really glad you called."

"Me too."

"Me too."

"Okay, bye."

"Bye."

And they both sit still in their bedrooms, waiting for their hearts to stop beating or to explode, and they wonder why they are not getting together right then, in the middle of the night. Why not? Anything, anything, can be. The world has come apart, and come back together, and come apart again. The world is crashing into itself like cymbals. Crash, crash, crash, crash. It is hard to sleep with all that noise in the universe. Crash, crash, crash, crash.

In the morning at breakfast with their respective mothers,

mothers as different as night and day, fat and thin, dark and blond, heavy and light, Vaclav and Lena sit, and say nothing to either mother about the Phone Call, and they fail to mention the existence of the Plan to Meet. Why? Why lie to these mothers? Why keep secret this thing that does not need secrecy? Vaclav and Lena do not know. But they keep their secrets in the safe pockets between their clasped palms, protecting them and wanting instinctively to shield them like tiny shiny frogs found in the wet grass, but wanting simultaneously to share them, to show and share such an exciting new thing. Their minds run irresistibly over and over and over the same thing, they chant the words silently: *Guess who I talked to last night? You won't believe who I talked to last night. Wait until you hear about this, you know what Lena said?* But they don't say these things, they keep them to themselves, carefully, carefully.

Does Vaclav think of telling Ryan, his girlfriend, about this big thing? No, he does not.

Vaclav can only think of meeting Lena on Monday. He does not think of Ryan at all.

Lena starts to work on her plan.

VACLAV IS A HEAD TALLER THAN EVERYONE ELSE

...

Lena never cuts school, but Monday morning, she decides that the idea of staying at school is untenable. Declaring that the argument to stay at school is untenable soothes Lena; she likes the simple categorization, the absolute quality of it: School absolutely cannot be tolerated today. The idea of staying, of sitting in calculus, is untenable today. All weekend her anxiety grew exponentially. She kept thinking of Vaclav's voice on the phone and losing her breath. Untenable.

Lena leaves school and takes two buses to Fort Greene, to sit across the street from Brooklyn Technical High School, to sit on a bench and wait for Vaclav for three hours. She looks at the building; she counts the stories, the windows, the doors. Vaclav is inside this building, inside a classroom, sitting in a chair, listening to a teacher; he is in there. He is alive. He is a real person. He is probably nervous to see her. Does this help calm her own electric nerves? Not really.

The day is fall, definitely fall, but warm. There is no fall crispness in the air; it is a soft baked day. The leaves are changing, barely, just the tips are turning orangey, losing a bit of green, nothing wild or dramatic yet.

There are bunches of kids already passing by on the sidewalk, even though school is not out yet. They have free periods, or they are leaving early, or they are cutting class. But what it seems like most of all is that these kids are just leakage, that a school the size of Brooklyn Tech is going to ooze some kids onto the neighboring sidewalk.

Lena's bench is under a maple tree that is sending down little whirlybirds, little brown two-winged fliers, like nature is just having a ball, designing trees that send their seeds down in a tailspin. Lena picks one up and peels it in two, folds back one of the halves of one of the wings, thinking *cotyledon,* from biology, thinking this thing is from a dicot plant but forgetting what the implications of being monocot or dicot are.

A bell rings inside the school, and this bell is so loud as to be audible to Lena. Within moments, doors are thrust open and kids are gushing out onto the street. Lena becomes agitated. There are too many kids. Their meeting is going to be impossible, he'll never see her, and she does not want to be looking eagerly at the crowd, craning her neck, guessing. She wants him to just find her, to just be there. There is an incredible amount of noise coming from these kids; some of them seem to be yelling, screaming, just to use their voices after the day of enforced quiet; everyone is talking loudly, laughing loudly, yelling to one another, and whooping. Some boys are actually making wild bird-whooping noises at one another.

Lena can't think of a time anyone at her school has ever been this loud. Maybe, she thinks, when you're part of it, it doesn't seem so loud to you. Lena's school is tiny, gorgeous, private, and quiet.

On the sidewalk alongside the school there are several clusters of kids, and they're all dressed in extreme ways. Instead of just people with accessories, they appear to be in costume, and it's too much. She thinks smugly about her small school, where everyone can just be, whatever they are, and then feels a wave of something. . . . Privilege? Luck? It feels unfamiliar. This school where you have to be so loud in every way, so big, would be exhausting to her. It would hurt.

In one of the little clumps of people she notices a boy who is taller than everyone else. He's taller by a head, or even by a foot, and he sticks out over the mass. He turns to talk to someone, and Lena sees his face. It's unmistakably Vaclav, but he looks completely different. He's an adult man, smiling Vaclav's smile. He hasn't seen her yet. Lena wonders about the coincidence of her attention settling on this one person, this one back of the head, and having the back of the head turn out to be Vaclav, but, of course, he's tall, so anyone would notice him. Who would have thought Vaclav would be so tall? But then again, what are the chances that the one person Lena is looking for, her one person who is so special to her, and is also so special in the whole universe, would stand so high above everyone else, that he is so obviously spectacular, luminous, charming, and magic?

She's sitting there wondering if Vaclav will recognize her in the same way when he starts walking across the street, charging straight through the crosswalk toward her. His hair is so dark—it is like Superman's hair from the comics—she expects almost to see flecks of electric blue highlighting its contours. It's wild, like he's been twisting it into horns all day. She's thrown by his hair, but most of all, she can't take her eyes off his eyebrows.

Vaclav's eyebrows are large, they are dark, but they separate from each other, they do not meld in the middle, they do not collapse into each other's weight. They are heavy and dense but somehow light, somehow airy, like charcoal but shinier, livelier, glowing? Could they be glowing? He is smiling with his whole face, a smile that is expanding and expanding even when it is at its maximum smiling capacity, his smile is expanding, impossibly, and she is smiling too, and she is standing up from the bench, because he is right there, in front of her, and she isn't sure if they are going to hug or not, but then, yes, they are hugging, and then, yes, she is up in his arms, and her feet are off the ground, and his face is in her hair, and she is laughing, laughing, laughing, and he is making a sound that is a little like a yell when you go down the steepest waterslide at the park, and they stay that way forever.

THEY DIDN'T STAY THAT WAY FOREVER, NOT REALLY. BUT SOME MOMENTS DO SEEM ETERNAL, NO?

...

Vaclav had already known that she was sitting there before he even saw her. He had felt her looking at him. He had known it was her, it had to be her, because he felt, suddenly, the compulsion to turn and look at that bench, to look in her direction, like there were magnets in his eyes and she was a supermagnetized hunk of some other planet, just fallen to earth.

She was still small, she was still dark, her eyes still unsettling, but now all the parts of her face were becoming graceful. She had a head of hair so curly, so frizzy, so unruly, it was like a mane around her head; it seemed a part of her like those collars on lizards, the ones that flare up their necks when it's time to do lizard battle. Everything else about her face had become more confident. *Here! I'm a nose, I'm a mouth; this is what I do.* It all seemed to have poise; it all seemed to belong. He couldn't have imagined her looking this way, but now that he's seen her he can't imagine anything else, anything else at all. And then he'd wanted just to hug her, but when he leaned down and she leaned up it was as if she was weightless and just wanted to spring into his arms, and then he was holding her, which he had not planned on at all, and he felt worried, because the moment he put her down, they would have to get a bit awkward, he is already feeling the awkwardness nibbling at their heels, just itching, itching to spread.

He puts her down, on the sidewalk, and there are other people trying to get around them, which is a surprise. A moment ago, while she was in the air, in his arms, there had seemed to be no one else in the world. She looks up at him and smiles, and her smile is toothy and goofy, but her lips are beautiful, and Vaclav smiles back.

"I want you to come to Russia with me," she says.

"Sure," he says.

"I'm serious," she says, smiling.

"I know," he says.

"Do you want to go somewhere?" she says.

"I thought we were going to Russia," he says.

She puts her hands on her hips and gives him a stern face, one eyebrow up, one eyebrow down, chin commanding attention, the same stern face she gave him the last time they saw each other.

"I meant now," she says.

"When are we going to Russia?" he says.

"Soon," she says.

"This afternoon?" he says.

"No," she says.

"Good, because I'm not packed."

"I'm serious," she says.

"When?" he says.

"We'll see," she says.

"Where are we going now?" he says.

"To eat something, maybe?" she says.

"Okay, cool. Because I'm really hungry," he says.

"I'm not," she says.

"I'm always hungry," he says.

"You must be growing," she says.

"You think?" he says. "We can get pizza. Do you like pizza?"

Such a strange question to ask the most important special secret person in your life, but he has to ask; he doesn't know. He's never seen Lena eat pizza.

"I'm not hungry," she says, "but I'll sit with you. We have a lot to talk about."

"No shit," he says. She is surprised to hear him curse but excited at this reminder that they are both grown-ups now. His saying "shit" makes Russia seem possible. The Russia plan is a thing she is holding in her head, and she pokes it, like a loose tooth, to see if it is real. Sometimes it is, sometimes it isn't. Sometimes it feels good, sometimes very bad. Today it's feeling really good. Really real.

They start walking down the sidewalk together, side by side, looking down at their feet. They are unused to navigating the sidewalk together; they do not have a pace for walking together, like couples in the city do, like old friends do. Vaclav walks slowly, to keep pace with Lena. They squeeze awkwardly past lampposts and groups of people, and find crossing the street awkward.

"What have you been up to?" Vaclav says.

Lena smiles at him mischievously.

"A lot," she says. "What have you been up to?" She smiles; it is so strange to ask him what he has been up to. Like meeting the president and saying, "Hey, how are you doing?"

"Same thing," he says, meaning same thing as when you left, meaning still magic, still trying to take care of you with my mind, still trying to control events using supernatural powers.

A SECRET MISSION

. . .

It's unbelievable to Lena and to Vaclav that they are sitting in a pizza dive, across from each other, just ordering pizza, like everything is normal.

Luckily for Lena and Vaclav, it is assumed by Vaclav, and unchallenged by Lena, that as Vaclav eats he cannot talk at all. Vaclav eats like a pig. Lena is afraid that she might be sprayed with pizza sauce, burned by hurtling molten cheese. While Vaclav eats his first three slices, Lena picks the cheese off a slice and explains to him the Russia plan.

"I want to find my parents," she says. "I mean my biological parents. I have a mom now, an actual mom, my real mom. She adopted me. I love her. I just want to know about my real parents." Vaclav notes the striking calm in Lena's voice when she talks about her new mom, her actual mom.

"I want you to come. It's going to be really hard to find them. I don't know yet how to go about doing that, but I'm sure we can find them. I mean, it can't be impossible. I'm sure they're there, so it's just about figuring out how to find them. Through documents and whatever."

Vaclav pauses eating, just momentarily, directs his eyes up at Lena; he wants to ask her a question, but his mouth is full and she's not stopping.

"We'll do as much research as possible here, before we leave, and we might be able to make some progress, but I'm sure that we'll hit a wall, and we'll need information that we won't be able to get unless we're actually there, you know? We might have to knock on doors and ask questions, or find records in some obscure place, or whatever."

It is becoming quickly very clear to Vaclav that much of Lena's concept of this plan is based on television shows. But then again, much of the brashness of her plan is based on the confidence of a straight-A student, the confidence that with diligence, with hard work, with dedication, with exhaustive research, questioning, planning, any result can be achieved. Vaclav too is a disciple of this method of living. It is precisely why he is sure that he will, someday, be a successful magician. "The problem is just getting there—specifically, the money to get there. But that's just a number; you count to all numbers one at a time. One dollar at a time," she says.

This is again the thinking of a person who is smart enough to know that they are smart, and that even in a very big world, there is no one significantly smarter, and so anything can be accomplished. There is nothing so childish about wanting to find your parents. This need, he thinks, must be innate, natural, eternal. Lena is like a homing pigeon, a boomerang. There is a motor inside her, always seeking them.

She isn't done talking.

"The main thing is, we can get there if we just decide to go, you know? And I know you understand that, that if we just decide to make it happen, then we can. Then it is done. Basically."

"You know what Houdini said? He said, 'I have done things which rightly I could not do, because I said to myself, *You must.*' "

"I like that," she says.

"I thought you might," he says, and they both blush. "First of all," he says, "yes, of course I'll go with you." Lena never doubted that Vaclav would come along. She nods.

"So I just want to get that out of the way, because of course I'll do it, I just have a few questions, and some ideas and stuff, about the plan. But I don't want you to worry that in any way I'm not on board, because I really am," he says. "First of all, are you completely sure that they're in Russia?" he asks.

"Yes."

"Why?" he asks. "If you don't know where they are, how can you be sure they're not here?"

"If they were here, in America, they would have contacted me. They would have found me. At some point." Lena says this as fact. Vaclav is less sure.

"How do you know they're still alive?" he asks, and then immediately wonders if this is a question he can ask. It seems like such a cruel question, such an awful question.

"Doesn't matter. If I find them and they're dead, that's still finding them. I just want to fill in the holes. I don't want anything from them. I just want to know. I want to know why they came here, and why they left me. I think anyone would want to know that."

Vaclav thinks about how his parents too came to America, brought him here. He thinks about how they haven't discussed it much, not in years. He hasn't asked his mother or father what their lives were like in Russia, why they left, anything. Their dinner table discussions are about school, about politics, about everything else. Vaclav remembers a little bit of living in Russia when he was little; he remembers a day he played with another little boy outside of their big apartment building, and a windup spaceman toy that he cried about when they landed in America and he realized he had left it behind. He remembers that he took his Houdini book with him on the plane. These are only vague memories he has from when he was little; life before Vaclav is never discussed. Vaclav wants to tell this to Lena, to say something like, "My parents live with me in my house, and I don't know these things that you think most people know. He does not say this. *I could know if I wanted,* he tells himself, *and that's the difference.*

"Are you going to tell your parents about this?" he asks, realizing, again, that the very basic things he does not know about Lena's life would make a long list.

"Parent. It's just my mom. And no, I'm not, because she would never let me travel alone. I mean, alone? To Russia? Never. It has to be a secret."

This is a mission. Vaclav understands missions, understands the need for secrecy when something is so important.

"I won't tell my mom either; she would flip out."

Lena almost cringes at this mention of Vaclav's mom, and wonders why. Why would the mention of Vaclav's mom make her feel anxious? Her brain is full of holes sometimes. Having Vaclav here feels good, but she feels like he's poking around in some dark soft spots. His questions are harder to answer, harder to hear, than she thought they would be, like he's pressing on some muscles that have atrophied.

"Yeah," she says. "I feel like it's best if no one knows. Easier."

"Okay," he says. He doesn't even wonder why they would have to go alone, why it therefore has to be a secret, he so much likes having a secret with Lena again.

They walk outside the pizza parlor, and Lena tells Vaclav that she has to go, she has a meeting. School council. Yes, it is boring. She's the president, and it's still boring. Yeah, good for college applications, she tells him. This conversation, this small talk about high school politics, it is all just words to fill the air while they stare at each other. They never want to leave each other's company, and they do not know how to say goodbye.

"Oh, wait!" Vaclav says. "What about your aunt? Would she be able to help us? Does she still live on Seventh?"

"She moved," Lena says. "Back to Russia."

"Oh, too bad," Vaclav says. "She probably knows, right?"

"Yeah," Lena says. "I wish I could just ask her, but she's gone."

There is a pause, and Vaclav fills it with "Can I see you tomorrow?" and Lena hops on the end of tomorrow with her yes. Here, after school. Okay, they say, too many times, okay, okay, okay, smiling, on the verge of goofy. They are about to turn and just walk away from each other, not knowing at all what to do with this departure, how it should go, and then they step forward into each other's hug space, which as soon as they are doing it seems like the reasonable thing to do. Two long-lost friends hugging. Reasonable. Except there is too much contact between necks, between the softness at the intersection of neck and jaw, not enough friendly vigor, too much of the world falling silent while they hold on to each other.

As Vaclav walks away, he realizes he meant to tell her about his newest trick, the Ancient Egyptian Sarcophagus of Mystery. She would be so excited, because they dreamed of building it together when they were little, and he's finally done it. It's a trick for two, and he hasn't been able to practice it yet. He was always waiting for Lena.

THE NEXT DAY

...

They sit under a tree in Fort Greene Park. They sit on the ground and run their fingers through the grass. It's good that the grass is there; it gives them something to pick at, to pull at, somewhere to put their eyes while they talk.

Lena is looking at the grass, and Vaclav is looking at her. He can't believe she's right there.

Lena tells Vaclav that she wants to tell him everything, and then she tells him almost everything.

She tells him what she knows about before she met him, which they never discussed when she was nine. She tells him about Radoslava Dvorakovskaya, and about the day she found her dead in the bathtub. She tells him she doesn't know where she was before Radoslava, or how she got there. She tells him about waiting for her aunt, about coloring, and about not being able to talk.

Vaclav feels so good, so good that she's telling him everything.

He asks her what she remembers about when she was taken away. She tells him about Child Protective Services, about going to live with Em. She tells him about the day Em announced that she was going to adopt Lena, which was the second day Lena was in Em's house. She tells him about how she and Em decided on what Lena would call her, how Em was the first two letters, the first syllable of her name, Emily, and also the first letter of Mom, how it was a way to call her Emily and Mom without saying either.

Vaclav notices that Lena is skipping things. She's skipping the part about his mom calling the police. He figures she's leaving it out because it's awkward to talk about, because it was his mom's fault that Lena was taken away. He's always blamed his mom, and he imagines Lena must too. Of course he's not angry anymore; he knows his mother thought she was helping when she overreacted, ruined everything, made them take Lena away. Just because she was home alone a lot, just because her aunt was a stripper and all of that, she called the police. He's really glad that Lena was happier with Em, that it all turned out better for her. Somehow he had always imagined that things got worse for Lena when she went away, maybe because it was so much worse for him.

The sun is going down, and a chill is coming on. He gives her his sweatshirt; he couldn't possibly feel cold. They talk until it's dark and the park is closing.

They get up and walk toward the subway, and he tells her he can't wait to work on the magic show again. He tells her that he never found a replacement assistant.

She smiles at him and tells him she can't wait to start planning their trip to Russia.

WHEN YOU ARE IN LOVE, IT FEELS LIKE YOU ARE FLOATING

...

Lena and Vaclav spend their time ecstatic in each other's company. They are wild-eyed like starving dogs, like recent converts. They both coast through school like zombies, and no one notices. For the first time, Lena does her homework in the hallway against a locker ten minutes before class is due to start, instead of meticulously, the afternoon it is assigned, at home, at the kitchen table, with Em keeping company, keeping watch, like a fire tower attendant.

Until now, homework was a bad place. A contaminated zone, a slash-fest, an all-out slaughter. Much pencil chewing and lead breaking. Much ripping up. Lena is surprised at her ability to break her own mold. Em is pleased too. Lena doing her homework for hours at the kitchen table, immersed, obsessive, was better than the screaming fights, but it was still just another version of being off balance.

Vaclav does his tests now without studying; he goes through lunch without making jokes, without entertaining his friends, without doing any magic tricks. He's busy writing notes, to read to Lena, to give to Lena, about how much he's thinking of her, about how amazing he feels. He's busy writing lists, planning the Russia trip. He's coming up with ways to raise money, questions to answer, places to look. His favorite new idea is to raise money by doing magic shows. It's so perfect, so perfectly full circle. He and Lena are together again—of course, they were meant to be, he the famous magician, she his lovely assistant.

A STORM WITH MANY EYES

...

Vaclav walks into school bleary-eyed. He slept not even one hour; he was on the phone all night with Lena. All night, making plans. He started to really picture getting on a plane with her, taking off, flying to somewhere they've never been. He knows they can do it, because they can do anything.

Vaclav doesn't see Ryan right away, he's so tired, and he's still thinking about Lena, about how easy it was to spend eight hours on the phone with her. Ryan's been watching Vaclav come down the hallway toward his locker, and she's not alone. All her friends are watching too.

"Hi," Vaclav says, realizing that something is wrong.

"You missed my show," she says.

"I'm so sorry," he says, realizing how completely he has forgotten about her.

"Lindsey saw you," she says.

"What?" Vaclav says.

"Lindsey saw you sitting with that girl. In Fort Greene Park."

"What?" he says.

"She saw you with some girl with frizzy hair." This is the first time that Vaclav has realized that Lena and Ryan might be mutually exclusive.

Ryan has tears in her eyes.

"She's just a friend. . . ." he starts, but Ryan is already walking away.

WHEN YOU ARE IN LOVE IT FEELS LIKE FALLING

. . .

Vaclav suddenly feels terrible about Ryan. The truth is that he hasn't thought one bit about her since Lena came back. Now here is a churning in his belly and a prickliness in his brain that is distinctively not productive, and he feels he can talk to Lena about anything, so he brings it up. He brings it up with Lena the next time they are sitting in the park, under their tree, which becomes the best, most special tree in the world the moment they sit together under its branches and pick at its acorns.

"Have you noticed that we've kind of not done anything except see each other since we, you know, met up again?" he says.

"Yeah," Lena says, her eyes shining, excited. "Isn't it crazy?"

"I haven't been doing anything for school."

"Me either! It's nuts." She racks her brain for an example, an example to show him, like a gift. "I turned in a lab yesterday that I worked on for like ten minutes, in the hall. Right before class." Her face is lit up like she's got a lightbulb in her skull, and she feels like light must be sneaking out from the corners of her eyes.

"I haven't talked at all to my mom; she doesn't even know about you. She doesn't know that you're back," he says.

"Yeah, I haven't really talked at all to my mom either. I just haven't felt like it." This seems to him to be an incomplete comment. There is more than this to the secrecy of their relations, and they both know it.

"I mean, until today, I hadn't talked to my girlfriend in a week," Vaclav says, and as the words take flight, he hears what he is saying and what the impact will be, and he tries to say it like he is dropping a tiny marshmallow into a cup of hot chocolate, but it drops like the boulder it is.

"Yeah. I didn't know you had a girlfriend," she says. Holding back tears? Fists? She doesn't know. She just knows she has to try to hold back, to hold on.

"Yeah. I'm sorry. I guess I should have told you that."

"Yeah. I guess you should have." She's angry. She's a comet crashing to earth. She's trying not to explode, he can see that, but she's going to make impact.

"Is there anything else you're not telling me?" Lena is fuming. Her words rattle in her throat.

"Well, I'm sorry about not telling you about the girlfriend, I'm sorry if it's such a big deal, I would have told you if I knew."

"Well it's not a big deal at all, then. It's like you said, it's not a big deal, right? Of course. It's fine." But she's irate.

"No, it is a big deal, I guess. I mean, you're a big deal. You're such a big deal I haven't practiced my magic at all since I saw you on that bench. . . ." Vaclav says.

"I can't believe . . ." she says with a smile, and stops.

"What?"

"I can't believe you still want to be a magician." She pauses. "Honestly, grow up." She says this like being a magician is both hilarious and pathetic.

Vaclav can only shake his head.

Lena stands, waiting.

"I can't believe you said that. You're exactly the same," he says.

How can I be exactly the same, she thinks, *I have never had any idea of who I am or who I was?*

"You only care about you, about your fucked-up life. About going to Russia, about your parents. You don't care about me."

"How can I care about you if you don't tell me anything about your life? You don't tell me about your girlfriend, you don't tell me anything. How can I know?" She picks up her bag and walks away.

I totally forgot about her, and about everything else, the moment you showed up, he thinks. *I love you, I'm coming to Russia with you, I'd go anywhere with you, I've been with you the whole time, I've been waiting for you the whole time, I'd do anything for you, it's always been that way,* he thinks, but she's already gone.

She has no idea what to do, or think, and she's thinking everything. She's thinking *I love him, I hate him, how could he not tell me about his girlfriend, I hate her, why do I hate her, I don't even know her, I can't believe I made it sound like I think it's stupid to still do magic, of course I don't think that, do I? Maybe I do think it's stupid that he still does magic. Is he right about me? About the way I was? How could he say any of those things?*

Lena's rage is new and strange to her, and confusing. She flies down the stairs to the subway, and the concrete steps feel strange beneath her feet. The subway feels odd, like a place she's never been before. Her mind is still racing, and she doesn't want to be away from Vaclav. It's been ninety seconds, and it feels too long. She wants to go back, but she doesn't go back.

Vaclav sits for a while, in case she's coming back. Then he walks to the subway station, goes slowly down the stairs, and sinks into a seat on the subway. He looks at the ground, looks at the window. He hasn't felt this lonely since the first time he lost Lena.

FALLOUT, OR FALLING OUT, OR FALLING IN

...

Rasia has already noticed that something is different with Vaclav, and the main thing that she has noticed is the absence of the girlfriend, what's-her-name. This is a good thing. This is a thing she is not questioning. Vaclav has been staying late at school, and the business of him and the girlfriend doing homework in his bedroom before she gets home from work, this has stopped.

Rasia worries, of course, that the girl has broken up with Vaclav and hurt his feelings. This is unacceptable. Rasia feels capable of tearing the girl apart with her teeth, spitting out the skinny bones.

Em has noticed that something is different too. Lena is happier, lighter. She's smiling. She's obsessing less, about homework and school and student council. Lena's even been late for school and staying out later with her friends. Em is always happy to see her be social. Always.

When Vaclav and Lena arrive at their respective homes early that night, slamming all doors, refusing meals, taking no phone calls, watching no television, both mothers chalk it up to the roller coaster of teenage hormones. Neither mother senses that this very day her child has learned that it is possible for a universe that is good and light and thrilling to tear at its seams suddenly and irreparably.

Lena races up to her room and sits on the floor, on soft carpet, with her fingers dug deep into the pile, her legs twisted beneath her, sobbing with her teeth clenched, her throat raw. She is so distraught she can't see ever feeling better, she can't see ever living happily in this human way, where everything good can come apart and go away, where terrible things have happened that cannot be erased, where more terrible things will happen after that, where good things will be defined by their endings.

Lena thought that Vaclav was a safe thing, and he wasn't.

Vaclav stomps into his room. He slams the door and paces. Back and forth. Trying to understand and trying to figure out what to do next. He wants to make a list, but the things he's thinking, he doesn't think he can write them down. He starts but then stops, over and over again, writing:

What to do about Lena?
What to do about Lena?
What to do about Lena?

FALLING UP AND DOWN AT THE SAME TIME

...

Lena lies on the floor, facedown, with the carpet irritating her cheek, half closing her eyes and enjoying, really enjoying, the exhaustion that is washing over her, the wet feel of her eyes, the tears on her face. She feels satisfied, and she falls asleep on the floor.

When she wakes up it is late, but Lena isn't tired anymore. She feels good. She starts to feel like everything is going to be good, or better. She sees an opening, an opportunity. She dials Vaclav's number.

When Lena calls, Vaclav almost forgets how bad he was feeling. When she apologizes, his anger seems to dissolve, and he forgets how hurt he was that she insulted his magic.

"I should never have gotten angry."

"It's okay, I understand."

"I never want to argue with you. I never want to be angry with you again."

"No, or me. That was horrible."

Lena sees, sees clearly through the whole thing, sees an opportunity. Because of this arguing and making up, there is room, there is shifting, there is fluidity. There is suddenly an opportunity to say things they weren't saying before.

"I love you," she says.

"I love you too," he says, feeling like he is falling up and down at the same time.

"I do," she says.

"I know. You don't have to explain it," he says. "I know. I feel the same way."

"I don't know what it is, but I don't want you to be with anyone else," she says.

He's silent.

"I know that's stupid," she says. "It's just a feeling."

"It's not stupid," he says. "It's not stupid." The way Lena is talking to him makes him feel like Ryan is about as appealing and important as an instruction manual to a game you don't have anymore, a game you can't imagine was ever fun for anyone. Vaclav forgets that a moment ago he was sure he didn't do anything wrong, that Lena's anger about Ryan was unfair. He should have mentioned Ryan, that was true, but he hadn't been trying to hide her or lie, he had just forgotten.

"I'm sorry," he says. "I don't want to be with anyone but you."

Lena smiles and says nothing.

"I want to see you now," he says. "I'm going to come over."

"It's the middle of the night," she says.

"I mean it," he says. "I want to be alone with you."

"I can't," she says.

"I'll come to your house tomorrow," he says.

"My mom will be home all day," she says.

"We'll go to my house. My mom won't be home until dinner," he says. "Meet me after school."

"Okay," she says, and she hangs up, feeling surprisingly calm, like she knew that this would happen, which she did.

TRY NOT TO TELL YOUR MOTHER AT BREAKFAST

...

Out the window the sun is bleeding into the sky and birds are waking up. The house is quiet except for the shower running, and the boom, boom, boom of Vaclav's heart pounding in his ears.

His alarm goes off an hour later, but he is already awake, unable to sleep for the adrenaline racing around his body, whirling dizzy in his brain.

Vaclav is so excited about being alone with Lena that it is all he can think about, and he is terrified that he might slip and tell his mother about it at breakfast. When she asks him what he is doing after school, he has to struggle to not say the thing that is constantly on the tip of his tongue.

In the middle of physics class, where his mind is wandering to Lena, Vaclav realizes that Ryan is still a problem. Ryan is sitting, sulking, two rows ahead of him.

How did it happen that Lena went, overnight, from a yearning to an addiction? She seems to have planted herself into his life and sprouted, almost instantly, without his knowing, from a tiny seed into an entire jungle.

Walking in the hallway, he finds that his friends are slightly out of step with him. They're talking about the morning's ethics lesson, which he practically slept through. They're raving about a television show he hasn't seen, isn't interested in seeing. He wonders how they could possibly care about these things; he's wishing he could tell them about his big, exciting news, and he's feeling that somehow they are sliding away from him, just like everything else.

Lena wakes up happy, excited. All day at school, she gets absorbed for a moment, conjugating verbs or making a timeline, and then a thought of Vaclav washes over her, and her head spins with anticipation. As the time approaches when they will see each other, kiss each other, hold each other, they both start forgetting everything that could possibly be bad. The minutes pass slowly, and everything else in the world is starting to matter less and less and less.

After school Lena rushes to meet Vaclav, and everyone on the sidewalk seems to be an old lady, worrying the cement with their canes, picking their way along, getting in Lena's way. Lena can't breathe for seeing Vaclav, and she weaves and bobs through the crowds to get there.

When Vaclav sees her he tries to contain the run in his gait like a giggle in class, like a sneeze at a funeral, but when he gets to her a little bit of the run escapes and there is a bit of a hop-skip, but he doesn't care, and he grabs her hand and says, "My mom isn't home until six, come on."

I REMEMBER THIS PLACE

...

Sometimes the feeling of holding hands is too much for one or the other or both, so they let go, drop their hands, and sit silently on the subway, like drunks trying to arrange their minds.

By the time they are at Vaclav's stop, they are both experiencing significant stress, significant anxiety, their skin unable to contain their nerves, to hold in ever-expanding galaxies of desire.

When they get off the subway, Lena finds that she is walking on a sidewalk she recognizes, on a street she recognizes. She feels like she is in an unfriendly place, as if in a bad dream, and her ears are getting hot, like when she has a blood test at the doctor's office. Also, she can't hear anything, not really, but then again, maybe she can; she hears a car go by, and then she can't hear at all, like someone is cupping their hands over her ears.

Vaclav looks at her, and she's sure he's going to see in her face that she's green, that her blood is turning to rubbing alcohol, light and harsh in her brain, that she's about to pass out.

He looks at her, and he smiles, a big, honest grin, and he says, "Can you believe you're here again?"

"Yeah," Lena hears herself say, far away. She wonders if that is enough to say, and she opens her mouth and says, "Yeah, I can't believe it." She's surprised that she is able to talk; her voice doesn't sound normal. She is surprised that Vaclav seems to think that she's fine, that nothing is wrong with her, and for a while she thinks she might actually be okay, putting one foot in front of the other on this familiar sidewalk. Step, step, step, step, and if she doesn't look up, at the trees, at the familiar houses, she can keep stepping, step in front of step in front of step. She watches her own two feet moving in their strange rhythm over the sidewalk.

Walking in this neighborhood, Lena feels like she is returning to the site of her own death. This is strange and paradoxical for a human being, a living, breathing thing, to look and say, *Oh, yes, I remember this place. This is where I died.*

Is it less paradoxical for Lena, who, after all, has been feeling of late that a part of her is missing, is rotted, is perhaps dead? Yes. It is slightly less paradoxical for Lena. Recently she discovered that something inside of herself was dead, and here she has come upon, unexpectedly, a crime scene. To her, it makes sense.

Vaclav is pulling her toward a door. Lena has to look up now, at the house, at the same brick, at the same windows, the same mailbox. All the same but sharper on her eyes than in her foggy memories. The house seems to announce its realness, its solidness, its actuality, with its obnoxious stance, with its lifelike details, the mortar between the bricks, the garage door, the pile of shoes outside the screen door, the same as she remembers.

Lena is not prepared today to be dusting off this part of her mind. She is not prepared for how this feels. She is dreading going into the house, she realizes, as Vaclav fumbles with the keys. The house looks mean, the way a knife that you cut yourself with once never looks the same.

THE FALL OF EMPIRES

...

Lena walks with Vaclav through the front door of the house, and it's all exactly the same, exactly. It has been here the whole time, and it was not just a memory. It was not just a big, fuzzy, dark, rotting memory, it was an actual place, and no matter how much she forgot, here it is just as big and powerful as ever. Vaclav's parents are frugal people, they're immigrants, they're ex-communists. They're refugees from a place and time when nothing was owned, when you battled the neighbor-woman for a mealy potato. Not really, but really. What is real is that they have been citizens of a great empire and watched it fall. They have felt the rug pulled out from under them. So even in America they save every penny, glue together the broken dishes, stitch together the rips in the couch, and they would never, never, throw away a good rug.

Because Vaclav is born of these two Soviet refugees, savers of everything, buyers of nothing, the house Lena walks into is identical to the house she last saw when she was nine.

She's taking it all in, wide-eyed, trying to breathe, afraid that she is about to lose control, when Vaclav grabs her and kisses her, and she wants to push him away and say, "No, I can't be here," but the words aren't coming.

Her knees buckle a little bit, but Vaclav takes this as her leaning into him, and he holds her and kisses her more.

Smells from the past are rushing into her nose, and pictures are rushing into her head. The smell of the leather cleaner on the couch. The smell of ammonia in the kitchen. The smell of the vodka in Oleg's glass, and Rasia, her perfume, her face, her chins, her mole.

TELL YOURSELF IT'S HAPPENING

...

Lena walks to the couch and sits down because she is sure that she is about to pass out. Vaclav comes close to her, and she opens her mouth to say something, but before she can, Vaclav is on her, his hands on the couch on either side of her head, his feet still firmly on the floor. He is in an incline push-up over her, and he kisses her, hard, then drops to his knees, one knee on either side of her hips. He is crouching above her, and kissing her and kissing her, and it is fantastic, and it is not hard enough, and he will never be able to kiss her enough, and it is torture.

He breaks away from her, sits on the couch next to her, breathes heavy, big athletic breaths, before he pulls her across his lap and kisses her more, more and more and more.

He stands up and says, "Let's go in my room." She stands up, dizzy, and takes his hand, and reminds herself that this is what she knew would happen all along, that this is what she wanted.

Lena follows Vaclav to his room and stands right in the middle, taking everything in. Above his bed he still has the poster of David Copperfield stuck to the wall with ticky-tack. There are large framed black-and-white photos of Vaclav in a top hat and a T-shirt, pulling a rabbit out of a hat. She wonders who took them. On his desk she recognizes *The Magician's Almanac,* which she gave him for his ninth birthday, and his Harry Houdini book. Tacked to the wall above his desk there is a brown paper bag. Written on the bag, in Vaclav's deliberate handwriting, is a list.

THINGS THAT *ARE:*

1. *One day being a famous magician*
2. *Lena being lovely assistant*
3. *Perseverance toward those goals in spite of any and every obstacle*

In the corner, there is a six-foot-tall wooden box painted in gold paint. The Ancient Egyptian Sarcophagus of Mystery. She knows what it is; she remembers when they were little, sitting on the floor and planning to build it, reading over and over again the detailed plans in *The Magician's Almanac*, and here it is, he's really done it. She wants to ask him about it, she wants to slow everything down and just talk, but Vaclav leans down and kisses her, his hands traveling from her shoulders down her arms to her hips.

Every time he touches her, Lena tries to figure out how it feels. She asks herself, over and over again, *How does this feel?* She gets no answer. There's a panic somewhere; somewhere inside she's yelling at herself to pay attention, to be present, something big is happening, but from some important part there's no answer, a phone ringing off the hook, no answer to this very important question. All of her selves are out to lunch.

Vaclav lifts her shirt swiftly up over her head. Lena, standing there topless, feels as if she's just surprised herself by counting to three and then jumping feetfirst into a cold lake. She's surprised at what her body can do, even when her mind is three steps behind. Or five steps behind. Or not there at all.

Lena is now very dizzy. The smells in the house seem to be coming up out of her own horrible rotten insides, big, shameful, embarrassing smells. She looks down, expecting to see fumes wafting from her belly button.

Lena has only sensations. His hands are all over her in a way that's entirely pleasant, in a way that suggests that he sees her body as some natural wonder or some perfect creation. There's awe in his hands, and she's the thing that's so awesome. She doesn't really feel naked. There is a draft from the windows. Vaclav is tall. He is fully dressed, and she is undressed.

Lena is trying to think, but she feels drunk, and her nose is full of a strange smell. It smells like her missing, rotted-out, dead piece. It smells like she has found it, or that it is nearby, stinking.

This place, which she is discovering today is a real place, a real place where a piece of her has been rotting all these years, is pulling on other strings of memory, knocking into other buried synapses, and things are starting to come back to Lena.

Vaclav leads her to his bed. There's more kissing, and they lower themselves down, and he seems to slow up. He's kissing her slowly, and his hands are lingering more, but not in a careful way, not in a gentle way. It feels like she is riding a roller coaster, not the crazy up-and-down part, the slow, chug-chug-chug up the steep incline part, where you are starting to feel afraid and realizing that there is no way out.

She's still trying over and over to get in touch with distant parts of her, and they're not answering. She wants to ask herself an important question: *Is this something I want to do? Am I saying yes? Yes to this very big thing? Get back to me as soon as possible, I need an answer.* Girls on television and in movies and books seem always to know if they are ready to have sex for the first time.

Lena does not know. Not in a way that she is unsure but in a way that she, as a person who wants and does not want things, does not exist. Like the part of her that is responsible for this decision is missing.

When they tangle together and they are both out of all their clothes, and his explorations bring them to the brink, she has to tell herself, *It's happening, watch, pay attention, it's happening.*

For Vaclav, it is what his body has been dreaming about without his permission. It is the missing piece, or he is the missing piece and he has just found his puzzle. It is exactly right and wonderful, and impossibly, he thinks, for all the poetry and song and painting and verse dedicated to it, underrated. The feeling, in fact, is so wonderful that Vaclav can feel himself in his body like he never has before; it is impossible to think, to step outside of pure physical wonder; all he feels is all he feels, and Lena, Lena is another planet, and he is a star shooting through the cold, black sky. He cradles her head in his hand, and he loves her so much he would shield her from a meteorite with his body, and he tries to be gentle, and he asks her if she is okay.

She is not okay. She feels something, finally, and it is bad. She feels as if she has unzipped herself from her belly button to her throat and found nothing inside. The feeling is like reaching for an orange and finding it hollow, rotted out, giving sickly beneath your fingers.

STOP

...

Lena grabs Vaclav's shoulder.

"Stop," she says, trying to scream, but it comes out only in a tiny whisper, and he doesn't hear her.

"Stop," she says again, louder, "please," and he stops, but he still hasn't heard her.

"I have to get out of here, Vaclav. You have to get me out of here. Something horrible is happening, and I need to go to the doctor or the hospital, and I need to go home, so please take me home." She talks as fast as possible, even though she can't hear her own voice. She tries to make herself shout, though she is not sure if any sound is coming out. She talks as fast as possible, even as she is getting less and less sound into her ears, less air into her lungs, less light into her eyeballs, and horrible, gruesome things are popping into her head.

Vaclav is frozen; he's not moving or saying anything at all. She's pinned beneath him. She is panicked and trapped, and when she turns to wriggle out, to free herself, she sees what he sees, which is Rasia, standing in the door.

WHAT RASIA HEARS AND SEES

...

At work, there was a fire alarm going off in the warehouse all morning. Over and over again, a faulty alarm. So loud your thoughts fell right out of your head. The fire department had to come to take apart the alarm and fix whatever was wrong to make it scream and scream when there is no fire, no nothing. The manager said, "Go home, the day is lost."

What Rasia hears when she walks in the house is the thing she has always dreaded hearing. Moving around in the bed and hushed voices. *Ryan's back*, she thinks. *That batonchik is back*. This is the truth. This is what she thinks. She does not like this, to think of the girl this way, but this is what she thinks. She walks slowly through the house; her intention is not to sneak up on them, but she is afraid also of embarrassing them, really of embarrassing Vaclav, and also, she wants confirmation that what she thinks is going on is what is really going on. So she goes a little bit closer, a little bit closer, down the hallway, her big body moving silently.

Outside the door of Vaclav's room she hears a girl talking, and this is not the big, horsey sound of the American girl. Not at all. She can hear sounds of the girl talking, and the sound is familiar and frightening—it is a sound like thieves in the nighttime.

This is not Ryan.

Rasia pushes open the door of Vaclav's room, which is just slightly ajar because he is not expecting her, and she sees her son, naked, on top of a girl with an explosion of hair that is so dark it has no color, like the black of darkness in a cave. Who is this girl that Vaclav has brought home? In her worry, her absorption, Rasia has forgotten about hiding and has pushed the door open all the way. Rasia stands in the doorway, mouth open, heart pumping, and Vaclav sees her, and their eyes connect.

The girl seems upset, and she starts trying to get out from under Vaclav, and she turns her head, and Rasia sees (as in a dream that you are having in which everyone wears the wrong faces, and doors open to the wrong thing, and your grandfather is alive again but with the body of a horse) that this girl, she is a person back from the dead, from another world, from another time.

Rasia is angry and scared. Lena should be far away for her own sake, far away from memories that must be so awful for her, they are hard enough for Rasia, who is a big woman and tough like she's made of frozen potatoes. Here is the little girl that she loved like her own, that she still wants to hold, and rock to sleep, and tell stories to, and protect. Here she is, little Yelena, back from outer space, from death, from her next life, from never-never land, from wherever they sent her.

LENA REMEMBERS

...

It all comes together when she sees Rasia's face. She remembers. She remembers, and she can't get her clothes on fast enough, and she runs.

Vaclav runs after her, but she is too fast. By the time he is at the door, she is gone.

THE PLANET AND THE DUST

...

Vaclav can't see where Lena has gone. He runs three blocks in one direction, then worries that she has gone the other way and runs three blocks in the other direction. She is gone; he has lost her. He runs as fast as he can. He runs one more block, one more block with tears stinging in his eyes, until he can't run anymore.

Rasia is sitting in the kitchen at the table, waiting, when he returns.

They don't know what to say to each other.

Rasia is so overwhelmed; where to begin? It must be talked about. Vaclav is not a not-talk person. This is because he is American; he can't not-talk about anything, he must talk about everything. Rasia can not-talk about anything. Still, she is trying to be, for his sake, an American mother. An American mother for an American son. This is what he wants and needs. To talk about this, though, this is too much.

First they make eye contact. She can hold it longer than he can. He can't hold it at all. He looks down at the floor and makes a sound, a tiny little sound, a sound Rasia can barely hear. Rasia's heart starts to break a little bit, because this is a sound like a baby makes when they are just making sounds, no words.

Then he says, "I don't think I can handle this, Mom," and when he says that word, *Mom,* his lip starts to tremble, and she can see it in his eyes that he is going to cry, and it has been a long time since she saw him cry. She can't remember when. Not since he was young enough to skin his knees.

"This is too much for me," he says now, and Rasia agrees. Lena was too much for her too.

She should have known that when Lena came back it would be secret, it would be sneaking and lying. With that girl, it was always sneaking and lying. Always. Not her fault, what could she do but sneak and lie, so much shame in her life and so much sadness. Always stealing and squirreling away things from Rasia's fridge, always her tiny hands trying to steal things, useful things from the bathroom, from Vaclav's room, from the linen closet, everywhere.

Whenever Rasia would take Lena home to tuck her in at night, after Lena fell asleep, Rasia would check her backpack and see the homework that Vaclav was doing for her, the toilet paper she was stealing from the house, the little bits of snacks, a tube of toothpaste, a notebook, a piece of bread. She wanted to help, so she used the backpack like a shopping list. She would leave toilet paper for her, toothpaste, a new toothbrush, snacks for school, extra sandwiches. She would leave these things at Lena's house when she fell asleep, and she would leave them out at her own house for Lena to take. Still, Lena snuck and stole. Maybe because there was an endless list of things that she needed, or maybe it was because shame and survival were already in her. Maybe the sneaking and lying and conniving were something she would do forever.

Still, Rasia is surprised. She thought that Lena would not be more powerful than Vaclav.

She is. Lena is like a planet, and Vaclav is like a little piece of dust. Lena is a bull, and Vaclav is a piece of string tied around its neck. Vaclav is a chip of paint on the exterior of the Sputnik satellite. Rasia tells herself that the power that Lena has over Vaclav is because she is a girl and he is a teenage boy. But she always had this power over him, even when she was a little scrawny weed and Vaclav had eyes only for David Copperfield. This power that Lena has, over a nice boy, it comes from the way that she learned to get power when she was young. Vaclav is a nice boy who struggles for nothing. Lena learned how to grab power early. Is this her fault? Rasia will be the first one to tell you that no, it is not. Rasia saw firsthand that this is not at all the little girl's fault. Does this, the fact that the girl is not to blame, mean that Rasia wants the girl (now even stronger, more powerful, more dangerous, armed with breasts and hips and lips and those eyes like oil slicks in a puddle) around her son? No, she does not.

But she cared so much for Lena, like her own child.

All of this crowds Rasia's mind, all at once, and she hasn't even scratched the surface. And still her son sits forlorn beside her, destroyed by sobbing, leaking snot onto a nice clean T-shirt.

THERE IS NOT PUNISH

...

Rasia realizes that she can no longer assume anything about her son when it comes to Lena.

"What has been going on between you two?" she asks. This seems like a good question, a good wide net. Vaclav looks at her like he's trying to decide what to tell her.

"Listen," she tells him, "no one is being angry at you, you are not in trouble, there is not punish. Stop making strategies, stop thinking like her. Just tell me what is going on here."

Vaclav's face shows that he is trying to strategize, to scoot his battleship into less dangerous waters, if he can find them.

"What do you mean, 'stop thinking like her'?" he says. He's stopped crying, and now he looks angry, at Rasia.

"With the strategies and the conniving! With lying and stealing and cheating, and making this and that happen in secret! Secrets! Vaclav, see! She is like a squirrel, always hiding some rotting secret under this rock, under that tree, under the bed, in the pillowcase! This is not the way!"

"What are you talking about, Mom?" he asks.

"How long she has been back?" she asks.

"She's not back, she's always been here! Always been in Brooklyn, she never left." He says this like Rasia is the jail master, some warden person who has been hiding Lena from him all this time.

"You are avoiding the question. Don't be stupid. I just found you, in my house, sneaking around when you thought I would be at work, doing sex, which I can't believe, and with Lena, who you should have told me you were seeing! Don't be stupid. I am getting answered. How long?"

"I don't know, a little while," he says, looking down at the table.

"You have been lying to me. You have been sneaking, and why? I ask you, how is your day today, my loving son, and you say *nothing*, you lying sack of I don't know what lies as much as you! Why do you hide this from me?"

"Why do you need to know? You need a full report, every day, on who I see, like Big Brother?" This reference is lost on Rasia. What is not lost is Vaclav's attempt at anger, at teenage rebellion. He wears it poorly, self-consciously, awkwardly. Rasia decides to retaliate with something she wears equally poorly, victimhood, sadness.

"'Need to know'? Oh, Vaclav. I thought that we were close; I thought that you could tell me anything, because you know that my love for you is bigger than the ocean I put between me and my own mother in order to give you this life. I thought, you, my only son—I thought we were close. I had no idea I was so wrong. . . ." Vaclav stops looking angry at Rasia, and tears come to his eyes again.

Is Rasia pleased that she has made Vaclav cry? No, but she is pleased that he has dropped the act of seeming somehow angry with her, of deflecting all her inquiries with misdirected fury.

"How did this happen?" she says. She lets some moments pass, because she knows he wants to tell her, but he is afraid.

"She called me. We met up after school, I dunno."

"What about Ryan?" she asks, remembering the name, saying it perfectly. Knowing she is, as they say, out of the picture. Vaclav only sobs harder.

Rasia is feeling very deeply for Ryan, because it is happening a lot to girls who are nice, and kind, and sweet, that they get their hearts pulped like a tomato in a can by boys who leave them for the wild ones who jump up on the beds and say "Woo-hoo, let's go."

"So why did you lie about this from me?" Rasia asks.

"It's *to* me, Mom. You should say 'lie about this *to* me.' "

"Listen," Rasia says, "it is a truth you are keeping away, so I say, from me. And stop with the English lesson, Mr. American, I'm asking you something. Why keep a secret? You think I wouldn't approve? You just hate me so much?"

"Obviously I don't hate you. She didn't want anyone to

know about going to find her parents and stuff, and I don't know, I don't know why it had to be a secret, but it did." He can't remember anymore why he agreed to keep Lena a secret from his mom, or how he started lying about it.

"What do you mean, 'going to find her parents'?" Rasia lowers her voice, and she says very, very gently, "Where were you planning to find her parents?"

Vaclav is too exhausted to lie.

"Russia," he says. Rasia takes a deep breath, calms herself, reminds herself to be glad that Vaclav has told her. She feels, though, like she has opened the freezer and found a land mine on top of the ice trays, and she is now carrying it gently out of her house.

"Russia?" Rasia asks, gently, evenly.

"Yeah."

Rasia thinks about the country she left, about what she went through to leave it, about all of the things that were awful, especially about all of the hard decisions to be made, and she thinks now about how in a few short days, this girl has dragged her son into a snake pit of lies, and sex, and beyond that, beyond that, she is planning to take him, with her, to Russia, to try to find missing people, the kind of people who abandon their baby, to go poking around the underbelly of a giant ex-Soviet monster.

"You were going to go with her? To Russia? When?"

"I don't know, Ma, we didn't buy the tickets yet."

"When were you going to tell me?" she asks.

"Eventually," Vaclav says, trailing off, because when he thinks about it, there was no "we'll tell them eventually" in Lena's plan. In Lena's plan, not explicitly but definitely, was the assumption that the mothers, the families, could not know, because they would not allow the plan to happen, and the plan had to happen, so the families had to be lied to. Vaclav remembers leaving the house to sneak out and take the train to Lena's house early in the morning. He can see now what Lena wanted him to do: to run away, to get on a plane, to not tell anyone, to disappear. *I could never do that to my mom,* he thinks, at the same time he is terrified because he was well on his way, and he knows it.

"She didn't want to tell her mom either," he says, to soften things.

"She has a mom?" Rasia says, aching with joy and sadness for Lena to have a mother who is not Rasia.

"She was adopted. She really likes her mom." Vaclav takes a deep breath. "I don't know what happened." Of course he doesn't. Lena comes back, and she whispers things and she makes him feel good, and she has secrets, and plans, and mystery and power. Rasia wonders, though, if Lena had any idea what was going on, what was happening. Lena is a hurt person. Lena is a sad person. Rasia has a whole section of her heart devoted to tender feelings for Lena.

Rasia knows—well, maybe not knows, but it is her best guess—that Lena had no idea what was going on either. It was not her idea to come and get Vaclav and break him down and make him lie and all this. She is a girl who is lost and is looking for something. Lena is thinking that maybe Vaclav can help her get this something. Beyond that, Lena is operating without full instructions.

FATHER KNOWS BEST

...

Vaclav puts his head down on the table. He tries to understand why Lena would run away from him. He cannot understand. He cannot imagine running away from Lena.

When the door opens, Vaclav knows who it is. He does not pick up his head. Vaclav's dad comes home at the same time every day.

Oleg, upon arrival in the kitchen, notices that there is nothing cooking for dinner, and that Vaclav and Rasia both look like they have been crying.

"What?" he says, looking at them, going to the freezer for vodka.

No one answers him.

"What is it? What is tragedy?"

"Lena's back," Vaclav says, through snot and tears.

"Lena?" Oleg says, as if she weren't the center of the universe.

"Yeah, Lena," says Vaclav.

"Oh, the little girl, with the Aunt's boyfriend who diddled her? This one? That guy was scum. They kill him in prison."

Rasia's face is frozen. Vaclav feels like his face is coming apart from his skull.

Oleg looks at Rasia, and he sees that he told something he was not supposed to tell.

"What?" Oleg says.

"He shouldn't know this," Rasia says, softly. "I don't want him to know."

"Why?" says Oleg. "He is old enough to understand."

"Oleg," Rasia says. "Enough."

"Mom, is that true?" says Vaclav, quietly, carefully. "You said that you called the police because her aunt wasn't taking care of her."

"I called the police," she says. "Because of what I saw."

"You saw?" he asks. "What did you see?"

"Not what I saw, what I knew. I knew for too long," she says, and then her head goes down because she is starting to cry. "I knew, and then I saw. So that I could not ignore anymore."

"What did you know?" Vaclav says. He says this because he is trying to disbelieve the diddling comment. He is wanting it to be something else. He is wanting it to be anything else.

"These are things that are unspeakable! You know what it is. Vaclav, to make me say this, don't punish me. I'm sorry, I had to do what I did. It's hard to live with, and who knows, I tried." Rasia and Vaclav are both crying now, and Oleg looks like he is watching a soap opera in a foreign language.

"What did you know?" Vaclav says quietly. "What did you see?" He is refusing to believe. He is refusing to understand. He is the silence before a bomb explodes. He is the tick, tick, tick, tick before the boom.

"Vaclav, she was a child and there was no one to care for her; it was a bad situation. What do you want me to tell you?"

"That's not it," Vaclav says.

"Vaclav, what does it matter now?" Rasia says.

"You have to tell me. When she left, you just wanted to pretend that she never existed, but I was just a little kid, and my heart was broken," Vaclav shouts, because he can't help it. He shouts, gasping for air, "She was gone, and my heart was broken. I just need to know; she was here and then she was so gone for so long, but I never stopped thinking about her, never, and then she was back, and now she's gone again and I can't stand it. Please, Mom, please, Mom, please, Mom, please . . ." His voice trails off because he has run out of air.

He is asking her what happened, but he knows what happened. He is asking her to make it not true.

"Vaclav," Rasia says.

"Please tell me what happened," Vaclav says.

"I told you," she says.

"No," he says.

"The man, he did terrible things to her. . . ."

"No," he says.

"I suspected," she says.

"No," he says.

"I was not sure. She stayed home sick from school, and I was worried about her, she had been so skinny, and she wasn't eating well. Do you remember? She would eat nothing, and then everything? I thought something might be wrong, and she had no one to take care of her, so I went over there to check on her, and I walked in, and I saw," she says.

"No," he says.

"I saw him." She chooses her words carefully, terrified. "I caught him."

"No," Vaclav shouts. *"No. No. No. No."* His shouts become screams, and his screams become lightning tearing apart ancient trees, and the lightning becomes continents ripping apart, and the ripping becomes the earth splitting in two pieces, and the sky tearing from the earth, the darkness from the light.

Vaclav runs out of the room, into his own room, leaving her there with his father, leaving her sitting there, alone.

Oleg sits next to Rasia at the table and takes her hand in his hand.

"I did the best I could," Rasia says, to the room, to her husband, to herself.

UN-FORGET, RE-REMEMBER, RE-FORGET, UN-REMEMBER

...

Lena can't catch her breath. Lena can't un-see what she is seeing. Lena decides on the train that she doesn't want to tell anyone ever. She doesn't want to tell Vaclav, or to ever talk to him again. To tell anyone would be impossible anyway; she could never give flight to the things she is seeing in her mind by attaching them to words, setting them loose. She decides to forget. She decides to forget again. She wishes she could turn off her brain. She tries not to think, not to think anything at all, but the feeling of hands holding her down, pulling her knees apart, is in her body, and it won't go away.

Lena keeps seeing Rasia's face, not her face today but her face in the doorway at her aunt's house, when Lena was nine. She can remember now that she knew that Rasia was there, to save her, and that the horror on Rasia's face terrified her.

She feels a familiar feeling, like she has done something hideous. She tries to tell herself that nothing is her fault. It's not Lena's fault that Rasia knew she was alone in that house, with Ekaterina, with the kind of people Ekaterina knew, vulnerable and unprotected, night after night. It's not Lena's fault that she was born Lena. She has stayed far away from that world, from that place, from that time, from all that hurt and all that mess, away from Vaclav, and Rasia, whose face is part of the disgusting loop playing in her mind; Rasia will only remind her of it. It was better before she went back, before she remembered. She should stay with Em and move brightly into the future. With chamomile tea and Em's friends, who bring lovely produce to the house. With Em's friends, who sit outside to watch the stars and drink wine and bitch about men. With Em's really great music, with the solid French farmhouse distressed wood furniture, with the quilts and the chandeliers.

Lena is on a train moving toward better, and she's already starting to forget. Emily is a god who came to earth and saved her. She is the sun around which Lena will orbit for the rest of her life. She is the center of Lena's new cosmology. Lena's parents don't exist. Vaclav does not exist; Rasia does not exist. Her aunt does not exist, and the man does not exist. Emily is a bastion of trust and warmth and safety, has always been and will always be. Lena is born again, and moving toward the sun on her train under the ground, she feels nothing.

When Lena gets home, the smell of her house hits her as she's opening the door, and it's bright and clear, like open windows and shampoo.

Lena finds Em in the kitchen. Reading in the window seat. Something is cooking on the stove, vegetable soup, not canned soup, not heavy winter soup, not borscht, just a light vegetable soup, which will be golden and perfect, and have some carrots, and squash, and bright green zucchini, and Em will put it in a big earthenware pot because she's such a hippie, and she'll put out a crusty bread, and there will be wine, which Lena can try.

The table is set, and there are flowers on the table. They're not regular flowers, they're a flowering branch from a tree. Em looks from her book and sees Lena looking at the flowers.

"I took a walk today, and I could not resist those. Aren't they just amazing? I tore them off a tree, and I immediately thought, *Well, if everyone did that, there would be no flowers for anyone, but still.* And I hid them in my shopping bag the whole way home, I was so afraid, like someone was going to arrest me."

Em sees the look on Lena's face and stands up. The moment she says, "What's wrong?" Lena is like an egg hitting the floor, she comes apart everywhere.

RING, RING

...

In his room, Vaclav dials the phone.

The person who picks up the receiver on the other end is laughing with someone else. She says hello, and her voice is warm and loose. There is music playing in the background.

"Hello, am I interrupting you?" Vaclav says. This is not proper phone manners. This is not what he meant to say.

"Oh, no," she says, "we just sat down to dinner! No worries. How can I help you?"

"Umm, this is Vaclav calling for Lena, please, if she's available," he says, but the lady doesn't respond; she didn't hear him.

"I'm sorry, honey, who is this?"

"My name is Vaclav," he says.

"Lena can't come to the phone," she says, her voice suddenly serious, but then she adds, softly, "I'm so sorry," and hangs up.

It occurs to Vaclav only after she has hung up that this sweet, warm voice must have been Lena's mom, her new mom, her real mom, her adoptive mom, whatever.

Vaclav is angry at her for not letting him talk to Lena. He has to remind himself that she's been Lena's mom for seven years, and she probably knows Lena better than he does, which is sad to him. And suddenly, everything is sad to him, his bedroom, lonely and dark, his mom crying in the kitchen, the cruel happiness at Lena's house, the darkness outside, and it all seems totally lonely, far too lonely.

Emily returns to Lena, who is wrapped in a blanket on the sofa. Although it broke Emily's heart when Lena told her that she could not bear what she had remembered, could not go on living, Emily knew that actually, Lena could go on living, that she might finally begin.

GO TO MOSCOW TO FIND OUT

...

Vaclav wakes up early the next morning and gets dressed in his room. He decides not to brush his teeth, not to shower, not even to pee. He does not want to talk to Rasia. If he goes into the bathroom, she will hear, she will know he is up and getting ready, and she will try to stop him. He will pee at McDonald's, he tells himself; he will buy a pack of gum. Nothing will stop him from going to Lena.

When he opens the door of his bedroom, she is there, like a wall, his mother.

"You are sneaking," she says. Her voice is extra-Russian, like she's KGB. He just glares at her. "You are planning to sneak to Lena's house, to talk to her."

"Mom, just let me go."

"Listen, wait. All I am saying is this is a big knot of problems, yes? You, me, Lena, her family, it is a mess. So don't think it is just one problem. That is all."

"Move," he says.

"Wait," she says. "Wait. Lena wants to know where her parents are, no? You don't need to go to Russia for this. We live, Vaclav, practically in Moscow."

"Mom, why are we talking about this? I'm going to go talk to Lena," he says.

"Because to go to Russia, it is stupid, when everyone is right here," she says.

"I'm not going to Russia, okay? I'm going to Park Slope," says Vaclav.

"If Lena wants to know about her parents, she should ask her aunt."

"What?" says Vaclav.

"Lena's aunt, Ekaterina; she lives on Seventh."

"I know that. I used to pick Lena up for school every day. Wait, she still lives there?"

"Yes. Of course." Rasia says this like no one has ever moved. Like Vaclav has asked if the Aunt has kept the same head, or if she traded it in for a better, nicer head.

"Lena said she was gone. . . . Lena said she was in Russia."

"Lena, she has many problems," says Rasia. She can see that Vaclav is starting to get a whiff of something. There is hurt on his face.

"She lied to me," he says. "I'm going to talk to Ekaterina."

"Okay," she says, not moving. "Okay. I want you to, I want you to find the truth, and to understand. I am not stopping you," she says, stopping him. "I just want you to take a deep breath and think about what to ask her, what to talk about, what you want to say. Because to talk out of anger, it is bad."

"Okay," he says.

"I want you to know that with this there is no fixing. There is not magic solution. Lena has many problems. You can't just make this all—"

He cuts her off. "I know, Mom," he says, and then he pauses before saying, "Thank you."

Vaclav pushes past her, and his long legs take him to the front door and out into the morning faster than even he expected.

On the street, walking to the Aunt's house, Vaclav realizes that he wishes the walk was longer. He wishes he didn't remember exactly where it was. He wishes a lot of things. He wishes he'd realized it was only seven-thirty in the morning.

The same question keeps dropping out from under him like a roller-coaster ride: *Why would she not start with the Aunt? Why lie? Why the trip to Russia?*

When he breathes in the morning air and thinks about what he now knows, it makes sense. It would be awful for Lena to go find the Aunt; it would be hard to talk to her and ask her questions. It makes perfect sense, total sense, that Lena would not want to go back there.

Lena's lie is burrowing around in his brain like maggots, turning things to maggot shit, turning solid brain cells into hot puddles of jealousy, of mistrust, of suspicion. He wonders if Lena has lied to him about anything else. How can you know anything, do anything, when you don't know what is true? He has never lied to Lena. Lena has made him lie for her. She has made him lie to his mother and maybe other times. Maybe. It is hard to say. When lying starts to turn your brain into maggot shit, it becomes hard to say what is up and what is down.

Vaclav doesn't know what to think, but he feels that if he puts together the pieces of the puzzle, Lena's puzzle, his mom's puzzle, then this will get better. He doesn't really even think it will get better, to tell the truth. He just thinks something will change, which is good, because he can't stand to have it stay like this.

Finding the truth will stop the big false search, take the steam out of her quest to get to Russia. Russia. It has become a word like . . . something disgusting. Something stupid and disgusting.

Walking outside so early in the morning feels good, in the same way that he is sure that talking to Lena's aunt will be good.

He feels that for Lena he is healing a wound; he is closing a door. It does not, to him, seem to be an enormous intrusion, an exceptional violation. Lena wanted something; he wants her to have it. He does not consider that he might be slightly, or completely, off base on the question of what Lena really wanted.

Maybe also, a little bit, he knows that if he does this, then Lena will talk to him, definitely, no matter what.

Vaclav charges up the stairs to Lena's aunt's house, and knocks hard on the door.

There is no response for a while. Vaclav checks his watch and then knocks again. He resolves to wait two minutes and then knock again. After his third knock, after six minutes, there is a rustling of the blinds next to the window. The door opens a crack, and the Aunt pours herself into this crack, slinks into it like a cat. She looks directly into Vaclav's eyes, not just at his eyes but into them, way too far. She looks at him in a way that tells him that she will have sex with him right now. There is no other way for him to describe this look.

She does not say hello, she just gives him this look. He is taken aback. He would like to speak. He would like to run away. It takes him a moment.

"Can I talk to you?" he asks.

"Talk," she says.

"I know you. I know Lena." There is a gigantic pause. There is a pause like Superman is holding the world still.

"Come in," she says, and she turns into the house.

TRINA

...

Vaclav follows her inside. He has never been inside before, even when he was younger. It's dark inside, and it smells stale. Everything is a mess; there are dirty dishes and take-out containers and empty cigarette packs everywhere.

"I'm sorry, did I wake you up? I know it's really early." Vaclav is standing just inside the door, and Lena's aunt is fumbling inside the kitchen. Putting on tea. He doesn't know what else to say.

"Wake me up? No. I'm not going to bed yet."

She's wearing a lot of makeup, heavy nighttime makeup, but it looks used, slept in. Her hair looks slept in. She's wearing gray sweatpants with big yellow-ringed white bleach blotches on them, and a tight black top with mesh parts, exposing her lower back, a portion of skin above her belly button, the cleavage between her breasts. She smells terrible, like old milk and cigarettes.

"You want tea?" she says.

"Yes, ma'am," he says.

"Fuck you, ma'am. Call me Trina," she says, from the kitchen. "Sit down," she says, sounding angry.

Vaclav sits on the couch feeling out of his league. His hands don't know where to go; he doesn't know where to put them.

She brings him the tea and sits down at the other end of the couch. She curls her legs underneath her in the same complicated way that Lena does. Vaclav's teacup is dirty, but she is looking at him, so he drinks. There is nowhere to put his tea bag. She takes out a cigarette and lights it, and Vaclav is acutely aware that there are no windows open, no fan, nothing. He wants to smoke one of her cigarettes, take it without asking, to show her that he is a man and not a child, that he is not afraid of her. He eyes the pack of cigarettes. He cannot do it.

She drops her tea bag into an ashtray, an ashtray that has another desiccated tea bag in it already.

"What is this about?" she says, glaring at him. She is like a cat, this way her eyes never leave him.

"I want to know about Lena," he says. She looks at him for a long time. A very long time. She is like a computer full of memory, loading information. Sorting files. *She knows everything I want to know,* he thinks.

"I know nothing," she says. "I haven't seen her for years."

"That's not what I care about. I care about before. When she lived with you."

"I will not talk about this," she says.

He knows that what she will not talk about is the man, the boyfriend.

"Before that," he says. "Before she went away. I don't care about that," he says. "I want to know what happened to Lena's parents. To her mother. To her father. How she got here."

"Why do you want to know?" she says.

"She wants to know," he offers, by way of correction. "Lena wants to know."

"And you give her what she wants." *How is it*, Vaclav thinks, *that these people, prostitutes, crazy street people, homeless men on the subway, they see sometimes straight to the truth, no matter what?*

"Why does she not come and see me herself?" Trina asks. Wouldn't it be obvious, to anyone, why Lena would not want to come back here?

"She doesn't know that I'm here."

The Aunt nods. He seems to have met all of her prerequisites, so she can tell him this story. She has decided to tell him, but she will make him wait. Vaclav can see that this is a story that part of her wants to tell but that she will tell it only on her own terms.

Trina knows from stripping about negotiations, about power struggles. She knows how to give a customer everything he wants, so that by the time she does, he wishes he could give it back.

She lights another cigarette, uncurls and recurls her body on the couch, arranges her bleached hair on top of her head. She's trying to make him uncomfortable. She is succeeding. He decides to speak.

"Where are Lena's parents?" he says.

"Dead," she says, without hesitation. She says it loud, and mean, and it startles him.

"Where?" he asks.

"What do you mean 'where'?" she says, finding humor in it. "They are dead! There is no place, it is not geography, no? Once you are dead you are nowhere, everywhere, yes?"

"I mean where did they die?" Vaclav asks. "Here? In Brooklyn?" he asks. She smiles.

"You know nothing of anything," she says. How could he know anything? Of course he knows nothing. She is taunting him, and he hates her.

"They were never here. They died in Russia. Both."

"How did it happen? They died together?"

"Listen, if you are wanting Romeo and Juliet, it is not happening. They were never together. They were fucking. Enough to make Lena and some dirty sheets. She didn't even know his last name."

"They were not in love?" he says, grasping. He's made many faulty assumptions. Already this is falling apart as a solution, as a story to take to Lena, wrapped up like a valentine.

"They were high," she says.

"What do you mean?" he asks.

"They were junkies, you know what this is? Criminals. Drug addicts. And stealing, she stole things. That was why she was killed. The street."

"She was killed on the street?" he says.

"She was killed in prison," she says.

"I'm sorry," he says, hating the sound of the words, because he wanted to interrogate her like he was a detective on television, like she had the information and it belonged to him; he would beat it out of her. But instead he was coddling her, being nice, apologizing, and it's just like him to do this. "Please tell this to me from beginning to end. I need to know the whole story. Please."

She nods.

"Okay, okay, it is fair. I start from the beginning. In Russia it was a bad time. It was, what, 1991? No, Lena was born in 1993. The country was coming apart, every day, the government crumbling. Everything was a mess. There was not food or jobs, and there was crime everywhere, and with the rationing, everyone was, what they say, dirty? You pay for this, you get this, you pay with vodka, with fuck, with whatever. Right?"

"Corrupt," says Vaclav.

"Right," she says. "So there was nothing. In our family, there was sadness and failing, and our father could not work, and he drank and sat with the other men. He was not bad. This was what was. Like your depression in this country. It makes men into nothing, into dogs or criminals or girls. Our father was like this. He was nothing.

"There was crime everywhere. To go out, to go to school, it was dangerous. Lena's mother—her name also it was the same as Lena's, but we called her Yelena—Yelena was older than me ten years. There was a dead baby in between us, a boy. He was born too soon. My mother, she would yell his name and offer us, her daughters, to have him back. A bloody lump who never spoke or cried or shat, but still, she would trade us in for a child with a dick. She would say, 'God, I would give you willingly these two little girls, if I could only have back my Aleck.'

"Yelena, with her it was a bad situation. There were girls who had things, clothes and food. And fun places to go where everyone was excited to see them there. And at home, it was like what I just told you. And me. I was at home, and anytime Yelena was there, my mother would make Yelena take care of me while she drank until she slept like death. Yelena would do her best to keep me happy, to make dolls and play around and enjoy ourselves, but she was sad. Even as a little girl I knew this. You know this about your sister." Trina takes a deep breath.

"So she went with the girls." The Aunt says this like it is the final word on the subject—like there is nothing more to say. Vaclav waits for her to continue, but she doesn't, she just smokes and looks at her fingernails.

"I'm sorry, I don't know what that means," Vaclav asks.

"She stopped going to school; she went to the street with these girls, to sell her pussy for money, to get nice things. I have to spell it out for you?" the Aunt barks. *It isn't easy to say that your sister became a whore,* Vaclav reminds himself.

"It sounds like she didn't have a choice," Vaclav says, by way of softening things. Trina doesn't like this either; she makes a face like there is a turd somewhere in the room that she can smell but cannot find.

"There is always choice," she spits.

"When did she get into drugs?" he asks.

"Selling pussy, drugs, it comes along with the territory, no?" She says this like Vaclav must be familiar with the situation. Vaclav has never before heard the word *pussy* spoken by a live woman in his presence. Never. The Aunt says it like *poo-see.*

"Girls need the drugs to keep selling themselves, and then they are selling suddenly only for the drugs."

Vaclav has a terrible thought.

"Was Lena's father one of these men? Who paid her, for . . ."

"For pussy? Probably he gave her drugs, not money. He was a drug dealer, a thug in a gang. Maybe he gave her nothing. Maybe he just took."

"So they were not together. Dating. Anything?"

"No."

"Okay. Did you know him?"

"No. Only from the trial, and when they were arrested."

"They were arrested together?" he asks.

"There was a bust of this drug ring. He was there; she was there. There had been a murder. A rich girl, the daughter of an important man. They were both arrested together for her murder."

"Did they kill her together?"

"Someone did. Who knows. Maybe they did. Yelena said she had nothing to do with it. Wrong place in time. At the trial she cried the whole time, but he never said a word. The police, they said that the two of them killed this girl for money. A mugging."

Vaclav is confused. It seems that the Aunt won't give him a straight answer on whether Lena's mother killed this girl, whether she was innocent or guilty, and it all seems so important, so huge to him. Every detail seems close to the one that will make sense, that will close the case, make the logic work.

"Wait . . . So she was innocent? And she was executed?" Vaclav's eyes are wild with fear that this could happen anywhere in the world, ever. Trina is used to this look on the faces of Americans. She is tired of this look, exhausted by it.

"No, not executed . . . It doesn't matter. She committed many crimes. Prostitution, theft, drugs. She could have been tried for any of these things. She was a criminal; to them she was dirt. It did not matter."

"Were you there? At the trial?"

"Yes. I went because my mother would not go. Yelena was dead already to her." Trina stands up and looks Vaclav directly in the eyes, and he does not understand how, but her look tells him that she will not answer any further questions about the trial, that there is something there that is still hurt.

"You want tea?" she says.

"I have tea, from before," he says. He looks at his cold tea.

She picks up a dish from the sink, runs water over it, and puts it back down.

"I did not know that she was pregnant then, at her trial. They didn't let me talk to her."

"So did you go see her in prison, after the trial?" Vaclav asks.

"No. There was the trial, she was guilty, and then they told me to go home, but there was no sentencing. They said she would be sentenced later. Now I know they were just waiting for her to have the baby. She delivered in prison, and then they kill her."

"Wait, what do you mean? When did you get Lena?"

"I was called to the prison; I am thinking Yelena asked to see me. I go in, expecting to see Yelena, and they give me this baby. I say, 'What is this baby and where is Yelena?' and they say, "This is her baby; she is in hospital.' I ask to see her and they say this is not possible."

"They just gave Lena to you?"

"Yelena requested that the baby be released to me. I did not know even that there was any baby."

"And then they killed her? Yelena?" Vaclav is trying desperately to put together the sequence of events.

"Yes, I know they did this. Six weeks later a letter comes that she is dead from tuberculosis. But that day at the prison, when they gave me this baby and say no, I cannot see Yelena, I know she is dead already."

"Do you think someone killed her, like executed her? And lied?"

"I think she is dead. Giving birth or with tuberculosis or with a gun to her head, doesn't matter. They wanted her dead; she died. They said there were prisoners dying with tuberculosis then. Maybe true, maybe not. Maybe it is true they have tuberculosis, maybe it is also true that the prison lets it spread and gives no medicine. Either way, someone wanted them dead, and they are dead."

"What did you do?"

"I brought the baby home." She stares at Vaclav, challenging him to ask for more.

"So her dad didn't want her?"

"The man who was tried with Yelena, who knows, maybe the man it wasn't even her father. Anyway, whoever her father is, either this man or some other drug dealer pimp whatever. Not someone to give a baby to, right?"

"Right."

"Forget the father," she says. "He is dirt or nothing. Dead. A criminal. A nothing. Forget."

"How did you get here?" asks Vaclav, promising nothing in the way of forgetting Lena's father.

"My mother didn't look at the baby or touch her or hold her, nothing. I could tell she wants only to forget Yelena. This baby, it was too much for her, this she did not want. I was buying formula and trying to take care of this baby and go to my job, and having girlfriends come over to watch the baby, my mother, she would do nothing.

"One day she gives me a passport with Yelena's name on it, and fake papers for the baby, and airplane tickets to New York John F. Kennedy International Airport. She tells me to pack and leave in the morning. She didn't pay for these tickets, there were men in the family already in Brooklyn, men who are involved, importing, exporting, whatever, drugs and girls and selling stolen things. Some of these people, we are related to them. So my mother gets in touch, and she says she has a girl and a baby to send to America, and we will be useful, and she puts us on a plane to America, and that is it."

"Why did the passport have Yelena's name?"

"This I think our mother was doing for her before she went to prison and died. Arranging for her to go to United States."

"She was trying to save her?" Vaclav asks, lost.

"She was tying to sell her," the Aunt says, "like she sold me."

"Sold you?"

"She sent me here to work for these men, and the lie is that you will work off the money that they have spent to get you here, the money spent on fake passport, on airplane flight, and they put you up in apartment and pay for green card, and do all sorts of other lying in your name so that you are trapped to them and you cannot go to police and escape. They make credit cards in your name, and a loan on a car in your name, because your credit is clean, and you cannot afford these things without them, and they are saying that you owe them money already for these things, and it is adding up every day. Some girls, they think they will work it off, and they count their dollars and every day they are thinking about how this work is getting them to freedom, but eventually they all give in to it being permanent slave to these men, and instead of dreaming to get out they start thinking this is the way their life will be always, and they start dating one of these men, and they take the drugs and let these men make their life into disaster."

Vaclav knows that this is not some girl's story, this is Trina's story.

"The man I was dating, he wasn't the one who touched Lena."

"What?" says Vaclav, stunned, confused.

"Some friend of his, some drunk thug from the club. He comes that day looking for me; I wasn't home, he finds Lena. I tried always to keep her out of the house, but this day she stays home sick, I did not know. Anyway, your mother comes, she sees, she sneaks away and phones 911. By the time they come, he is gone. So when the police come, they say, 'Who did this,' I gave them the name of my boyfriend, the man who has my debt. I say that he is always beating us, always touching Lena."

"What? You lied?" Vaclav asks.

"The man your mama saw, he went away free. The man who was my boyfriend, they put him in prison and I am free, and they take away Lena, and I am free of her too."

"But he never touched Lena?" Vaclav asks.

"No. He would never do this. I would never let this happen to Lena; it happened once, this man who comes and barges in, drunk, looking for me. But I knew if I said that my boyfriend is always touching her, and they see the evidence on Lena, and what your mama said she saw, that he would go to prison forever, and we would both be safe."

"But the man who did it . . . he got off?" Vaclav says, enraged.

"He escaped the police on that day, yes. Now he is dead," Trina says.

Vaclav tries to understand.

"I was trying always to keep Lena only fed and going to school and to not see anything of these things that are happening to me, to us. When we came to this country, I gave her to the old woman, but then she died. I did not want Lena. I want her not to see or be seen by these men, these scum, to see these things, the club where I am working or the drugs or these criminals or anything. I want her and me to get out of this horrible place that my sister made us go to."

Trina stops; she relights a cigarette that is already lit.

"I love my sister. I want to make something good from her, for her."

Vaclav lets her stop for a moment. He looks away while she wipes her eyes with the backs of her hands.

"When they take Lena away, I know she will finally be happy. She will live in a place that is clean. She will be safe from seeing me and my life; she will be safe from these men and this way of living. This is what I always want for her. I am glad that this happens, you see?

And then this man goes to prison, and I am free from him. I am going to school now all the time to be a nurse. I am dancing only to pay for this; this is the only way. And that will be my freedom, when I am RN—and making salary and benefits and all this. I have only one year to go. Starting salary for nurse is ninety thousand. Is good. Then I will see Lena, when I am good for her. When she is grown up and safe. That is all. That is all I have to tell you; you know the whole story."

Vaclav does not know what to say.

"You want to go tell Lena this, and I will ask you one thing and then you will do whatever you will do. I know this, you are a boy, and with your ideas you will do whatever you are thinking is the right thing." She pauses, and smokes.

"But this is this thing. Lena does not know any of this. She is protected from all of this horrible things. I protected her. I sent her away from this. And now you will bring it to her. I am thinking you know that she is not ready for this. She is still soft and not a happy and ready grown-up person. I do not know. I have not seen her. You know the best. Maybe she is ready."

Vaclav searches her face and sees that she is toying with him, that there is something that she wants him to do or not to do but that she is not going to say it.

"I am thinking that since you are here, and she is not here, this is a sign that she is most definitely not ready. Now you will go from my house. I am done talking with you."

She turns her back on him and goes to the kitchen, runs the water. Then she turns around, looks at Vaclav, and tries to soften.

"I am very tired. Goodbye."

BROOKLYN IS ONLY A BOROUGH

...

Vaclav walks to Lena's house. It is far to Lena's house; all of Brooklyn is between them. But Brooklyn is only a borough, it is not a country. Lena's house is six miles away, and Vaclav can walk every step. Vaclav must put one foot down and then another foot down and push the sidewalk behind him; he must move himself over the ground, and feel that he is a person moving himself through the world. First he walks up Ocean Parkway, and he walks through all of Midwood, through the gaggles of Hassidic girls in their navy skirts, the mothers with their strollers and matching hair. He walks through Ditmas Park, where one side of the street is big Victorian mansions, holding forth proud porches and manicured lawns, and the other side is bodegas with their signs painted over eight times. He walks through Prospect Park, where the trees are exploding in color and all the people running or walking their dogs or talking on cellphones underneath seem not to notice.

Vaclav walks and walks and walks some more.

By the time he gets to Lena's house he knows what to do.

Lena's neighborhood is beautiful in a way that Vaclav's is not. The houses are big, tall row houses, they have big stately windows that look like wise old eyes. They look knowing and old. They look solid and beautiful. They don't look smushed in and small, like crowded crooked teeth, like the houses in Vaclav's neighborhood. There are trees here, perfect trees that arch across the street and make a little canopy. Vaclav's feet land not on the bare sidewalk but on a carpet of perfect fallen leaves.

Lena's house has accomplished the easy Americanness that his house never could. His house always has the wrong smell, the wrong mat at the door, the wrong stance.

The doorbell makes a wonderful sound, a deep ringing, like an actual bell, and there are two long, slow, grand tones, ding, dong. Ding, dong. There is laughing inside; there is yelling inside. "I gooooooot it!" Laughing on the way to get it.

A woman opens the door with great effort; it is a heavy door. The inside of the house is full of a warm light, like Lena's mom has somehow learned to magically make lightbulbs out of clementines.

Lena's mom is small, maybe the same height as Lena, shorter than Vaclav for sure. Her hair is long, and gray or blond, or graying blond, but she looks young; her chin is young and she has bangs cut straight across her forehead. Her eyes are crinkled at the edges, as if she knows things, but she still looks young. She is wearing a black dress, and her arms are showing, and she's wearing a scarfy thing even though she's inside. She has bracelets on, a lot of bracelets, like armor, from her wrists halfway up her forearms. She has rings on her thumbs. She is smiling at Vaclav, he realizes, and she knows who he is, and she grabs his shoulders and hugs him as she pulls him into the house.

"Vaclav," she says, like she has been expecting him. She takes his hand and brings him inside. Vaclav realizes that Lena must have told Emily everything.

"Come," she says, "come." She leads him through the house, which is weird but still normal. This house is not trying to be normal; it has weird things all around. There are colorful pieces of fabric everywhere, and nothing matches, and there are so many paintings on the walls that there is no empty space, but it still looks nicer than his house.

The kitchen is nothing like his kitchen. It is big, and there are books in stacks on the counters, and there are three different bunches of flowers in three different vases, and there are pots hanging from the ceiling.

Lena is sitting at the kitchen table, reading. When she sees Vaclav, her face freezes.

"Lena," Emily says. "Let's not be dramatic about it, let's not be *Days of Our Lives*. Let's just be people. He is here because he cares about you. It's okay, we can all just talk, right?" She looks at Vaclav.

He hesitates, staring at Lena. Lena is wearing pink plaid pajama pants and is hiding her arms inside of an oversized fisherman-knit sweater. She looks smaller than ever, huddled at the table.

"Yes," he says. "I want to tell you the truth."

Lena can say nothing.

"About your parents," he says, "I know."

Lena looks at her mom, like a toddler the moment after she's been stung by a bee, just as it starts to sting and burn.

"Vaclav," Em says, "why don't you sit down?"

Vaclav sits down, feeling awkward in the chair, feeling like he does not know what to do with his face, with his hands, with anything. No one talks.

"I'm here to tell you the truth about your parents," Vaclav says, and Lena looks him right in the eyes.

"I went to see your aunt, your mom's sister. The one you lived with when we were little. She still lives in the same apartment. I remember now how nervous it used to make me to go there. She told me about your mom and dad, all about them."

Lena's eyebrows show him how desperate she is to know, and also how terrified. Emily sits down at the kitchen table next to Lena, and nods at Vaclav.

"I know you didn't want to go there, and I know you didn't want me to go there. I know why you didn't tell me about it, and it's fine. I went, and everything is fine." Vaclav takes a breath.

THE TRUTH

...

They were students. Your mom and dad were both Ph.D. students at the University of Moscow, both there on scholarship, they were so brilliant. Your aunt said that everyone knew they were the smartest people; everyone talked about it.

She was a scientist, and he was a poet. They were in love from the first moment they saw each other in the university cafeteria. They saw each other across the room, and they just went to each other. They both knew instantly. They walked out of the cafeteria together, silently, and then they both saw the sky and the trees and the grass and the domes above the buildings for the first time ever. They held hands only for the first month, not out of duty or respect or ideals or religion or to abstain but because they knew that anything else would be too much too fast, would destroy them, would kill them, would explode their hearts and their skulls and their fingertips.

Of course, they didn't wait forever.

There were protests all the time, then, there. Student protests, uprisings, against the government, against the tyranny, against the bread lines and the concrete and the grayness of the sky. Against the terrible oppressive architecture of all the buildings. They went out together to protest, with the other brilliant writers and poets and scientists and sculptors, writers of papers and explorers of new things, new ideas, and new theories. They stood in the street and held signs, they marched and they chanted songs, wonderful uplifting songs of the strength and the beauty of the world.

They were rounded up and beaten by policemen. They were brought to jail for their beliefs, for their conviction, for the pure beauty of their ideas. At this time, you have to realize, people disappeared for thinking the wrong thing, they were made to disappear by the government. Getting thrown in jail, no one got a fair trial or anything like that.

She sent him a final message, through the prison, to tell him she was pregnant, with you. It said: We will be together, in the stars, in the grass, in the concrete, in the sound of the trees at night, in our daughter.

He sent her a final message. It said: I love you. I had the most beautiful life anyone could have. They can take nothing from us; we had everything.

He received her message the day before he was executed. She received his the day before she gave birth.

They took her away as soon as you were born, and they gave you to her sister. They gave you her name, a beautiful name, Yelena. Light.

Your aunt did the best that she could. She brought you here; your grandparents helped her get you safely to America. She was young; she tried her best. It was hard; you reminded her of the sister she lost; her beauty, her brilliance, are all in you. She knew she could not take good care of you, that's why she left you with that old woman for a little while. She's so glad that you're safe now. She loves you. She is so sorry, her heart is breaking all the time.

PEOPLE WHO KNEW HE WAS LYING

...

Lena's real mom, Emily, knew that this was not the truth, but she also knew that Vaclav was not lying.

Vaclav knew that he was telling the truth.

Lena knew that it was a lie, but she loved it and believed it, like a fairy tale, like a song, like a bedtime story, like a magic trick.

She loved Vaclav until it became the truth, and so it was.

ACKNOWLEDGMENTS

...

Thank you, first and foremost, to my parents, the best parents in the universe, bar none. You gave me everything.

Colin. You are my best friend, my right-hand man, and the safest place I could fall. Thank you, little brother.

Lindsey. Thank you for everything that you are. Thank you for always sticking up for me, even when I am being stupid. I love you desperately. Thank you, little sister.

Thank you to my grandparents, who taught me what it means to love someone forever and ever. It is one of the great secrets of the universe, and I will be forever grateful.

Enormous thanks to Molly Friedrich, Lucy Carson, and Paul Cirone for their wild enthusiasm, their brilliant advice, and their limitless patience.

Susan Kamil and Noah Eaker helped this book become everything it could be. Any imperfections that remain are mine.

William Tapply taught me how to write, and told me that I must; his memory is with me every time I put pen to paper.

Spasibo to Sebastian Schulman for last-minute Russian translation.

Julie Sarkissian read this book before it was a book, and she is the only reason I survived writing it. She is my best friend and soul mate, and I am lucky that she also happens to be such a brilliant writer and reader.

All my friends in Brooklyn, with your beautiful minds and hearts, and my extended family in Tennessee, the very best people in the world, you keep me dancing and laughing and surrounded by love. Thank you.

Finally, I have taken a few liberties with facts concerning Coney Island. I won't list them here, but instead encourage you to take the Q train to Coney Island, ride the Wonder Wheel, watch the lovely and talented Heather Holliday perform at the sideshow, and find out for yourself.

ABOUT THE TYPE

This book is set in Fournier, a typeface named for Pierre Simon Fournier, the youngest son of a French printing family. He started out engraving woodblocks and large capitals, then moved on to fonts of type. In 1736 he began his own foundry and made several important contributions in the field of type design; he is said to have cut 147 alphabets of his own creation. Fournier is probably best remembered as the designer of St. Augustine Ordinaire, a face that served as the model for Monotype's Fournier, which was released in 1925.